TM SERIES

Horror Stories

COMPILED BY

PATRICIA MOORE

MAANU
GRAPHICS
(PUBLISHERS OF GENERAL BOOKS)

Horror Stories

Published by
MAANU GRAPHICS
(PUBLISHERS OF GENERAL BOOKS)
5FF, Ganpati Bhawan, 21 Ansari Road,
Darya Ganj, New Delhi-110002
Ph: 65285220, 64138266
E-mail : maanugraphics@yahoo.com

ISBN 978-93-80078-50-2

Printed at
New Z. A. Printers, Delhi

CONTENTS

THE DARK LAND

MICHAEL MARSHALL SMITH

1991 WAS A good year for Michael Marshall Smith. Not only did his story "The Man Who Drew Cats" win the British Fantasy Award for Best Short Story, but he was also presented with the Icarus Award for Best Newcomer.

Smith was born in Knutsford, Cheshire, and grew up in the United States, South Africa and Australia, before returning with his family to England in 1975. His stories have appeared in *Dark Voices 2* and *4, Darklands 1* and 2, and *Best New Horror 2,* and his first novel, *Only Forward,* will be published by HarperCollins in 1993. He is currently working on more short stories, gearing up for a second novel, co-writing a situation comedy for BBC-TV and developing a feature treatment based loosely on the very strange story that follows . . .

FOR WANT OF ANYTHING BETTER TO DO, and in the spirit that keeps my room austerely tidy when there are other things I should be doing, I decided to move my bed. After returning from college I'd redecorated my room, as it had been the same since I'd been about ten, and I'd moved just about everything round except for the bed. I knew it was largely an excuse for not doing anything more constructive but pulled it away from the wall and tried it in another couple of positions.

It was hard work, as one of the legs is rather fragile and the thing had to be virtually lifted off the floor, and after half an hour I was hot and irritated and becoming more and more convinced that its original position had been the optimal, and indeed the only, place to put it. And it was as I struggled to shove it back up against the wall that I began to feel a bit strange. When it was finally back in place I sat down on it, feeling light-headed and a bit ill and I suppose basically I just drifted off to sleep.

I don't know if the bed is pan of it in some way. I only mention it because it seems important, and because I guess that it was while I was asleep on it that it all began. After a while I woke up, half-remembering a dream in which I had been doing nothing more than lying on my bed remembering that my parents had said that they were going to extend the wood panelling on the downstairs hall walls. For a few moments I was disorientated, confused by being in the same place in reality as I had been in the dream, and then I drifted off again.

Some time later I awoke again, feeling very sluggish and slightly nauseous. I found it very difficult to haul my mind up from sleep, but eventually stood up and lurched across the room to the sink to get a glass of water, rubbing my eyes and feeling very rough. Maybe I was going down with something. I decided that a cup of tea would be a good idea, and headed out of the bedroom to go downstairs to the kitchen to make one.

As I reached the top of the stairs I remembered the dream about the panelling and wondered vaguely where a strange idea like that could have come from. I'd worked hard for my psychology paper at college, and was fairly confident that Freud hadn't felt that wood panelling was even worth a mention. I trudged downstairs, still feeling a bit strange, my thoughts dislocated and confused.

Then I stopped, open-mouthed, and stared around me. They really *had* extended the panelling. It used to only go about eight feet up the wall, but it now soared right up to the front hall ceiling, which is two floors high. And they'd done it in exactly the same wood as the original panelling: there wasn't a join to be seen. How the hell had they managed that? Come to that, *when* the hell had they managed that? It hadn't been there that morning, both my parents were at work and would be for hours and . . . well, it was just impossible, wasn't it? I reached out and touched the wood, marvelling at how even the grain was the same, and that the new wood looked just as aged as the original, which had been there fifty years.

As I struggled to get my still sluggish mind in gear surprise suddenly gave way to astonishment. Wait a minute, I thought, that isn't right. There hadn't used to be *any* panelling in the hall. It used just to be white walls. Sure, the stairs were panelled in wood, but the walls were just plain white plaster. How the hell could I have forgotten that? What had made me think that the front hall had been panelled, and think it so unquestioningly? I could now remember that I'd recently noticed, sensitised to these things as I was by having recently repainted my room, that the white paint in the hall was rather dirty, especially round the light switches. So what was all this panelling doing here? Where had it come from, and when, for Christ's sake? And why had I been so sure that at least some of it had always been there?

I walked slowly into the kitchen, casting bewildered backward glances at the walls. I heard a soft clinking sound outside and walked to the back door, too puzzled about the front hall to even notice that it was rather late for a milk delivery. The back door, which like the front door opens out onto the driveway, is in a little corridor full of gardening implements, shoes and tools which leads off the kitchen to the garage. I threaded my way through these and wrenched the stiff door open.

As soon as it was open I reeled backwards from the light and unthinkingly crouched just inside the back hall. Then I realised that it wasn't even that bright outside: it was late afternoon and the light was muted, but everything seemed very intense, like colours before a storm. Odd, but not odd enough to throw yourself to the ground over, I thought as I stood up. But it had been the milkman after all, for there was our milk bottle holder with four bottles of milk in it. Only they weren't milk bottles, but large American-style quart containers somehow jammed into slots meant to take pints. And someone had taken the silver tops off.

Something at the edge of my vision caught my attention and I looked up towards the top of the driveway. There, about thirty yards away, were two children, one fat and on a bike, the other slim and standing. I was seized with a sudden irrational fury and started quickly up the drive towards them, convinced that the clinking sound I'd heard was them stealing the tops off the milk.

I had covered scarcely five yards when from behind me someone who'd been at my school walked quickly and inexplicably past me up the drive, staring straight ahead. I couldn't remember his name, had barely known him, in fact. He'd been two or three years older than me, and I'd completely forgotten that he'd existed, but as I stared after him I remembered that he'd been one of the more amiable seniors. I could recall being proud of having some small kind of communication with one of the big boys and how it had made me feel a bit older myself, more a man of the world, less of a kid. And I remembered the way he used to greet my yelling a nickname greeting at him, a half-smile and the raising of an eyebrow.

All this came back with the instantaneous impact of memory, but something wasn't right. He didn't smile at all, or even seem to register that I was there. I felt oddly disturbed and chilled, not by the genuinely strange fact that he was there at all, or that he was wearing school athletic gear when he must have left the school seven years ago, but because he didn't smile and tilt his head back the way he used to. It was so bizarre that I wondered briefly if I was dreaming, but if you can ask yourself the question you always know the answer, and I wasn't.

My attention was distracted on the other side by a reflection in the glass of the window in the back hallway. A man with glasses, a chubby face and blond hair that looked as if it had been cut with a basin seemed to be standing behind me, carrying a bicycle. I whirled round to face where he should have been, but he wasn't there. Then I remembered the kids at the top of the driveway and, seeing that they were still standing motionless, began to shout at them again, needing something to take my bewilderment out on.

Almost immediately a tall slim man in a dark suit came walking down the drive. I don't know if it was a trick of the light in the gathering dusk, but I couldn't seem to fix on his face. In retrospect it was as if an unnatural shadow hung there but at the time my eyes just seemed to slide off it as if it were slippery, or made of ice.

"Stop shouting at them," the man said as he passed me, walking towards the back door. I stared at him open-mouthed. "They're not doing anything wrong. Leave them alone."

The kids took themselves off, the one walking beside the other on the bike, and I turned to the suited man, anxious, for some reason, to placate him, and yet at the same time slightly outraged at his invasion of our property.

"I'm sorry," I said. "It's just, well, I'm a bit thrown. I thought I saw someone I knew in the drive. Did you see him? Sort of wavy brown hair, athletics gear?"

For some reason I thought that the man would say that he had, and that that would make me feel better, but all I got was a curt "No". I was by now looking at his back as he entered the back hallway.

"Shall we go into your old house then?" asked another voice, clearly talking to the suited man, and I saw that someone else was in the back hall: the man with the blond hair and glasses. And he really was carrying a bicycle, for God's sake.

"What?" I said incredulously, and hurried after them, catching a glimpse of the suited man's face. "But it's you ..." I continued, baffled, as I realised that the man in the suit was the man who had been in athletics gear. The two men walked straight into the kitchen and I followed them, quietly, and seemingly impotently, enraged. *Was* this his old house? Even if it was, wasn't it customary to ask the current occupants if you fancied a visit?

The suited man was by now peering round the kitchen, where for some reason everything looked very messy. He poked at some fried rice I'd left in a frying pan on the stove, or at least I seemed to have left it there, though I wasn't sure when I would have done so. Again I felt the urge to placate and hoped he would eat some, but he just grimaced with distaste and joined the other man at the window looking out onto the drive, hands on hips, his back to me.

"Dear God," he muttered, and the other man grunted in agreement.

I noticed that I'd picked up the milk from outside the back door, and appeared to have spilt some of it on the floor. I tried to clean it up with a piece of kitchen roll which seemed very dirty and yellowed as if with age, my mind aching under the strain of trying to work out what the hell was going on. I felt that there must be some sense to it somewhere, some logic of the situation that I was missing. Even if he had lived here once he had no right to just march in here with his friend like that, but I realised as I continued ineffectively trying to swab up the milk before he noticed it (why?) that there was something far wronger than a mere breach of protocol going on here. The suited man looked about thirty-five, far older then he should have been if he was indeed the man I'd been to school with, and yet far too young to ever have lived here, as between our family and the people we'd bought it from, the house's last 40 years were accounted for. So how the hell could it be his house? There was no way. And was it him anyway? Apart from being too old, it looked like him, but was it actually *him?*

As I straightened up, having done the best I could with the milk, I staggered slightly, feeling very disorientated and strange, my perception both heightened and jumbled at the same time, as if I was very drunk. Everything seemed to have a nightmarish intensity and exaggerated emotional charge, and yet there also seemed to be gaps in what I was perceiving, as if I was only taking in an edited version of what was going on. Things began to appear to jump from one state to another, with the bits in between, the becoming, missed out like a series of jump cuts. I felt hot and dizzy and the kitchen looked small and indescribably messy and the orange paint of the walls seemed to jump in at me beneath a low swaying ceiling. I wondered confusedly if I was seeing the kitchen as they saw it, and then immediately wondered what I meant by that.

All the time they just stood there, turning round occasionally to stare balefully at me, radiating distaste and impatience. Obviously they were waiting for something. But what? What was going on? Noticing I still had the piece of kitchen roll in my hand I stepped over all the rubbish on the floor–what the hell had been going on in this kitchen?–to put it in the overflowing bin. Then, squeezing my temples with my fingers and struggling both to concentrate and to stand upright against the weight of the air I turned towards the men.

"L-look", I stuttered, "what the hell is going on?" and immediately wished I hadn't. There was a pause and then the suited man turned his head very slowly towards me and it kept turning and turning until he was facing me while his body stayed facing the other way. I could feel my stomach trying to crawl away and fought against the gagging. He'd done that deliberately, done it because he knew it would make me want to throw up, and I thought he might just be right.

"Why don't you just shut up?" he snarled, the words squirming from his mouth like rats out of the stomach of something recently dead, and twisted his head slowly back round through 180 degrees until he was looking out onto the drive once more.

Meanwhile, the mess in the kitchen seemed to be getting worse. Every time I looked there were more dirty pans and bits of rubbish and old food on the floor. My head was getting thicker and heavier and felt like it was slipping away from me. I half fell against the fridge and clung to it, almost pulling it off the wall, and began to cry, my tears cutting channels in the thick grime on the fridge door. I dimly remembered that we'd bought a new fridge the week before but they must have changed it because this one looked like something out of the fifties, but it was hard to tell because it was swimming back and forth and there was a lot of white in my eyes and I couldn't see past it. They were both watching me now.

Suddenly a terrible jangling pierced my ear, as if someone were hammering a pencil into it. It happened again and I recognised it first as a sound and not a blow after all, and then as the doorbell. Someone was at the front door.

The two men glanced at each other and then the blond one nodded. The suited man turned to me.

"Do you know what that is?" he asked.

"Yes, it's the front door," I said, trying to please him.

"Yes. So you'd better answer it, hadn't you? Answer the *door.*"

"Should I answer it?" I said, stupidly. I just couldn't seem to remember what words meant any more.

"Yes" he grated and then picked up a mug, my mug, the mug I came down, I remembered randomly, to put tea in, and hurled it at me. It smashed into the fridge door by my face. I struggled to stand upright, my head aching and ears ringing, hearing a soft crump as a fragment of the mug broke under my foot. Then the doorbell jangled again, its harsh sharpness making me realise how muted sounds had been becoming. I fell rather than stepped towards the kitchen door, sliding across the front of the fridge, my feet tangling in the boxes and cartons that now seemed to cover the filthy floor. I could feel the orange of the walls seeping in through my ears and mouth and kept missing whole seconds as if I was blacking out and coming to like a stroboscope. As I banged into the door and grabbed the handle to hold myself up I heard the blond man say, "He may not go through. If he does, we wait." But it didn't mean anything to me. None of it did. Stepping clumsily over more piles of rubbish I headed for the front door. The chime of the doorbell had pushed the air hard and I could see it coming towards me in waves. Ducking, I slipped on the mat and almost fell into the living room on hands and knees. But it was getting dark in there, I could see, really dark, and

I could hear the plants talking. I couldn't catch the words, but they were there, beneath the night sounds and a soft rustling which sounded a hundred yards away. The living room must have grown, I thought groggily, picking myself up and turning myself to the front door as the bell clanged again. It should be about four paces across the hall from the living room door to the front door but I thought it was only going to take one and then it took twenty, past all the panelling and over the huge folds in the mat. And then I had my hand on the doorknob and then the door was open and I stepped out of the house.

"Oh hello Michael. I thought someone must be in, because all the lights were on."

"Wuh?" I said, blinking in the remnants of sunlight, breathless with the feeling of my mind soaring up towards normality like a runaway lift. Then "Sorry?"

"I hope I didn't disturb you?" the woman standing in front of me said, and I now recognised her to be Mrs Steinburg, the woman who brings us our catfood in bulk.

"No, no, that's fine. Fine," I said, looking covertly behind me into the hall, which was solid and unpanelled and four paces wide and led to the living room which was light and about ten yards deep. Good. Think about that later. Deal with the cat woman.

"I've brought your delivery," she said. "Look, are you all right?"

"Yes. I'm fine," I replied, smiling broadly. "I . . . er . . ." I . . . er . . . what? "I . . . er . . . just nodded off for a moment, in the kitchen. I still feel a bit, you know ..."

"Of course." Mrs Steinburg smiled. I followed her up the drive and heaved the box of catfood out of the back of her van, looking carefully back at the house. There was nothing to see. I thanked her and then carried the box back down the drive as she drove off.

I walked back into the house and shut the front door behind me. I felt absolutely fine. I walked into the kitchen. Normal. It didn't even occur to me to wonder if the two men would still be there. They weren't. I must just have fallen asleep making tea, and then struggled over to the front door to open it while still half asleep. I could remember asking myself if it was a dream and thinking it wasn't but that just showed how wrong you could be, didn't it? It had been unusually vivid, and it was odd how I'd been suddenly awake and all right again as soon as I stepped out of the front door. Odd, and a bit disconcerting. But here I was in the kitchen again and everything was normal, clean and tidy, spick and span, with all the rubbish in the bin and the pans in the right places and the milk in the fridge and a smashed mug on the floor.

Suddenly I didn't feel quite so good. It was my mug, and it was smashed, on the floor, at the bottom of the fridge. Now how had that happened? Maybe I'd fallen asleep holding it (fallen asleep standing up with a mug in my hand? Now how likely was that?), maybe I'd knocked it over waking up and incorporated the sound into my dream (better, better, but where exactly was I supposed to have fallen asleep? Just leaning against the counter, or actually stretched out on it with the kettle as a pillow?). Then I noticed the fridge door.

There was a little dent in it, with a couple of flecks of paint missing. At about head height.

That wasn't good. That wasn't good at all. In fact it felt as if someone had just punched a hole in my chest and poured icy water into it. But everything else was all right, wasn't it? I cleared up the mug and switched the kettle on and while it was boiling wandered into the hall and the living room. Everything was fine, tidy, normal. Super. Back into the kitchen. The same. Great. Apart from a little dent in the fridge door at about head height.

I made my cup of tea, though not in my mug of course, and drank it standing looking out of the kitchen window at the drive, feeling unsettled and nervous, and unsure of what to do with either of those emotions. Even if it had been a dream, it was odd, particularly the way it had fought so hard against melting away. Maybe I was much more tired than I realised. Or maybe I was ill. But I felt fine, physically at least.

I carried the box of catfood into the pantry, unpacked it, and stacked the cans in the corner. Then I switched the kettle on for another cup of tea. Suddenly my heart seemed to stop and before I had time to realise why, the cause repeated itself. A soft chinking noise outside the back door.

I moved quickly to the window and looked out. Nothing. I craned my neck, trying to see round to the back door, but could only see the large pile of firewood that lay to one side of it. The noise again.

Clenching my fists I walked slowly into the back hallway and listened. Silence, except for the sound of blood beating in my ears. My stomach knotting and hands moist with perspiration. Then I grabbed the knob and swung the door open. Stillness. Just a rectangle of late afternoon light, a patch of driveway, a dark hedge waving quietly. I stepped out into the drive.

A very faint crunching noise. And then again. Sounded almost like pebbles rubbing against each other. Again. I looked more closely at the drive, peering at the actual stones, and then noticed that a very small patch about ten yards in front of me appeared to be moving slightly, wriggling, almost. As I watched they stopped, and then the sound came again and another patch, about a yard closer than the first, stirred briefly. As if registering the weight of invisible feet. I was so engrossed that I didn't notice the whistling straight away. When I did, I looked up.

The blond man was back. Standing at the top of the driveway, carrying a bicycle with the wheels slowly spinning in the dusk, whistling the top line of two in perfect harmony, the lower line just the wind. As I stared at him, backing slowly towards the house, the crunching noise got louder and louder and then the suited man was standing with his nose almost touching mine.

"Hello again," he said.

The blond man started down the driveway, smiling.

"Hello again indeed," he said. "Come on, in we go."

Suddenly I realised that the very last thing in the world I should do was let those two back into the house. I leapt through the back door back into the hallway. The suited man, caught by surprise, started forward but I was quick and whipped the door shut in his face and locked it. That felt very good but then he started banging on the door very hard, ridiculously hard, grotesquely hard, and I noticed that to my right the kitchen was getting messy again and the fridge was old and I could barely see out of the window because it was so grimy and a slight flicker made me think that maybe I'd missed the smallest fraction of a second and I realised that it really hadn't been a fucking dream and I was back there, and I was back there because I'd come in through the back door again. As I backed into the kitchen I tripped and fell, sprawling amongst the cartons and bacon rind and the dirt and was that puke, for Christ's sake? The banging on the back door got louder and louder and louder. He was going to break it. He was going to break the fucking door down. I'd let them back and they had to come in through the back door. I'd come in through the wrong door . . .

Suddenly realising what I must do, I scrambled up and lucked my way through the rubbish towards the door to the front hall. The fridge door swung open in my way and the inside was dark and dirty and there was something rotted in there but I slammed it out of the way, biting hard on my lip to keep my head clear. I had to get to the front door, I had to open it, step out, and then step back in again. That was the right door. And I had to do it soon, before the back door broke and let them in. As I ran out of the kitchen into the front hall I could already hear a splintering quality to the sound of the blows. And the back door was about two inches thick.

The hallway was worse than I expected. I came to a halt, at first unable to even see the front door. Then I thought that I must be looking in the wrong direction but I wasn't, because there it was over to the left where it was supposed to be, but the angles were all wrong and to see it I had to look behind me and to the right, although when I saw it I could see that it was still over there to the left. And it looked so close, could it really be less than a yard away, but when I held my hand out to it I groped into nothing, my hand still in front of the door when it should have been past it. I stared wildly around me, disorientated and unsure somehow even of which way to go.

Then the banging behind me got even louder, probably as the blond man joined in, and this helped marginally to restore my sense of direction. I found the door again, concentrated hard on its apparent position and started to walk towards it. I immediately fell over, because the floor was much lower than I expected, and in fact must be tilted in some way as one of my legs reached it easily enough, although it looked flat and level. I pulled myself up onto my knees and found I was looking at a sort of sloped wall between the wall and the ceiling, a wall which bent back from the wall and yet out from the ceiling. And the door was still over there on the left, although to see it I now had to look straight ahead and up.

Then I noticed another sound beneath the eternal banging and whirled round to face the direction it was coming from. I found that I was looking through the living room door and that it gave into sheer darkness, a darkness which was seeping out into the hallway like smoke, clinging to the angles in the air like the inside of a dark prism. I heard the noise again and it was a deep rumbling growling far far away in there, almost obscured by the night noises and the sound of vegetation moving in the wind. It didn't seem to be getting any closer but I knew that was because the living room now extended out far beyond, into hundreds and hundreds of miles of dense forest jungle, and as I listened carefully I could hear the gurgling of some dark river far off to the right, mixing with the warm rustling of the breeze in the darkness. It sounded very peaceful and for a moment I was still, transfixed.

Then the sound of a violently splintering crack wrenched me away and I turned my back on the living room and flailed towards where the front door must be. The hall table loomed above me and I thought I could walk upright beneath it but tripped over it trying and fell again, headlong onto the cool floorboards. The mat had moved, no, was moving, sliding slowly up the stairs like a draft and as I rolled over and looked at the ceiling I saw the floor coming towards me, the walls shortening in little jerks. Another splintering thud and now I had no idea which way was up.

As I lay there panting a clear cool waft of air stroked my cheek. At first I thought that it must have come from the living room, although it had been warm in there, but then I remembered rather than saw that I was lying on the floor and that the breeze must be a draught coming under the front door. I must nearly be there. I looked all around me but all I could see was panelling and floor and what was behind me. I closed my eyes and tried to grope for it but it was even worse inside so I opened them again. Then I caught a glimpse of the door, far away, obscured from view round a comer but visible once you knew where to look. On impulse I reached my hand out in not quite the opposite direction and felt it fall upon warm grainy wood. The door, the bloody door. I'd found the front door.

I pulled myself along the floor towards it and tried to stand up. I got no more than a few inches before I fell back down again. I tried again with the same result, feeling as if I was trying to do something very unnatural and bizarre. Again, and this time I reached a semi-crouching position, muscles straining. I started to slump down again but as I did so I threw myself forwards and found myself curled up, my feet a couple of feet from the floor, lying on the door. Forcing my mind not to even try to come to terms with this I groped by my side and found the doorknob. I tried to twist it but the sweat on my hands made them spin uselessly on the shiny metal. I wiped them on my shirt and tried again and this time I got some purchase and heard the catch withdraw as the knob turned. Exultantly I tugged at it as with a tremendous crash the back door finally gave way.

The door wouldn't budge. Panicking, I tried again. Nothing. By peering down the crack I could see that no lock or bolt was impeding it, so why wouldn't it bloody move?

Footsteps in the back hall. Suddenly I realised that I was lying on the door, and trying to pull it towards me against my own weight. Silly me. The footsteps reached the kitchen.

I rolled over off the door onto the wall beside it and reached for the handle but I'd gone too far. As the footsteps came closer, towards the kitchen door into the hall, I scrambled across the slippery wall, grabbed and twisted the doorknob with all my strength. It opened just as they entered the hall and I rolled out through it, fell and landed awkwardly and painfully on something hard and bristly and for a few moments had no clear idea of where or who I was and just lay there righting for breath.

After some time I sat up slowly. I was sitting on the doormat, my back to the front door. At the top of the drive a passing couple were staring at me curiously. I stood up and smiled, trying to suggest that I often sat there and that they ought to try it as it really was a lot of fun, hoping to God that they hadn't seen me fall there from about two-thirds of the way up the door. They smiled back and carried on walking, mollified or maybe even hurrying off home to try it for themselves, for all I knew. I turned hesitantly back towards the door and looked in.

It had worked. It was all all right again. The mat was on the floor, right angles looked like 90 degrees again and the ceiling was back where it was supposed to be. I stepped back a pace and looked across at the back door. It had been utterly smashed and now looked like little more than an extension of the firewood pile.

I walked back into the hall through the front door, the right door, and shut it behind me. I wandered carefully and quietly into the living room and the kitchen. Everything was fine, everything was normal. Just a nice normal house. If you came in through the right door.

The wrong door was in about a thousand pieces now, of course. I thought about that for some time, with a cup of tea and what felt like my first cigarette in months. Less than an hour had elapsed, I saw with frank disbelief, since I'd first come downstairs.

The wrong door. It was coming in through there that took me to wherever or whatever it was that the house became. Coming in through the front door brought me back to wherever it was that I normally lived. So presumably I was safe so long as I didn't leave the house and come back in through the back door. They couldn't get me.

Presumably. But I didn't like having that door in pieces. The wrong door, the door through which they had to come, was in pieces. Being safe was only part of the problem. I wasn't going to feel *secure* until that portal was well and truly closed. It wasn't precisely clear, however, what I could do about that.

I walked into the back hall and looked nervously out through the wreckage onto the drive. Everything was fine. There was nothing I needed protecting from. But I didn't like it. Did it have to be me who came through it, or what if maybe a falling leaf or even just a soft breeze came inside? Would that be enough? Could I take the risk?

As I stood there indecisively I noticed once more the pile of firewood propped up against the outside wall of the back hall. I probably still wouldn't have thought of it had not a very large proportion of the pile been old thick planks. I looked at the tool shelf on the inside wall and saw a hammer and a big box of good long nails. Then I looked at the wood again.

I could nail the damn thing shut.

I flicked my cigarette butt out onto the drive and rolled up my sleeves. The hammer was big and heavy, which was just as well because when I nailed the planks across the door frame I'd be hammering into solid brickwork. I was going to have to board right the way up but that was all right as there were loads of planks, and if I reinforced it enough it should be well-nigh impregnable. Feeling much better now that I had a way of sealing off the door, I set to work. I may even have hummed.

Kneeling just inside the door, I reached out and began pulling planks in, taking care to select the thickest and least weathered. I judged that I'd need about thirty-five to make the doorway really secured, although that was largely guesswork as I'd never tried to turn the back hall into a fortress before. Getting the planks in was heavy work as I had to stretch out to reach them, and I began to get hot and tired, and anxious to begin the nailing. Outside it was getting darker as the evening began, and the air was very cool and still.

As the pile in the back hall increased in size it became more difficult still, and I had to lean further and further out to reach the next plank, and this made me nervous. I was still inside, my feet were still on the ground in the back hall. I wasn't "coming back in", I was just leaning out and then, well, sort of coming back in but not really, because my feet never left the back hall, did they? But it made me nervous, and I began to work quicker and quicker, perspiration running down my face and arms as, clinging to the doorframe with my left hand, I stretched out to bring the last few boards in. I felt tired and irritated and was dying for a smoke but couldn't take the time: I was anxious to start nailing. Thirty-one, thirty-two, just a couple more. Now the last one I could possibly reach: that would have to be enough. Hooking my left foot behind the frame and gripping it hard with my left hand I stretched out towards the plank, my waving fingers little more than an inch from the end. Just a little further forward: I let my hooking foot slide round slightly, let my fingers slip round half an inch and tried to extend my back as far as it would go. My fingers just scraping the end I tried a last yearning lunge.

And then suddenly a stray thought struck me. Here I was, pulled out as if on some invisible rack: why on earth hadn't I just gone out of the front door, picked up piles of wood and brought them back into the house through the front door? It would have been easier, it would have been quicker, and it wouldn't have involved all this monkeying around at the wrong door. Not that it mattered now, because as it happened even if I didn't get this last plank I'd probably have plenty, but I wouldn't have been so hot and tired and it was also a bit worrying that in my haste I'd been putting myself in needless danger. I'd better slow down, calm down, take a rest.

An unimportant, contemplative thought. But one that distracted me for a fraction of a second too long. As I finally got the tips of my fingers round the plank I realised with horror that my other fingers, the ones on the doorframe, were slipping. I was slowly sliding forwards. Desperately I tried to scrabble with my fingers, but my hands were too sweaty and the doorframe itself was slippery now. I felt the tendons in my hand stretch as I tried to defy my centre of gravity and think my weight backwards, and then suddenly my forehead walloped onto the ground and I was lying flat on my face.

I was up in a second, and I swear to God that both feet never left the hall floor at once. I hurled myself back into the hallway, clutching that last bloody piece of wood without even noticing it.

Panting and almost sobbing with nervous hysteria I crouched in the doorframe, looking out. Everything looked normal. The driveway was quiet, the pebbles were still and there was none of the faint deadening of sound that I associated with the other place. I was furious with myself for having taken the risk, for not having thought to bring them in through the front door, and especially for falling, which had been bloody painful quite apart from anything else. But I hadn't fallen out, not really. I hadn't come back in, as such. The drive was fine, the kitchen was fine. Everything was fine.

Soothed by the sounds of early evening traffic in the distance, my heart gradually slowing down to only about twice its normal rate, I began to feel a bit better and had a quiet cup of tea, perched on the pile of planks. In falling over my right foot had caught the tool shelf and there were nails all over the place, inside and out, but there were plenty left and the ones outside could bloody stay there. I wasn't going to make the same damnfool mistake twice.

Gathering up the hammer and a fistful of nails I laid a plank across the door and started work. Getting the nails through the wood and into the masonry was even harder than I'd expected, but in a couple of minutes it was in place, and felt very solid. I heaved another plank into place and set about securing it. This was actually going to work.

After half an hour I was into the swing of it and the wood now reached almost halfway up the doorframe. My arms aching and head ringing from the hammering, which was very loud in the confined space of the back hall, I had a cigarette leaning on the completed section, staring blankly out onto the drive. I was jolted back from reverie by the realisation that a piece of dust or something must have landed in my eye, slightly distorting my vision, and I blinked to remove it. But it didn't go. It didn't hurt, just made a small patch of the drive up near the road look a bit ruffled. I rubbed and shut both eyes individually and discovered with mounting unease that the distortion was present in both.

I stood upright. Something was definitely going on at the top of the drive. The patch still looked ruffled, as if seen through a heat haze, and whichever way I turned my head it stayed in the same place. It was flickering very slightly now too, like a bad quality film print. But the flecks weren't white, they were dark. I rubbed my eyes hard again, but once I'd stopped seeing stars I saw that the effect was still there, and I stared hard at it, trying to discern something that I could interpret. The flecks seemed to organize into broken and shifting vertical lines as I watched, as if something were hidden behind a curtain of rain, rain so coloured as to make up a picture of that patch of the drive. This impression gradually strengthened until it was like looking at one of those plastic strip "doors", where you walk through the hanging strips. It was as if there was one of those at the top of the drive with a patch of driveway pictured on it in living three dimensions, with something moving just the other side of it.

Then suddenly the balance shifted, like one of those drawings made up of black and white dots where if you stare at it long enough you can see a Dalmatian. I dropped to my knees behind the partially completed barrier. Fear was no longer a word I had any use for. They were back.

Standing at the top of the drive, their images somehow both underlying and superimposed on it as if the two were woven together, were the man in the suit and the blond man. They were standing in a frozen and unnatural position, like a freeze-frame in a very old home movie, their faces pallid and washed out, the colouring uneven, the image flickering and dancing in front of my eyes. And still they stood, not there, and yet in some sense there.

As I stared, transfixed, I noticed that the suited man's foot appeared to be moving. It was hard to focus on, and happening bizarrely slowly, but it was moving, gradually leaving the ground. Then, as over the course of several minutes it was raised and then lowered back onto the ground a couple of feet in front of its original position, leaving the man's body leaning slightly forward, I realised what I was seeing. In extraordinary and flickering slow motion, somehow projected onto the drive, the suited man was beginning to walk down towards the house. Except that the image wasn't flickering so much any more, the colours were stronger, and I could no longer see the driveway through them. Somehow they were coming back through. I thought I'd got away with it, but I hadn't. I'd fallen out. Not very far by anyone's standards, but far enough. Far enough to have come back in through the wrong door. And now they were tearing their way back into the world, or hauling me back towards theirs. And very very slowly they were getting closer.

Fighting to stay calm I grabbed a plank, put it into position above the others and nailed it into place. Then another, and another, not pausing for breath or thought. Through the narrowing gap I could see them getting closer and they didn't look anything like two-dimensional photographs any longer and they were moving quicker now too. Then as I leaned towards the kitchen for a plank I saw that there was a single dusty carton on the floor. It had started.

I smacked another plank into place and hammered it down. The suited man and the blond man were now real again, and they were also much closer, though still moving at a weirdly graceful tenth of normal speed. Hammering wildly now, ignoring increasingly frequent whacks on the fingers, I cast occasional monitoring glances aside into the kitchen. The fridge was beginning to look a bit strange, the stark nineties geometry softening, regressing, and the rubbish was gathering. I never saw any of it arrive, but each time I looked there was another piece of cardboard, a few more scraps, one more layer of grime. It had barely started, and was still happening very slowly, maybe because I'd barely fallen out, but it was happening. The house was going over.

And I kept right on hammering. Obviously what I had to do at some point was run to the front door, go out and come back in again, come in through the right door. But that could wait, would have to wait. It was all developing very slowly this time and I still felt completely clear-headed. What I had to do first was seal off the back door, and soon. The two men, always at the vanguard of the change, were well and truly here, and getting closer all the time. I had to make sure that the back door was secure against anything those two could do to it for long enough for me to get to the front door. I had no idea what the front hall would be like by the time I got there and if I left the back door unfinished and got caught up in the front hall trying to get to the door I'd be in real trouble.

So I slammed planks into place as fast as I could. Outside they got steadily closer and inside another carton appeared in the kitchen. As I jammed the last horizontal board into place the suited man and the blond man were only a couple of yards away, now moving at full pace, and I'd barely nailed it in before the first blow crashed into it, bending it and making me leap back with shock. I hurriedly picked up more wood and started to place planks over the barrier in vertical slats and crosses, nailing them in hard, reinforcing and making sure that they were securely fastened to the wall on all sides, furiously hammering and building. After a while I couldn't feel the ache in my back or see the blood on my hands: all I could hear was the beating of the hammer, and all I could see were the heads of the nails as I piled more and more wood onto the barrier. I had wood to spare–I hadn't even needed that last bloody plank–and by the time I finished it was four planks thick in some places, and the reinforcing strips spread several feet either side of the frame. I used the last three pieces as bracing struts, forcing them horizontally across the hallway, one end of each lodged in niches in the barrier, the other jammed tight against the opposite wall.

Finally it was finished and I stood back and looked at it. It looked pretty damn solid.

"Let's see you get through that then, you bastards," I said quietly, half sitting and half collapsing to the ground.

After a moment I noticed how quiet it was. At some point they must have stopped banging against the door. How long ago I had no idea. I'd been making far too much noise to notice, and my ears were still ringing. I put my ear against the barrier and listened. Silence. I lit a cigarette and let tiredness and a blessed feeling of safeness wash over me. The sound of the match striking was slightly muted, but that could've been the ringing in my ears as much as anything and the kitchen looked pretty grubby but no more than that. And I felt fine.

Vaguely wondering what the two outside were up to, whether there was any chance that they might, not realising that I understood about the right door and the wrong door, have given up and be waiting for the change to take its course, I sat and finished my cigarette, actually savouring the feeling of being balanced between two worlds, secure in the knowledge that in a moment I would just walk out that front door and the house would come back and none of it would matter a damn.

Eventually I stood up. I was really going to ache tomorrow, I thought as I stepped into the kitchen, narrowly avoiding a large black spider that scuttled out of one of the cartons. The floor was getting very messy now, with scraps of dried-up rotted meat covered with the corpses of dead maggots and small piles of stuff I really didn't want to look at too closely. Skirting the rubbish I walked over to the door past the now bizarrely misshapen fridge and into the front hall.

The hallway was still clear, and as far as I could see, utterly normal. As I crossed it towards the front door, anxious now to get the whole thing over with, and wondering how I was going to explain the state of the back door to my family, I noticed a very faint tapping sound in the far distance. After a moment it stopped, and then restarted from a slightly different direction. Odd, but scarcely a primary concern. Right now my priority was getting out of that front door before the hall got any stranger.

Feeling like an actor about to bound onto stage, and looking forward very much to looking out onto the real world, I reached out to the doorknob, twisted it and pulled it towards me, smiling.

At first I couldn't take it in. I couldn't understand why instead of the driveway all I could see was brown. Brown flatness.

Then as I adjusted my focal length, pulling it in for something much closer than the drive I'd been expecting, I began to realise, because the view looked rather familiar. I'd seen something like it very recently.

It was a barrier. An impregnable wooden barrier nailed across the door into the walls from the outside. Now I knew what they'd been doing as I finished nailing them out. They'd been nailing me in.

I tried everything I could think of against that barrier, my fists, my shoulder, a chair. It was there to stay. I couldn't get out. I couldn't come back in through the right door and for the moment they couldn't get in through the wrong door. A sort of stalemate. But a very poor sort for me, because they were much the stronger and getting more so all the time, because the house was still going over and now I couldn't stop it.

I walked into the kitchen, rubbing my bruised shoulder and thinking furiously. There had to be something I could do, and I had to do it fast. The change was speeding up. Although the hall still looked normal the kitchen was now filthy, and the fifties fridge was back. In the background I could still hear the faint tapping noise. Maybe they were trying to get in through the roof.

I had to get out, had to find a way. Come on, lateral thinking. You leave a house by a door. How else? No other way. You always leave by a door. But is there any other way you *could* leave? The doors . . . Christ. The windows. What about the windows? If there was a right door and a wrong door, maybe there were right and wrong windows too, and maybe the right ones looked out onto the real world. Maybe, just maybe, you could smash one and then climb out and then back in again. Maybe that would work.

I had no idea whether it would or not, I wasn't kidding myself that I understood anything, and God alone knew where I might land if I chose the wrong window. Perhaps I'd go out the wrong one and then be chased round the house by the two maniacs outside as I tried to find a right window to break back in through. That would be a barrel of laughs, wouldn't it? That would be just Fun City. But what choice did I have? Through the square window today, children, I thought crazily, and ran into the living room, heading for the big picture window.

I don't know how I could not have made the connection. Maybe because the taps were so quiet. I just stood in the living room, my mouth open. This time they were one jump ahead. They'd boarded up the bloody windows.

I ran into the hall, the dining room, upstairs to the bedrooms. Every single window was boarded up. I knew where they'd got the nails from, I'd spilt more then enough when I fell, but how . . . Then I realised how they'd nailed them in without a hammer, why the tapping had been so quiet. With sudden sickening clarity I found I could imagine the suited man clubbing the nails in with his fists, smashing them in with his forehead and grinning while he did it. Oh Jesus.

I walked downstairs again. Every single window. Even the ones that were too small to climb through. Then as I stood in the kitchen amidst the growing piles, the pounding on the back door started. There was no way I could get out of the house. I couldn't stop it. This time it was going over all the way and taking me with it. And they were going to smash their way in to come along for the ride. To get me. I listened, watching the rubbish, as the pounding got louder and louder.

It's still getting louder, and I can tell from the sound that some of the planks are beginning to give way. The house stopped balancing long ago, and the change is coming on more quickly. The kitchen looks like a bomb site and there are an awful lot of spiders in there now. Eventually I left them to it and came through the hall into here, only making one or two wrong turnings. Into the living room.

And that's where I am now, just sitting and waiting. There is nothing I can do about the change, nothing. I can't get out. I can't stop them getting in.

But there is one thing I can do. I'm going to stay here, in the living room. I can see small shadows now, gathering in comers and darting out from under the chairs, and it's quite dark down by the end wall. The wall itself seems less important now, less substantial, less of a barrier. And I think I can hear the sound of running water somewhere far away, and smell the faintest hint of dark and lush vegetation.

I won't let them get me. I'll wait, in the gathering darkness here in the living room, listening to the coming of the night sounds, feeling a soft breeze on my face and sensing the room opening out as the walls shade away, as I sit here quietly in the dark warm air. And then I'll get up and start walking, walking out into the dark land, into the jungle and amidst the trees that stand all around behind the darkness, smelling the greenness that surrounds me and hearing the gentle river off somewhere to the right. And I'll feel happy walking away into the night, and maybe far away I'll meet whatever makes the growling sounds I begin to hear in the distance and we'll sit together by running water and be at peace in the darkness.

THE MIRACLE MILE

ROBERT R. McCAMMON

"THE MIRACLE MILE" atmospherically sets the scene for Robert McCammon's anthology *Under the Fang,* in which vampires have usurped humans as the dominant race on earth.

McCammon was only 26 years old when his first novel, *Baal,* was published in 1978. Since then he has followed it with a string of commercially successful books including *Bethany's Sin, The Night Boat, They Thirst* (more vampires). *Mystery Walk, Usher's Passing, Swan Song, Stinger, The Wolfs Hour,* and the collection *Blue World and Other Stories.*

More recently he has moved away from the horror genre with the novels *Mine* and *Boy's Life.* However, the following story proves that he has not lost the ability to take what has almost become a genre cliche and turn it into a very effective dystopian nightmare.

THE CAR DIED OUTSIDE PERDIDO BEACH. It was a messy death, a wheeze of oil and a clatter of cylinders, a dark tide spreading across the sun-cracked pavement. When it was over, they sat there for a few minutes saying nothing, just listening to the engine tick and steam, but then the baby began to cry and it came to them that they had to get moving. Kyle got the suitcase, Allie took the bag of groceries in one arm and the baby in the other, Tommy laced up his sneakers and took the thermos of water, and they left the old dead car on the roadside and started walking south to the Gulf.

Kyle checked his watch again. It was almost three o'clock. The sun set late, in midsummer. July heat crushed them, made the sweat ooze from their pores and stick the clothes to their flesh. The road, bordered by pine woods, was deserted. This season there would be no tourists. This season there would be no lights or laughter on the Miracle Mile.

They kept walking, step after step, into the steamy haze of heat. Kyle took the baby for a while, and they stopped for a sip of water and a rest in the shade. Flies buzzed around their faces, drawn to the moisture. Then Kyle said, "I guess we'd better go on," and his wife and son got up again, the baby cradled in Kyle's arm. Around the next curve of the long road they saw a car off in a drainage ditch on the left-hand side. The car's red paint had faded, the tires were flat, and the driver's door was open. Of the car's occupants there was no sign. Allie walked a little closer to Kyle as they passed the car; their arms touched, wet flesh against wet flesh, and Kyle noted she looked straight ahead with that thousand-yard stare he'd seen on his own face as he'd shaved in the mirror this morning at dawn.

"When are we gonna get there?" Tommy asked. He was twelve years old, his patience wearing thin. It occurred to Kyle that Tommy asked that question every year, from his seat in the back of the car:

Hey, Dad, when are we gonna get there?

"Soon," Kyle answered. "It's not far." His stock reply. They'd never walked the last few miles into Perdido Beach, not once in all the many years they'd been coming here for summer vacation. "We ought to see the water pretty soon."

"Hot," Allie said, and she wiped her forehead with the back of her arm. "Hot out here."

Over a hundred, Kyle figured. The sun reflecting off the pavement was brutal. The road shimmered ahead, between the thin pines. A black snake slid across in front of them, and up against the blue, cloudless sky hawks searched for currents. "Soon," Kyle said, and he licked his dry lips. "It's not far at all now."

It was four o'clock when the pine woods fell away and they saw the first wreckage from Hurricane Jolene. A motel with pink walls had most of its roof ripped away. A twisted sign lay in the parking lot amid abandoned cars. Curtains, cigarette butts, deck chairs, and other debris floated in the swimming pool. "Can we get out of the sun for a few minutes?" Allie asked him, and he nodded and led his family toward the pink ruins.

Some of the doors remained, but most of them had been torn from their hinges by the storm. The first unit, without a door, had a bed with a bloodstained sheet and the flies spun above it in a dark, roiling cloud. He opened the door of the next unit, number eight, and they went into a room where the heat had been trapped but the sun and the flies turned away. The room's bed had been stripped to the mattress and a lamp with flamingoes on the shade had been overturned, but it looked safe. He opened the blinds and the windows, and in his inhalation of air he thought he could smell the Gulf's salt. Allie sat down on the bed with the baby and took a squeeze tube of sun block from the grocery bag. She began to paint the infant's face with it, as the baby's pink fingers grasped at the air. Then she covered her own face and arms with the sun block. "I'm already burning," she said, as she worked the stuff into her skin. "I didn't used to burn so fast. Want some?"

"Yeah." The back of Kyle's neck was stinging. He stood over his wife and looked at the baby, as Tommy sprawled on the bed and stared at the ceiling. "She needs a name," Kyle said.

"Hope," Allie answered, and she looked up at her husband with heat-puffed eyes. "Hope would be a good name, don't you think?"

It would be a cruel name, he decided. A name not suited for these times or this world. But saying no would be just as cruel, wouldn't it? He saw how badly Allie wanted it, so he said, "I think that's fine," and as soon as he said it he felt the rage surge in him like a bitter flood tide and he had to turn away before she saw it in his face. The infant couldn't be more than six months old. Why had it fallen to him, to do this thing?

He took the thermos and went into the bathroom, where there was a sink and a shower stall and a tub with a sliding door of smoked plastic. He pulled the blind up and opened the small window in there too, and then he turned on the sink's tap and waited for the rusty water to clear before he refilled the thermos.

Something moved, there in the bathroom. Something moved with a long, slow, and agonized stretching sound.

Kyle looked at the smoked plastic door for a moment, a pulse beating in his skull, and then he reached out and slid it open.

It was lying in the tub. Like a fat cocoon, it was swaddled in bed sheets and tacky beach towels covered with busty cartoon bathing beauties and studs swigging beer. It was impossible to determine where the head and feet were, the arms bound to its sides and the hands hidden. The thing in its shroud of sheets and towels trembled, a hideous involuntary reaction of nerves and muscles, and Kyle thought, *It smells me.*

"Kill it."

He looked back at Allie, who stood in the doorway behind him with the baby in her arms. Her face was emotionless, her eyes vacant as a dreamer's. "Kill it, Kyle," she said. "Please kill it."

"Tom?" he called. He heard his voice crack. "Take your mother outside, will you?" The boy didn't respond, and when Kyle peered out from the bathroom he saw his son sitting up on the bed. Tommy was staring at him, with the same dead eyes as his mother. Tommy's mouth was halfopen, a silver thread of saliva hanging down. "Tom? Listen up!" He said it sharply, and Tommy's gaze cleared. "Go outside with your mother. Do you hear me?"

"Yes sir," Tommy said, and he did as he was told. When he was alone, Kyle opened his suitcase, reached beneath the socks and underwear and found the .38 pistol hidden there. He loaded it from a box of shells, cocked the gun, and walked back into the bathroom where the wrapped-up thing at the bottom of the tub awaited.

Kyle tried to get a grip on the towels and pull them loose, but they were held so tightly they wouldn't give. When he pulled with greater determination, the shape began thrashing back and forth with terrible strength, and Kyle let go and stepped back. The thing's thrashing ceased, and it lay still again. Kyle had once seen one that had grown a hard skin, like a roach. He had seen one with a flat, cobralike head on an elongated neck. Their forms were changing, a riot of evolution gone insane. In these times, in this world, even the fabric of nature had been ripped asunder.

He didn't have time to waste. He aimed the gun at the thing's midsection and squeezed the trigger. The noise of the shots was thunderous in the little bathroom. When he was through shooting, there were six holes in the towels and sheets but no blood.

"Chew on those," Kyle said.

There was a wet, splitting noise. Reddish black liquid soaked the towels and began to stream toward the drain. Kyle thought of a leech that had just burst open. He clenched his teeth, got out of the bathroom and closed the door behind him, and then he put the pistol back into the suitcase and snapped the suitcase shut.

His wife, son, and the baby called Hope were waiting for him, outside in the hot yellow sunshine.

Kyle checked the cars in the motel's parking lot. One had keys in the ignition, though its windshield was shattered. He got in and tried the engine; the dead battery wouldn't even give out a gasp. They started walking again, toward the south, as the sun moved into the west and the afternoon shadows began to gather.

Tommy saw them first: sand dunes rising between the palmettos. He cried out with joy and ran for the beach, where the Gulf's waves rolled up in lathery foam and gulls skimmed the blue water. He took off his sneakers and socks, threw them aside and rushed into the sea, and behind him came his father and mother, footsore and drenched with sweat. Kyle and Allie both took off their shoes and waded into the water, the baby in Allie's arms, and as the waves rolled around them onto the sand Kyle inhaled a chestful of salt air and cleansed his senses. Then he looked down the beach, its crescent curving toward the east, and the motels that stood at the edge of the Gulf.

They were alone.

Gulls darted in, screaming. Two of them fought over a crab that had been flipped onto its back. Broken shells glittered where the sand turned brown and hard. And all along the beach the motels—the blocky violet, sea green, periwinkle, and cream-colored buildings that had stood there since Kyle and Allie were teenagers—were without life, like the structures of an ancient civilization. Hurricane Jolene had done its damage; some of the motels—the Spindrift, the Sea Anchor, the Coral Reef—had been reduced to hulks, their signs battered and dangling, their windows broken out, whole walls washed away. A hundred yards down the beach, a cabin cruiser lay on its side, its hull ripped open like a fish's belly. Where Kyle recalled the sight of a hundred sunbathers tanning on their towels, there was nothing but white emptiness. The lifeguard's station was gone. There was no aroma of coconut-scented tanning butter, no blare of radios, no volleyball games, nobody tossing a Frisbee to a dog in the surf. The gulls strutted around, fat and happy in the absence of humanity.

Kyle had expected this, but the reality gnawed at his heart. He loved this place; he had been young here, had met and courted Allie here. They'd come to Perdido Beach on their honeymoon, sixteen years ago. And they'd come back, every year since. What was summer, without a vacation at the beach? Without sand in your shoes, the sun on your shoulders, the sound of young laughter, and the smell of the Gulf? What was life worth, without such as that?

A hand slid into his.

"We're here," Allie said. She was smiling, but when she kissed him he tasted a tear.

They were going to cook, out in this sun. They needed to find a room. Check in, stow the suitcase and the groceries. Think about the future.

Kyle watched the waves coming in. Tommy went underwater, clothes and all, and rose up sputtering and yelling for the sake of it. Allie's hand squeezed Kyle's, and Kyle thought, *We're standing on the edge of what used to be, and there's nowhere left to run.*

Nowhere.

"I love you," Kyle told his wife, and he drew her tightly against him. He could feel the heat of her skin. She was going to have a bad sunburn. Hope's cheeks were red. Pick up some Solarcaine somewhere. God knows *they* don't need it.

Nowhere.

He walked out of the water. The wet sand sucked around his ankles, trying to hold him, but he broke free and trudged up across the hard sand, leaving footprints all the way to where he'd left his suitcase. Allie was following him, with the red-cheeked Hope. "Tom?" Kyle called. "Tommy, let's go!" The boy splashed and romped for a moment more, gulls spinning around his head either in curiosity or thinking he was a rather large fish, and then Tommy came out of the water and picked up his socks and sneakers.

They began to walk eastward on the beach toward the Miracle Mile. A skeleton lay half-buried in the sand just past the wrecked cabin cruiser. A child's orange pail was caught by the surf, pulled out and thrust onto shore again, the sea playing a game with the dead. The sun was getting lower, the shadows growing. The suitcase was heavy, so Kyle changed hands. The tires of a dune buggy jutted up from the waves, and farther on a body with some flesh on it was drifting in the shallow water. The gulls had been at work; it was not pretty.

Kyle watched his wife, her shadow going before her. The baby began to cry, and Allie gently shushed her. Tommy threw shells into the water, trying to get a skimmer. They had found the infant in a gas station south of Montgomery, Alabama, near nine o'clock this morning. There had been an abandoned station wagon outside at the pumps, and the child had been on the floor in the women's room. On the driver's seat of the station wagon was a great deal of dried blood. Tommy had thought the blotch looked like the state of Texas. There had been dried blood on the doorknob of the women's room too, but what had happened at that gas station was unknown. Was the mother attacked? Had she planned to come back for the baby? Had she crawled off into the woods and died? They'd searched around the gas station, but found no corpses.

Well, life was a mystery, wasn't it? Kyle had agreed to take the baby with them, on their vacation to the beach. But he cursed God for doing this to him, because he'd finally got things right in his soul.

Hope. It had to be a cosmic joke. And if God and the devil were at war over this spinning ball of black sorrows, it was terribly clear who had control of the nuclear weapons.

Biological incident.

That was the first of it. How the government tried to explain. A biological incident, at some kind of secret—up until then—testing center in North Dakota. That was six years ago. The biological incident was worse than they'd let on. They had created something from their stew of gene manipulation and bacteriological tampering that had sent their ten test subjects out into the world with a vengeance. The ten had multiplied into twenty, the twenty to forty, the forty to eighty, and on and on. They had the wrath of Hell in their blood, a contamination that made AIDS look like a common cold. The germ boys had learned how to create—by accident, yes—weapons that walked on two legs. What foreign power were we going to unleash that taint upon? No matter; it had come home to live.

Biological incident.

Kyle shifted the suitcase again. *Call them what they are,* he thought. They craved blood like addicts used to crave heroin and crack. They wrapped themselves up and hid in closets and basements and any hole they could winnow into. Their skin burst and oozed and they split apart at the seams like old suits in the sunlight. Call them what they are, damn it.

They were everywhere now. They had everything. The television networks, the corporations, the advertising agencies, the publishing houses, the banks, the law. Everything. Once in a while a pirate station broke in on the cable, human beings pleading for others not to give up hope. Hope. There it was again, the cosmic joke. Those bastards were as bad as fundamentalist preachers; their role models were Jim Bakker and Jerry Falwell, seen through a dark glass. They wanted to convert everybody on earth, make them see the "truth," and if you didn't choose to join the fold they battered you in like a weak door and chewed the faith into you.

It wasn't just America. It was everywhere: Canada, the Soviet Union, Japan, Germany, Norway, Africa, England, South America, and Spain. Everywhere. The contamination–the "faith"–knew no racial nor national boundaries. It was another cosmic joke, with a hideous twist: The world was moving toward a true brotherhood.

Kyle watched his shadow loom before him, its darkness merging with Allie's. If a man couldn't take a vacation in the sun with his family, he thought, then what the hell good was living?

"Hey, Dad!" Tommy said. "There it is!"

Kyle looked to where his son was pointing. The motel had stucco walls painted pale blue, its roof of red slate. Some of the roof had collapsed, the walls and windows broken. The motel's sign had survived the hurricane, and said THE DRIFTWOOD.

It was where Kyle and Allie had spent their honeymoon, and where they'd stayed–cabana number five, overlooking the Gulf–every summer vacation for sixteen years. "Yes," Kyle answered. "That's the place." He turned his back to the sea and walked toward the concrete steps that led up to the Driftwood, and Allie followed with Hope and the grocery bag. Tommy paused to bend down and examine a jellyfish that had washed up and been caught by the sun at low tide, and then he came on too.

The row of oceanview cabanas had been demolished. Number five was a cavern of debris, its roof caved in. "Watch the glass," Kyle cautioned them, and he continued on around the brackish swimming pool and the deck that caught the afternoon's sea breeze. He climbed another set of stairs from the pool's deck to the major portion of the Driftwood, his wife and son behind him, and he stood facing a warren of collapsed rooms and wreckage.

Summer could be a heartless thing.

For a few seconds he almost lost it. Tears burned his eyes, and he thought he was going to choke on a sob. It had been important, so vitally important, that they come to Perdido Beach again, and see this place where life had been fresh and good and all the days were ahead of them. Now, more than anything, Kyle could see that it was over. But then Allie said, in a terribly cheerful voice, "It's not so bad," and Kyle laughed instead of cried. His laughter spiralled up, was taken by the Gulf breeze and broken like the walls of the Driftwood. "We can stay right here," Allie said, and she walked past her husband into an opening where a door used to be.

The room's walls were cracked, the ceiling blotched with water stains. The furniture—bed, chest of drawers, chairs, lamps, all ticky-tacky when they were new—had been whirled around and smashed to kindling. Pipes stuck up where the sink had been in the bathroom, but the toilet remained and the shower stall—empty of intruders—was all right. Kyle tried the tap and was amazed to hear a rumbling down in the Driftwood's guts. A thin trickle of rusty water flowed from the shower head. Kyle turned the tap off and the rumbling died.

"Clear this stuff away," Allie told Tommy. "Let's get this mattress out from underneath."

"We can't stay here," Kyle said.

"Why can't we?" Her eyes were vacant again. "We can make do. We've been making do at home. We can make do on vacation too."

"No. We've got to find somewhere else."

"We've always stayed at the Driftwood." A childlike petulance rose up in her voice, and she began to rock the baby. "Always. We can stay right here, like we do every summer. Can't we, Tommy?"

"I guess so," he said, and he nudged the shattered television set with his foot.

Kyle and Allie stared at each other. The breeze came in around them through the doorway and then left again.

"We can stay here," Allie said.

She's out of it, he thought. Who could blame her? Her systems were shutting down, a little tighter day after day. "All right." He touched her hair and smoothed it away from her face. "The Driftwood it is."

Tommy went to find a shovel and broom, because there was a lot of glass on the linoleum-tiled floor. As Allie unpacked the groceries, the baby laid to rest on a pillow, Kyle checked the rooms on either side. Nothing sleeping in them, nothing folded up and waiting. He checked as many rooms as he could get into. There was something bad—neither skeleton nor fully fleshed, but bloated and dark as a slug—wearing a flower-print shirt and red shorts in a room nearer the pool, but Kyle could tell it was a dead human being and not one of them. A Gideon's Bible lay close at hand, and also the broken beer bottle with which the sunlover had slashed his wrists. On a countertop, next to the stub of a burned-out candle, was a wallet, some change, and a set of car keys. Kyle didn't look at the wallet, but he took the keys. Then he put the shower curtain over the corpse and continued his search of the Driftwood's rooms. He walked through a breezeway, past the Driftwood's office and to the front of the motel, and there he found a half-dozen cars in the parking lot. Across the street was Nick's Pancake House, its windows blown in. Next to it, the Goofy Golf place and the Go-Kart track, both deserted, their concession stands shuttered and storm ravaged. Kyle began to check the cars, as gulls cried out overhead and sailed in lazy circles.

The keys fit the ignition of a blue Toyota with a Tennessee license tag. Its engine, cranky at first, finally spat black smoke and awakened. The gas gauge's needle was almost to the E, but there were plenty of gas stations on the Strip. Kyle shut the engine off and got out, and that was when he looked toward the Miracle Mile.

It was a beautifully clear afternoon. He could see all the way to the amusement park, where the Ferris wheel and the roller coaster rose up, where the Sky Needle loomed over the Hang Out dance pavilion and the Super Water Slide stood next to the Beach Arcade.

His eyes stung. He heard ghosts on the wind, calling in young voices from the dead world. He had to look away from the Miracle Mile before his heart cracked, and he walked back the way he'd come, the keys gripped in his palm.

Tommy was at work clearing away debris. The mattress had been swept free of glass. A chair had been salvaged, and a table on which a lamp had sat. Allie had put on her swimsuit–the one with aquamarine fish on it that she'd found in a Sears store last week–and she wore sandals so her feet wouldn't be cut. The flesh of her arms and face were blushed with Florida sun. It dawned on Kyle how much weight Allie had lost. She was as skinny as she'd been their first night together, here at the Driftwood a long, long time ago.

"I'm ready for the beach," she told him. "How do I look?" She turned around for him to appreciate the swimsuit.

"Nice. Really nice."

"We shouldn't waste the sunshine, should we?"

She'd had enough sun for one day. But he smiled tightly and said, "No."

Beneath one of the yellow beach umbrellas, Kyle sat beside his wife while she fed Hope from a jar of Gerber's mixed fruit. The groceries had come from a supermarket in the same area they'd found the baby, and Allie had stocked up on items she hadn't even thought about since Tommy was an infant. Out in the Gulf, Tommy splashed and swam as the sun sparkled golden on the waves.

"Don't go too far!" Kyle cautioned, and Tommy waved his *don't worry* wave and swam out a little farther. There was a boy for you, Kyle thought. Always testing his limits. Like me, when I was his age. Kyle lay down on the sand, his hands cupped behind his head. He had been coming to Perdido Beach since he was five years old. One of his first memories was of his father and mother dancing at the pavilion, to "Stardust" or some other old tune. He recalled a day when his father had taken him on every ride on the Miracle Mile: the Ferris wheel, roller coaster, mad mouse, tiltawhirl, scrambler, and octopus. He remembered his father's square brown face and white teeth, clenched in a grin as the mad mouse shot them heavenward. They had feasted on popcorn, cotton candy, candied apples, and corn dogs. They had thrown balls at milk jugs and rings at spindles and come away empty-handed but wiser in the ways of the Miracle Mile.

It had been one of the happiest days of his life.

After Kyle's mother had died of cancer eight years ago, his father had moved out to Arizona to live near his younger brother and his wife. A little over a week past, a midnight call had come from that town in Arizona, and through the static-hissing phone line the voice of Kyle's father had said, *I'm coming to visit you, son. Coming real soon. Me and your uncle Alan and aunt Patti Ann. I feel so much better now, son. My joints don't ache anymore. Oh, it's a wonderful life, this is! I sure do look forward to seeing my sweet grandboy . . .*

They had left their house the next morning and found another house in a town ten miles away. There were still some humans left, in the little towns. But some of them were crazy with terror, and others had made fortresses out of their homes. They put bars on the windows and slept in the daylight, surrounded by guns and barbed wire.

Kyle sat up and watched his son throwing himself against the waves, the glittering water splashing high. He saw himself out there; he hadn't changed so much, but the world had. The rachet gears of God's machine had slipped, and from here on out the territory was treacherous and uncharted.

He had decided he couldn't live behind bars and barbed wire. He couldn't live without the sun, or Perdido Beach in July, or without Tommy and Allie. If those things got hold of him–if they got hold of any of his family–then what would life be? A scuttling in the dark? A moan from gore-wet lips? He couldn't think about this anymore, and he blanked his mind: a trick he'd learned, out of necessity.

He watched his wife feeding the baby. The sight of Allie cradling the child made him needful; the need was on him before he could think about it. Allie was skinny, sure, but she looked good in her new swimsuit, and her hair was light brown and pretty in the reflected sunlight and her gray eyes had the shine of life in them again, for a little while. He said, "Allie?" and when she looked at him she saw the need in his face. He touched her shoulder, and she leaned over and kissed him on the lips. The kiss lingered, grew soft and wet and his tongue found hers. She smiled at him, her eyes hazy, and she put the child down on a beach towel.

Kyle didn't care if Tommy saw. They were beyond the need for privacy. A precious moment could not be turned aside. Kyle and Allie lay together under the yellow umbrella, their bodies damp and entwined, their hearts beating hard, and out in the waves Tommy pretended not to see and went diving for sand dollars. He found ten.

The sun was sinking. It made the Gulf of Mexico turn the color of fire, and way out past the shallows dolphins played.

"It'll be getting dark soon," Kyle said at last. The moon was coming out, a slice of silver against the east's darkening blue. "I've got somebody's car keys. Want to ride up to the Miracle Mile?"

Allie said that would be fine, and she held Hope against her breasts.

The wind had picked up. It blew stinging sand against their legs as they walked across the beach. Tommy stopped to throw a shell. "I got a skimmer, Dad!" he shouted.

In the room, Allie put on a pair of white shorts over her wet suit. Tommy wore a T-shirt with the computer image of a rock band on the front, and baggy orange cutoffs. Kyle dry-shaved with his razor, then dressed in a pair of khaki trousers and a dark blue pullover shirt. As he was lacing up his sneakers, he gave Tommy the car keys. "It's a blue Toyota. Tennessee tag. Why don't you go start her up?"

"You mean it? Really?"

"Why not?"

"Allll *right!*"

"Wait a minute!" Kyle cautioned before Tommy could leave. "Allie, why don't you go with him? I'll be up in a few minutes."

She frowned, reading his mood. "What's wrong?"

"Nothing. I just want to sit here and think. I'll be there by the time you get the car ready."

Allie took the baby, and she and Tommy went around to the parking lot. In the gathering dark, Kyle sat on the mattress and stared at the cracks in the wall. This was their honeymoon motel. It had once seemed like the grandest place on earth. Maybe it still was.

When Kyle opened the Toyota's door and Tommy slid into the back seat, he was wearing his poplin windbreaker, zipped up to his chest. He got behind the wheel, and he said, "Let's go see it."

Theirs was the only car that moved on the long, straight road called the Strip. Kyle turned on the headlights, but it wasn't too dark to see the destruction on either side of them.

"We ate there last summer," Tommy said, and pointed at a heap of rubble that used to be a Pizza Hut. They drove past T-Shirt City, the Shell Shack, and the Dixie Hot Shoppe, where a cook named Pee Wee used to make the best grouper sandwiches Kyle had ever eaten. All those places were dark hulks now. He kept going at a slow, steady speed. "Cruising the Strip," he and his buddies used to call it, when they came looking for girls and good times on spring break. His first roaring drunk was in a motel called the Surf's Inn. His first poker game had been played at Perdido Beach. He'd lost his first real fight behind a bar here, and ended up with a busted nose. He'd met the first girl he'd . . . well, there had been a lot of firsts at Perdido Beach.

God, there were ghosts here.

"Sun's almost gone," Tommy said.

Kyle turned the car to a place where they could watch the sunset over a motel's ruins. It was going down fast, the Gulf streaked with dark gold, orange, and purple. Allie's hand found her husband's; it was the hand with her wedding ring on it. The baby cried a little, and Kyle knew how she felt. The sun went away in a last scarlet flash, and then it was gone toward the other side of the world and the night was closing in.

"It was pretty, wasn't it?" Allie asked. "Sunsets are always so pretty at the beach."

Kyle started driving again, taking them to the Miracle Mile. His heart was beating hard, his palms damp on the wheel. Because there it was, the paradise of his memories. He pulled the car to the side of the road and stopped.

The last of the light glinted on the rails of the roller coaster. The Ferris wheel's cars were losing their paint, and rocked in the strengthening wind. Another casualty of Jolene was the mad mouse's maze of tracks. The long red roof of the Hang Out dance pavilion, the underside of which was painted with Day-Glo stars and comets, had been stripped to the boards, but the open-air building still stood. Within the smashed windows of the Beach Arcade, the pinball machines had been overturned. Metal rods dangled down from the Sky Needle, its foundation cracked. The concession stand that used to sell foot-long hot dogs and flavored snow cones had been flattened. The water slide had survived, though, and so had a few of the other mechanical rides. The merry-go-round—a beauty of carved, leaping lions and proud horses—remained almost unscathed. Fit for the junkyard were the haunted house and hall of mirrors, but the fun house with its entrance through a huge red grin was still there.

"We met here," Allie said. She was talking to Tommy. "Right over there." She pointed toward the roller coaster. "Your father was in line behind me. I was with Carol Akins and Denise McCarthy. When it came time for us to get on, I had to sit with him. I didn't know him. I was sixteen, and he was eighteen. He was staying at the Surf's Inn. That's where all the hoods stayed."

"I wasn't a hood," Kyle said.

"You were what a hood *was* then. You drank and smoked and you were looking for trouble." She stared at the roller coaster, and Kyle watched her face. "We went around four times."

"Five."

"Five," she recalled, and nodded. "The fifth time we rode in the front car. I was so scared I almost wet my pants."

"Aw, Mom!" Tommy said.

"He wrote me a letter. It came a week after I got home. There was sand in the envelope." She smiled, a faint smile, and Kyle had to look somewhere else. "He said he hoped we could see each other again. Do you remember that, Kyle?"

"Like yesterday," he answered.

"I dreamed about the Miracle Mile, for a long time after that. I dreamed we would be together. I was a silly thing when I was sixteen."

"You're still that way," Tommy said.

"Amen," Kyle added.

They sat there for a few more minutes, staring down the darkening length of the Miracle Mile. Many lives had crossed here, many had come and gone, but this place belonged to them. They knew it, in their hearts. It was theirs, forever. Their linked initials cut into a wooden railing of the Hang Out said so. It didn't matter that there might be ten thousand more initials carved in the pavilion; they had returned here, and where were the others?

The wind made the Ferns wheel's cars creak, but otherwise silence reigned. Kyle broke it. "We ought to go to the pier. That's what we ought to do."

The long fishing pier just past the Miracle Mile, where the bait used to be cut and reeled out every hour of the day and night. He and his father used to go fishing there, while his mother stretched out on a folding chair and read the forms from the dog track up the highway.

"I'm going to need some Solarcaine," Allie said as they drove past the Miracle Mile. "My arms are stinging."

"And I'm thirsty," Tommy said. "Can we get something to drink?"

"Sure. We'll find something."

The pier–LONGEST PIER ON THE PANHANDLE, the battered metal sign said–was a half mile past the amusement park. Kyle parked in front of it, in a deserted lot. A soft drink machine stood inside the pier's admission gate, but without electricity it was useless. Tommy got his arm up inside it and grasped a can but he couldn't pull it out. Kyle turned the machine over and tried to break it open. Its lock held, a last grip on civilization.

"Damn," Tommy said, and kicked the machine.

Next door to the pier, across the lot, was the rubble of what had been a seafood restaurant. The sign remained, a swordfish riding a surfboard. "Why don't we try over there?" Kyle asked, placing his hand on his son's shoulder. "Maybe we can find some cans. Allie, we'll be right back."

"I'll go with you."

"No," he said. "You wait on the pier."

Allie stood very still. In the deepening gloom, Kyle could only see the outline of her face. "I want to talk to Tommy," Kyle told her. She didn't move; it seemed to him she was holding her breath. "Man talk," he said.

Silence.

Finally, she spoke. "Come right back. Okay?"

"Okay."

"And don't step on a nail. Be careful. Okay?"

"We will be. Watch where you walk too." He guided Tommy toward the ruins, and the wind shrilled around them.

They were almost there when Tommy asked what he wanted to talk about. "Just some stuff," Kyle answered. He glanced back. Allie was on the pier, facing away from them. Maybe she was looking at the sea, or maybe at the Miracle Mile. It was hard to tell.

"I got too much sun. My neck's burning."

"Oh," Kyle said, "you'll be all right."

The stars were coming out. It was going to be a beautiful night. He kept his hand on Tommy's shoulder, and together they walked into the wreckage beneath the surfing swordfish. They kept going, over glass and planks, until Kyle had the remnant of a cinder block wall between them and Allie.

"Dad, how're we going to find anything in here? It's so dark."

"Hold it. See that? There beside your right foot? Is that a can?"

"I can't see it."

Kyle unzipped his windbreaker. "I think it is." A lump had lodged in his throat, and he could hardly speak. "Can you see it?"

"Where?"

Kyle placed one hand against the top of his son's head. It was perhaps the most difficult movement of flesh and bone he had ever made in his life. "Right there," he said, as he drew the .38 from his waistband with his other hand. *Click.*

"What was that, Dad?"

"You're my good boy," Kyle croaked, and he put the barrel against Tommy's skull.

No. This was the most difficult movement of flesh and bone.

A spasm of his finger on the trigger. A terrible *crack* that left his eardrums ringing.

It was done.

Tommy slid down, and Kyle wiped his hand on the leg of his trousers.

Oh Jesus, he thought. A sense of panic swelled inside him. *Oh Jesus, I should've found him something to drink before I did it.*

He staggered, tripped over a pile of boards and cinder blocks and went down on his knees in the dark, the after sound of the shot still echoing. *My God, he died thirsty. Oh my God, I just killed my son.* He shivered and moaned, sickness burning in his stomach. It came to him that he might have only wounded the boy, and Tommy might be lying there in agony. "Tommy?" he said. "Can you hear me?" No, no; he'd shot the boy right in the back of the head, just as he'd planned. If Tommy wasn't dead, he was dying and he knew nothing. It had been fast and unexpected and Tommy hadn't had a chance to even think about death.

"Forgive me," Kyle whispered, tears streaking down his face. "Please forgive me."

It took him a while to find the strength to stand. He put the pistol away and zipped his windbreaker up again, and then he wiped his face and left the ruins where his son's body lay. Kyle walked toward the pier, where Allie stood with the baby in the deep purple dark.

"Kyle?" she called before he reached her.

"Yes."

"I heard a noise."

"Some glass broke. It's all right."

"Where's Tommy, Kyle?"

"He'll be here in a few minutes," Kyle said, and he stopped in front of her. He could feel the sea moving below him, amid the pier's concrete pilings. "Why don't we walk to the end?"

Allie didn't speak. Hope was sleeping, her head against Allie's shoulder.

Kyle looked up at the sky full of stars and the silver slice of moon. "We used to come out here together. Remember?"

She didn't answer.

"We used to come out and watch the fishermen at night. I asked you to marry me at the end of the pier. Do you remember?"

"Yes." A quiet voice.

"Then when you said yes I jumped off. Remember that?"

"I thought you were crazy," Allie said.

"I was. I am. Always will be."

He saw her tremble, violently. "Tommy?" she called into the night. "Tommy, come on now!"

"Walk with me. All right?"

"I can't . . . I can't . . . think, Kyle. I can't . . ."

Kyle took her hand. Her fingers were cold. "There's nothing to think about. Everything's under control. Do you understand?"

"We can . . . stay right here," she said. "Right here. It's safe here."

"There's only one place that's safe," Kyle said. "It's not here."

"Tommy?" she called, and her voice broke.

"Walk with me. Please." He gripped her hand tighter. She went with him.

Jolene had bitten off the last forty feet of the pier. It ended on a jagged edge, and below them the Gulf surged against the pilings. Kyle put his arm around his wife and kissed her cheek. Her skin was hot and damp. She leaned her head against his shoulder, as Hope's head was against her own. Kyle unzipped his windbreaker.

"It was a good day, wasn't it?" he asked her, and she nodded.

The wind was in their faces, coming in hard off the sea. "I love you," Kyle said.

"I love you," she answered.

"Are you cold?"

"Yes."

He gave her his windbreaker, and zipped it up around her shoulders and the baby. "Look at those stars!" he said. "You can't see so many stars anywhere else but the beach, can you?"

She shook her head.

Kyle kissed her temple and put a bullet into it.

Then he let her go.

Allie and the baby fell off the pier. Kyle watched her body go down and splash into the Gulf. The waves picked her up, closed over her, turned her on her stomach and made her hair float like an opening fan. Kyle looked up at the sky. He took a deep breath, cocked the pistol again and put the barrel into his mouth, pointed upward toward his brain.

God forgive me there is no Hell there is no—

He heard a low humming sound. The noise, he realized, of machinery at work.

Lights came on, a bright shock in the sky. The stars faded. Multicolored reflections scrawled across the moving waves.

Music. The sound of a distant pipe organ.

Kyle turned around, his bones freezing.

The Miracle Mile.

The Miracle Mile was coming to life.

Lights rimmed the Ferris wheel and the roller coaster's rails. Floods glared over the Super Water Slide. The merry-go-round was lit up like a birthday cake. A spotlight had been pointed upward, and combed the night above the Miracle Mile like a call to celebration.

Kyle's finger was on the trigger. He was ready.

The Ferris wheel began to turn: a slow, groaning process. He could see figures in the gondolas. The center track of the roller coaster started moving with a clanking of gears, and then the roller coaster cars were cranked up to the top of the first incline. There were people in the cars. No, not people. Not human beings. Them.

They had taken over the Miracle Mile.

Kyle heard them scream with delight as the roller coaster's cars went over the incline like a long, writhing snake.

The merry-go-round was turning. The pipe organ music, a scratchy recording, was being played from speakers at the carousel's center. Kyle watched the riders going around, and he pulled the pistol's barrel from his mouth. Light bulbs had blinked on in the Hang Out, and now the sound of rock music spilled out from a jukebox. Kyle could see them in the pavilion, a mass of them pressed together and dancing at the edge of the sea.

They had taken everything. The night, the cities, the towns, freedom, the law, the world.

And now the Miracle Mile.

Kyle grinned savagely, as tears ran down his cheeks.

The roller coaster rocketed around. The Ferris wheel was turning faster.

They had hooked up generators, of course, there in the amusement park. They'd gotten gasoline to run the generators from a gas station on the Strip.

You could make bombs out of gasoline and bottles.

Find those generators. Pull the plug on the Miracle Mile.

He had four bullets in the gun. The extras had been in case he screwed up and wounded instead of killed. Four bullets. The car keys had been in the windbreaker. *Sleep well, my darling,* he thought.

I *will be joining you.*

But not yet. Not yet.

Maybe he could find a way to make the roller coaster's cars jump the tracks. Maybe he could blow up the Hang Out, with all of them mashed up together inside. They would make a lovely bonfire, on this starry summer night. He gritted his teeth, his guts full of rage. They might take the world, but they would not take his family. And they would pay for taking the Miracle Mile, if he could do anything about it.

He was insane now. He knew it. But the instant of knowing was pulled away from him like Allie's body in the waves, and he gripped the pistol hard and took the first step back along the pier toward shore.

Careful. Keep to the darkness. Don't let them see you. Don't let them smell you.

Screams and laughter soared over the Miracle Mile, as a solitary figure walked back with a gun in his hand and flames in his mind.

It came to Kyle that his vacation was over.

THE BACCHAE

ELIZABETH HAND

"I THINK I have seldom encountered a story as repulsive as The Bacchae'", wrote a disgruntled reader of *Interzone,* who continued: "It was a vile parade of anti-male hatred, an exhibition of baroque man-killing justified, so it seems, by the crimes of discarded beer cans and a dying fish." He (of course it was a he) concluded, ". . . I hope that you'll never again subject the magazine's readers to similar chuckling depictions of agony (male or female)".

The test of all good horror fiction is for it to have some kind of impact on the reader, and the author of the above letter was obviously greatly disturbed by Elizabeth Hand's story, which is as it should be. She knows what she's doing, as her story "On the Town Route" in *Best New Horror 2* proved.

The author of the novels *Winterlong, Aestival Tide, The Eve of Saint Nynex* and *Waking the Moon,* her short fiction has appeared in numerous magazines and anthologies, including several "Year's Best" collections. Her literary criticism and articles appear regularly in the *Washington Post Book World, Detroit Times* and *Penthouse,* among other publications, and she is a contributing editor to *Reflex* magazine and *Science Fiction Eye.*

As to whether "The Bacchae" is, as our letter writer complained, "nothing more than a snuff movie in prose, heaped with feathers, jewels and furs", we'll leave you to decide . . .

SHE GOT INTO THE ELEVATOR WITH him, the young woman from down the hall, the one he'd last seen at the annual Coop Meeting a week before. Around her shoulders hung something soft that brushed his cheek as Gordon moved aside to let her in: a fur cape, or pelt, or no, something else. The flayed skin of an animal, an animal that when she shouldered past him to the corner of the elevator proved to be her Rottweiler, Leopold. He could smell it now: the honeyed stench of uncured flesh, a pink and scarlet veil still clinging to the pelt's ragged fringe of coarse black hair. It had left a crimson streak down the back of her skirt, and stippled her legs with pink rosettes.

Gordon got off at the next floor and ran all the way down the hall. When he got into his own apartment he locked and chained the door behind him. For several minutes he stood there panting, squinting out the peephole until he saw her turn the corner and head for her door. It still clung to her shoulders, stiff front legs jouncing against the breast of her boiled-wool suit jacket. After the door closed behind her Gordon walked into the kitchen, poured himself a shot of Jameson's, and stood there until the trembling stopped.

Later, after he had changed and poured himself several more glasses of whisky, he saw on the news that the notorious Debbie DeLucia had been found not guilty of the murder of the young man she claimed had assaulted her in a parking garage one evening that summer. The young man had been beaten severely about the face and chest with one of Ms. DeLucia's high-heeled shoes.

When he was found by the parking lot attendant most of his hair was missing. Gordon switched off the television when it displayed photographs of these unpleasantries followed by shots of a throng of cheering women outside the courthouse. That evening he had difficulty falling asleep.

He woke in the middle of the night. Moonlight flooded the room, so brilliant it showed up the tiny pointed feathers poking through his down comforter. Rubbing his eyes Gordon sat up, tugged the comforter around his shoulders against the room's chill. He peered out at a full moon, not silver nor even the sallow gold he had seen on summer nights but a colour he had never glimpsed in the sky before, a fiery bronze tinged with red.

"Jeez," Gordon said to himself, awed. He wondered if this had something to do with the solar shields tearing, the immense satellite-borne sails of mylar and solex that had been set adrift in the atmosphere to protect the cities and farmlands from ultraviolet radiation. But you weren't supposed to be able to see the shields. Certainly Gordon had never noticed any difference in the sky, although his friend Olivia claimed she could tell they were there. Women were more sensitive to these things than men, she had told him with an accusing look. There was a luminous quality to city light that had formerly been sooty and grey at best, and the air now had a russet tinge. Wonderful for outdoor setups—Olivia was a noted food photographer—or would be save for the odd bleeding of colours that appeared during developing, winesap apples touched with violet, a glass of Semillon shot with sparks of emerald, the parchment crust of an aged camembert taking on an unappetizing salmon glow.

It would be the same change in the light that made the moon bleed, Gordon decided. And now he had noticed it, even though he wasn't supposed to be sensitive to these things. What did that he mean, he wondered? Maybe it was better not to notice, or to pretend he had seen nothing, no sanguine moon, no spectral colours in a photograph of a basket of eggs. Strange and sometimes awful things happened to men these days. Gordon had heard of some of these on television, but other tales came from friends, male friends. Near escapes recounted in low voices at the gym or club, random acts of violence spurred by innocent offers of help in carrying groceries, the act of holding a door open suddenly seen as threatening. Women friends, even relatives, sisters and daughters refusing to accompany family on trips to the city. An exodus of wives and children to the suburbs, from the suburbs to the shrinking belts of countryside ringing the megalopolis. And then, husbands and fathers disappearing during weekend visits with the family in exile. Impassive accounts by the next of kin of mislaid directions, trees where there had never been trees before. Evidence of wild animals, wildcats or coyotes perhaps, where nothing larger than a squirrel had been sighted in fifty years.

Gordon laughed at these tales at first. Until now. He pulled a feather from the bed-ticking and stroked his chin thoughtfully before tossing it away. It floated down, a breath of tawny mist. Gordon determinedly pulled the covers over his head and went back to sleep.

He was reading the paper in the kitchen next morning, a detailed account of Ms. DeLucia's trial and a new atrocity. Three women returning late from a nightclub had been harassed by a group of teenage boys, some of them very young. It was one of the young ones the women had killed, turning on the boys with a ferocity the newspaper described as "demonic." Gordon turned to the section that promised full photographic coverage and shuddered. Hastily he put aside the paper and crossed the room to get a second cup of coffee. How could a woman, even three women, be strong enough to do that? He recalled his neighbour down the hall. Christ. He'd take the fire stairs from now on, rather than risk seeing her again. He let his breath out in a low whistle and stirred another spoonful of white powder into his cup.

As he turned to go back to the table he noticed the MESSAGE light blinking on his answering machine. Odd. He hadn't heard the phone ring during the night. He sipped his coffee and played back the tape.

At first he thought there was nothing there. Dead silence, a wrong number. Then he heard faint sounds, a shrill creaking that he recognized as crickets, a katydid's resolute twang, and then the piercing, distant wail of a whippoorwill. It went on for several minutes, all the way to the end of the message tape. Nothing but night sounds, insects and a whippoorwill, once a sharp yapping that, faint as it was, Gordon knew was not a dog but a fox. Then abrupt silence as the tape ended. Gordon started, spilling coffee on his cuff, and swearing rewound the tape while he went to change shirts.

Afterward he played it back. He could hear wind in the trees, leaves pattering as though struck by a soft rain. Had Olivia spent the night in the country? No: they had plans for tonight, and there was no country within a day's drive in any direction from here. She wouldn't have left town on a major shoot without letting him know. He puzzled over it for a long while, playing back the gentle pavane of wind and tiny chiming voices, trying to discern something else there, breathing or muted laughter or a screen door banging shut, anything that might hint at a caller. But there was nothing, nothing but crickets and whippoorwills and a solitary vixen barking at the moon. Finally he left for work.

It was the sort of radiant autumn day when even financial analysts wax rapturous over the colour of the sky–in this case a startling electric blue, so deep and glowing Gordon fancied it might leave his fingers damp if he reached to touch it, like wet canvas. He skipped his lunchtime heave at the gym. Instead he walked down to Lafayette Park, filling his pockets with the polished fruit of horsechestnuts and wondering why it was the leaves no longer turned colours in the fall, only darkened to sear crisps and then clogged the sewers when they fell, a dirty brown porridge.

In the park he sat on a bench. There he ate a stale ersatz croissant and shied chestnuts at the fearless squirrels. A young woman with two small children stood in the middle of a circle of duncoloured grass, sowing crusts of bread among a throng of bobbing pigeons. One of the children pensively chewed a white crescent. She squealed when a dappled white bird flew up at her face, dropped the bread as her mother laughed and took the children's hands, leading them back to the bench across from Gordon's. He smiled, conspiratorially tossed the remains of his lunch onto the grass and watched it disappear beneath a mass of iridescent feathers.

A shadow sped across the ground. For an instant it blotted out the sun and Gordon looked up, startled. He had an impression of something immense, immense and dark and moving very quickly through the bright clear air. He recalled his night-time thoughts, had a delirious flash of insight: it was one of the shields torn loose, a ragged gonfalon of Science's floundering army. The little girl shrieked, not in fear but pure excitement. Gordon stood, ready to run for help; saw the woman, the children's mother, standing opposite him pointing at the grass and shouting something. Beside her the two children watched motionless, the little girl clutching a heel of bread.

In the midst of the feeding pigeons a great bird had landed, mahogany wings beating the air as its brazen feathers flashed and it stabbed, snakelike, at the smaller fowl. Its head was perfectly white, the beak curved and as long as Gordon's hand. Again and again that beak gleamed as it struck ferociously, sending up a cloud of feathers grey and pink and brown as the other birds scattered, wings beating feebly as they tried to escape. As Gordon watched blood pied the snowy feathers of the eagle's neck and breast until it was dappled white and red, then a deeper russet. Finally it glowed deep crimson. Still it would not stop its killing. And it seemed the pigeons could not flee, only fill the air with more urgent twittering and, gradually, silence. No matter how their wings flailed it was as though they were stuck in bird-lime, or one of those fine nets used to protect winter shrubs.

Suddenly the eagle halted, raised its wings protectively over the limp and thrashing forms about its feet. Gordon felt his throat constrict. He had jammed his hands in his pockets and now closed them about the chestnuts there, as though to use them as weapons. Across the grass the woman stood very still. The wind lifted her hair across her face like a banner. She did not brush it away, only stared through it to where the eagle waited, not eating, not moving, its baleful golden eye gazing down at the fluttering ruin of feather and bone.

As her mother stared the little girl broke away, ran to the edge of the ruddy circle where the eagle stood. It had lifted one clawed foot, thick with feathers, and shook it. The girl stopped and gazed at the sanguine bird. Carelessly she tossed away her heel of bread, wiped her hand and bent to pluck a bloodied feather from the ground. She stared at it, marvelling, then pensively touched it to her face and hand. It left a rosy smear across one cheek and wrist and she laughed in delight. She glanced around, first at her mother and brother, then at Gordon.

The eyes she turned to him were ice-blue, wondering but fearless; and absolutely, ruthlessly indifferent.

He told Olivia about it that evening.

"I don't see what's so weird," she said, annoyed. It was intermission of the play they had come to see: Euripides' "The Bacchae" in a new translation. Gordon was unpleasantly conscious of how few men there were at the performance, the audience mostly composed of women in couples or small groups, even a few mothers with children, boys and girls who surely were much too young for this sort of thing. He and Olivia stood outside on the theatre balcony overlooking the river. "Eagles kill things, that's what they're made for."

"But here? In the middle of the city? I mean, where did it come from? I thought they were extinct."

All about them people strolled beneath the sulfurous crimelights, smoking cigarettes, pulling coats tight against the wind, exclaiming at the full moon. Olivia leaned against the railing and stared up at the sky, smiling slightly. She wore ostrich cowboy boots with steel toes and tapped them rhythmically against the cement balcony. "I think you just don't like it when things don't go as you expect them to. Even if it's the way things really are supposed to be. Like an eagle killing pigeons."

He snorted but said nothing. Beside him Olivia tossed her hair back. Thick and lustrous darkbrown hair, like a caracal's pelt, hair that for years had been unfashionably long. Though lately it seemed that more women wore it the way she did, loose and long and artlessly tangled. As she pulled a lock away from her throat he saw something there, a mark upon her shoulder like a bruise or scrape.

"What's that?" he wondered, moving the collar of her jacket so he could see better.

She smiled, arching her neck. "Do you like it?"

He touched her shoulder, wincing. "Jesus, what the hell did you do? Doesn't it hurt?"

"A little." She shrugged, turned so that the jaundiced spotlight struck her shoulder and he could see better. A pattern of small incisions had been sliced into her skin, forming the shape of a crescent, or perhaps a grin. Blood still oozed from a few of the cuts. In the others ink or coloured powder had been rubbed so that the little "moon, if that's what it was, took on the livid shading of a bruise or orchid: violet, verdigris, citron yellow. From each crescent tip hung a gold ring smaller than a teardrop.

"But why?" He suddenly wanted to tear off her jacket and blouse, search the rest of her to see what other scarifications might be hiding there. "Why?"

Olivia smiled, stared out at the river moving in slow streaks of black and orange beneath the sullen moon. "A melted tiger," she said softly.

"What?" The electronic ping of bells signalled the end of intermission. Gordon grasped her elbow, overwhelmed by an abrupt and unfathomable fear. He recalled the moon last night, not crescent but swollen and blood-tinged as the scar on her shoulder. "What did you say?"

A woman passing them turned to stare in disapproval at his shrill voice. Olivia slipped from him as though he were a stranger crowding a subway door. "Come on," she said gently, brushing her hair from her face. She flashed him a smile as she adjusted her blouse to hide the scar. "We'll miss the second act." He followed her without another word.

After the show they walked down by the river. Gordon couldn't shake a burgeoning uneasiness, a feeling he might have called terror were it not that the word seemed one he couldn't apply to his own life, this measured round of clocks and stocks and evenings on the town. But he didn't want to say anything to Olivia, didn't want to upset her; more than anything he didn't want to upset her.

She was flushed with excitement, smoking cigarette after cigarette and tossing each little brand into the moonlit water snaking sluggishly beside them.

"Wonderful, just wonderful! The Post really did it justice, for a change." She stooped to pluck something from the mucky shadows and grimaced in distaste. "Christ. Their fucking beer cans– "

She glared at Gordon as though he had tossed it there. Smiling wanly he took it from her hand and carried it in apology. "I don't know," he began, and stopped. They had almost reached the Memorial Bridge. A path curved up through the tangled grasses toward the roadway, a path choked with dying goldenrod and stunted asters and Queen Anne's Lace that he suspected should not be such a luminous white, almost greenish in the moonlight. Shreds of something silver clung to the stunted limbs of lowgrowing shrubs. The way they fluttered in the cold wind made him think again of the atmospheric shields giving way, leaving the embarrened earth beneath them vulnerable and soft as the inner skin of some smooth green fruit. He squinted, trying to see exactly what it was that trembled from the branches. His companion sighed loudly and pointedly where she waited on the path ahead of him. Gordon turned from the shrubs and walked more quickly to join her.

"We should probably get up on the street," he said a little defensively.

Olivia made a small sound showing annoyance. "I'm tired of goddam streets. It's so peaceful here ..."

He nodded and walked on beside her. A little ways ahead of them the bridge reared overhead, the ancient iron fretwork shedding green and russet flakes like old bark. Its crumbling concrete piers were lost in the blackness beneath the great struts and supports. The river disappeared and then materialized on the other side, black and gold and crimson, the moon's reflection a shimmering arrow across its surface. Gordon shivered a little. It reminded him of the stage set they had just left, all stark blacks and browns and greens. Following a new fashion for realism in the theatre there had been a great deal of stage blood that had fairly swallowed the monolithic pillars and bound the proscenium with bright ribbons.

"I thought it was sort of gruesome," he said at last. He walked slowly now, reluctant to reach the bridge. In his hand the beer can felt gritty and cold, and he thought of tossing it away. "I mean the way the king's own mother killed him. Ugh." The scene had been very explicit. Even though warned by the *Post* critic Gordon had been taken aback. He had to close his eyes once. And then he couldn't block out their voices, the sound of knife ripping flesh (and how had they done that so convincingly?), the women chanting *Evohe! evohe!,* which afterwards Olivia explained as roughly meaning "O ecstasy" or words to that effect. When he asked her how she knew that she gave him a cross look and lit another cigarette.

No wonder the play was so seldom revived. "Don't you think we should go back? I mean, it's not very safe here at night."

"Huh." Olivia had stopped a few feet back. He turned and saw that she didn't seem to have heard him. She squatted at the river's edge, staring intently at something in the water.

"What is it?" He stood behind her, trying to see. The water smelled rank, not the brackish reek of rotting weeds and rich mud but a chemical smell that made his nostrils burn. The ruddy light glinted off Olivia's hair, touched her steel boot-tips with bronze. In the water in front of her a fish swam lethargically on its side, sides striped with scales of brown and yellow. Its mouth gaped open and closed and its gills showed an alarming colour, bright pink like the inside of a wound.

"Ah," Olivia was murmuring. She put her hand into the water and lifted the fish upon it. It curled delicately within her palm, its fins stretching open like a butterfly warming to the sun as the water dripped heavily from her fingers. It took him a moment to realize it had no eyes.

"Poor thing," he said; then added, "I don't think you should touch it, Olivia. I mean, there's something wrong with it– "

"Of course there's something wrong with it!" Olivia spat, so vehemently that he stepped backward. The mud smelled of ammonia where his heels slipped through it. "It's dying, poisoned, everything's been poisoned– "

"Well then for Christ's sake drop it, Olivia, what's the sense in *playing* with it– "

Hissing angrily she slid her hand back through the water. The fish vanished beneath the surface and floated up again a foot away, fins fluttering pathetically. Olivia wiped her hand on her trousers, heedless of the dark stain left upon the silk.

"I wasn't playing with it," she announced coldly, shaking her head so that her jacket slipped to one side and he glimpsed the gold rings glinting from her shoulder. "You don't care, do you, you don't even notice anymore what's happened. There'd be nothing left at all if it was up to people like you– "

He swore in aggravation as she stormed off in the direction of the bridge, then hurried after her. Muck covered his shoes and he stumbled upon another cache of beer cans. When he looked up again he saw Olivia standing at the edge of the bridge's shadow, hands clenched at her sides as she confronted two tall figures.

"Oh fuck," Gordon breathed. He felt sick with apprehension but hurried on, finally ran to stand beside her. "Hey!" he said loudly, pulling at Olivia's arm.

She stood motionless. One of the men held something small and dark at his side, a gun, the other wore a tan trenchcoat and looked calmly back and forth, as though preparing to cross a busy street. Before Gordon could take another breath the second man was shoving at his chest. Gordon shouted and struck at him, his hand flailing harmlessly against the man's coat. His other hand tightened around the beer can and he felt a sudden warm rush of pain as the metal sliced through his palm. He glanced down at his hand, saw blood streaming down his wrist and staining the white cuffs of his shirt. He stared in disbelief, heard a thudding sound and then a moan. Then running, stones rattling down the grassy slope.

The man in the trenchcoat was gone. The other, the man with the gun, lay on the ground at river's edge. Olivia was kicking him in the head, over and over, her boots scraping through the mud and gravel when they missed him and sending up a spume of gritty water. The gun was nowhere to be seen. Olivia paused for an instant. Gordon could hear her breathing heavily, saw her wipe her hands upon her trousers as she had when she freed the dying perch. "Olivia," he whispered. She grunted to herself, not hearing him, not looking; and suddenly he was terrified that she *would* look and see him there watching her. He stepped backwards, and as he did so she glanced up. For an instant she was silhouetted against the glimmering water, her white face spattered with mud, hair a coppery nimbus about her shoulders. Behind her the moon shone brilliantly, and on the opposite shore he could see the glittering lights of the distant airfield. It did not seem that she saw him at all. After a moment she looked down and began to kick again, more powerfully, and this time she would bring her heel back down across the man's back until Gordon could hear a crackling sound. He looked on paralyzed, his good hand squeezing tighter and tighter about the wrist of his bleeding hand as she went on and on and on. One of her steel boot-tips tore through his shoulder and the man screamed. Gordon could see one side of his face caved in like a broken gourd, dark and shining as though water pooled in its ragged hollows. Olivia bent and lifted something dark and heavy from the shallow water. Gordon made a whining noise in his throat and ran away, up the hill to where the crimelights cast wavering shadows through the weeds. Behind him he heard a dull crash and then silence.

A crowd had gathered in front of his apartment building when he finally got there. He shoved a bill at the cab driver and stumbled from the car. "Oh no," he said out loud as the cab drove off, certain the crowd had something to do with Olivia and the man by the river: policemen, reporters, ambulances.

But it didn't have anything to do with that after all. There was music, cheerful music pouring from a player set inside one of the ground floor windows. Suddenly Gordon remembered talk of this at the Coop meeting last week: a party, an opportunity for the tenants to get to know one another. It had been his neighbour's idea, the one with the dog. Someone had strung Christmas lights from another window, and several people had set up barbecues on the gray front lawn. Flames leaped from the grills, making the shadows dance so it was impossible to determine how many people were actually milling about. Quite a few, Gordon thought. He smelled roasting meat, bitter woodsmoke with the unpleasant reek of paint in it—were they burning *furniture?*—and a strange sweetish scent, herbs or perhaps marijuana. The pain in his hand had dulled to a steady throbbing. When he looked down he closed his eyes for a few seconds and grit his teeth. There was so much blood.

"Hi!" a voice cried. He opened his eyes to see the woman from down the hall. She was no longer wearing her Rottweiler, nor the expensively tailored suits she usually favoured. Instead she wore faded jeans and the kind of extravagantly beaded and embroidered tunic Gordon associated with his parents' youth. These and the many jingling chains and jewels that hung from her ears and about her wrists and ankles (she was barefoot, in spite of the cool evening) gave her a gypsy air. In the firelight he could see that her face *sans* makeup was childishly freckled. She looked very young and very happy.

"Mm, hi," Gordon mumbled, moving his bloodsoaked arm from her sight. "A block party." He tried to keep his tone polite but uninterested as he pushed through the crowd of laughing people, but the young woman followed him, grinning.

"Isn't it great? You should come down, bring something to

throw on the grill or something to drink, we're running out of hooch– "

She laughed, raising a heavy crystal wineglass and gulping from it something that was a deep purplish colour and slightly viscous, certainly not wine. When she lowered the goblet he saw there was a small crack along its rim. This had cut the girl's upper lip which spun a slender filament of blood down across her chin. She didn't notice and threw her arm around his shoulders. "Promise you'll come back, mmm? We need more guys so we can *dance* and stuff, there's just never enough guys anymore– "

She whirled away drunkenly, swinging her arms out like a giddy spinning child. Whether purposely or not the goblet flew from her hand and shattered on the broken concrete sidewalk. A cheer went up from the crowd. Someone turned the music up louder. A number of people by the glowing braziers seemed to be dancing as the girl was, drunkenly, merrily, arms outstretched and hair flying. Gordon heard the tinkling report of another glass breaking, then another; then the sharper crash of what might have been a window. He put his face down and fairly ran through the swarm to the front door, which had been propped open with an old stump overgrown with curling ivy. The neatly lettered sign warning against strangers and open doors had been yanked from the doorframe and lay in a twisted mass on the steps inside. Gordon kicked it aside and fled down the hall to the firestairs.

There were people in the stairwell, sitting or lying on the steps in drunken twos and threes. One couple had shed their clothes and stood grunting and heaving in the darkened corner near the fire extinguisher. Gordon averted his eyes, stepping carefully among the others. A small pile of twigs had been ignited on the floor and sweet-smelling smoke trailed upward through the dimness. And other things were scattered upon the steps: branches of fir-trees scenting the air with balsam, sheaves of goldenrod, empty wine bottles. One of these clattered underfoot, nearly tripping him. Gordon looked over his shoulder to see it roll downstairs, bumping the head of a woman passed out near the bottom and then spinning across the floor, finally coming to rest beside the couple in the comer. No one noticed it; no one noticed Gordon as he flung open the door to the fifth floor and ran to his apartment.

He walked numbly through the kitchen. The answering machine blinked. Mechanically he reset it as he passed, paused between the kitchen and living room as the tape began. A sound of wind filled the room, wind and the rustle of many feet in dead leaves. Gordon swallowed, pressed his shaking hands together as the tape played on behind him. The wind grew louder, then softer, swelled and whispered. And all the while he heard beneath the faint staticky recording the ceaseless passage of many feet, and sometimes voices, murmurous and laughing, eerie and wild as the wind itself. The tape ended. The apartment was silent save for the dull insistent clicking of the answering machine begging to be switched off, that and the muffled sound of laughter from outside.

Gordon stepped warily into the next room. He had forgotten to leave a light on. But it was not dark: moonlight flooded the space, glimmering across the dark wooden floor, making the shadowed bulk of armchairs and sofa and electronic equipment seem black and strange and ominous. On the sill of the picture window that covered an entire wall the moonlight gleamed upon one of his treasures, a fish of handblown Venetian glass, hundreds of years old. Its mauve and violet swirls glowed in the milky light, its gaping mouth and crystalline eyes reminding him of the perch he had seen earlier, eyeless, dying. He stepped across the living room and stood there at the window staring down at the glass fish. And suddenly his head hurt, his chest felt heavy and cold. Looking at the glass fish he was filled with a dull puzzling ache, as though he were trying to remember a dream. He pondered how he had come to have such a thing, why it was that this marvel of spun glass and pastel colouring had ever meant more to him than a blind perch struggling through the poisonous river. His hand traced the delicate filigree of its spines. They felt cold, burning cold in the cloudy light spilling through the window,

There was a knock at the door. Gordon started, as though he had been asleep, then crossed the darkened room. Through the peephole he saw Olivia, her hair atangle, a streak of black across one cheek. Her expression was oddly calm and untroubled in the carmine glare of the EXIT light. He tightened his hand about the doorknob, biting his lip against the pain that shot up through his arm as he did so. He wondered dully how she had gotten into the building, then remembered the chaos outside. Anyone could come in; even a woman who had seemingly just kicked a man to death by the polluted river. Perhaps it was like this all across the city, perhaps doors that had been locked since the riots had this evening suddenly sprung open.

"Gordon," Olivia commanded, her voice muffled by the heavy door that separated them. He was not surprised to feel the knob twist beneath his throbbing palm, or see the door swing inward to bump against his toe. Olivia slipped in, and with her a breath of incense-smelling smoke, the muted clamour of voices and laughter and pulsing music.

"Where'd you go?" she asked, smiling. He noticed that behind her the door had not quite closed. He reached to pull it shut but before he could grasp it, she took him by the hand, the one that hurt. Grunting softly with pain he turned from the door to follow her into the living room.

"What's happening?" he whispered. "Olivia, what is it?" Without speaking she pulled him to the floor beside her, still smiling. She pulled his jacket from him, then his shoes and trousers and finally his bloodstained shirt. He reached to remove her blouse but Olivia pushed him away ungently, so that he cried out. As she moved above him his hand began to bleed again, leaving dark petals across her blouse and arms. The pain was so intense that he moaned, tried in vain to slow her but she only tightened her grip about his upper arm, tossing her hair back so that it formed a dark haze against the window's milky light. The blouse slipped from her shoulder and he could see the scars there, the little golden rings against her skin, drops of blood like rain flashing across her throat. Behind her the moon shone, bloated and sanguine. He could hear voices chanting counterpoint to the blood thudding in his temples. It took him a long time to catch his breath afterward. Olivia had bitten him on the shoulder, hard enough to bruise him. The pain coupled with that from his cut hand had suddenly made everything very intense, made him cry out loudly and then fall back hard against the cold floor as Olivia slipped from him. Now only the pain was left. He rubbed his shoulder ruefully. "Olivia? Are you angry?" he asked. She stood impassively in front of the window. The torn blouse had slipped from her shoulder. She had kicked her silk trousers beneath the sofa but pulled her boots back on, and moonlight glinted off the two wicked metal points. She seemed not to have heard him, so he repeated her name softly.

"Mmmm?" she said, distracted. She stared up at the sky, then leaned forward and opened the casement. Cold air flooded the room, and a brighter, colder light as well, as though the glass had ceased to filter out the lunar brilliance. Gordon shivered and groped for his shirt.

"Look at them," whispered Olivia. He got unsteadily to his feet and stood beside her, staring down at the sidewalk. Small figures capered across the broken tarmac, forms made threatening by the lurid glow of myriad bonfires that had sprung up across the dead grey lawn. He heard music too, not music from the radio or stereo but a crude raw sound, thrumming and beating as of metal drums, voices howling and forming words he could not quite make out, an unknown name or phrase—

"Evohe," whispered Olivia. The face she turned to him was white and merciless, her eyes inflamed. *"Evohe."*

"What?" said Gordon. He stepped backwards and stumbled on one of his shoes. When he righted himself and looked up he saw that there were other people in the room, other women, three four six of them, even more it seemed, slipping silently through the door that Olivia had left open behind her. They filled the small apartment with a cloying smell of smoke and burning hair, some of them carrying smoking sticks, others leather pocketbooks or scorched briefcases. He recognized many of them: though their hair was matted and wild, their clothes torn: dresses or suits ripped so that their breasts were exposed and he could see where the flesh had been raked by their own fingernails, leaving long wavering scars like signatures scratched in blood. Two of them were quite young and naked and caressed each other laughing, turning to watch him with sly feral eyes. Several of the older women had golden rings piercing their breasts or the frail web of flesh between their fingers. One traced a cut that ran down her thigh, then lifted her bloodied finger to her lips as though imploring Gordon to keep a secret. He saw another grey-haired woman whom he had greeted often at the newstand where they both purchased the *Wall Street Journal*. She seemingly wore only a furtrimmed camel's-hair coat. Beneath its soft folds Gordon glimpsed an undulating pattern of green and gray and gold. As she approached him she let the coat fall away and he saw a snake encircling her throat, writhing free to slide down between her breasts and then to the floor at Gordon's feet. He shouted and turned to flee.

Olivia was there, Olivia caught him and held him so tightly that for a moment he imagined she was embracing him, imagined the word she repeated was his name, spoken more and more loudly as she held him until he felt the breath being crushed from within his chest. But it was not his name, it was another name, a word like a sigh, like the whisper of a thought coming louder and louder as the others took it up and they were chanting now:

"Evoke, evoke . . ."

As he struggled with Olivia they fell upon him, the woman from the newstand, the girl from down the hall now naked and laughing in a sort of grunting chuckle, the two young girls encircling him with their slender cool arms and giggling as they kissed his cheeks and nipped his ears. Fighting wildly he thrashed until his head was free and he could see beyond them, see the open window behind the writhing web of hair and arms and breasts, the moon blazing now like a mad watchful eye above the burning canyons. He could see shreds of darkness falling from the sky, clouds or rain or wings, and he heard faintly beneath the shrieks and moans and panting voices the wail of sirens all across the city. Then he fell back once more beneath them.

There was a tinkling crash. He had a fleeting glimpse of something mauve and lavender skidding across the floor, then cried out as he rolled to one side and felt the glass shatter beneath him, the slivers of breath-spun fins and gills and tail slicing through his side. He saw Olivia, her face serene, her liquid eyes full of ardour as she turned to the girl beside her and took from her something that gleamed like silver in the moonlight, like pure and icy water, like a spar of broken glass. Gordon started to scream when she knelt between his thighs. Before he fainted he saw against the sky the bloodied fingers of eagle's wings, blotting out the face of a vast triumphant moon.

THE SUICIDE ARTIST

SCOTT EDELMAN

SCOTT EDELMAN'S short fiction and poetry have been published in *The Twilight Zone Magazine, fantasy Book, Amazing Stories, Isaac Asimov's Science Fiction, Eldritch Tales, Weirdbook* and the Necronomicon Press chapbook. *Suicide Art.*

He has also written comic books for both Marvel and DC *(House of Mystery, Weird War Tales, Welcome Back Kotter* etc.) and various television scripts ranging from Saturday morning cartoons for Hanna-Barbera to *Tales from the Darkside.* His novel *The Gift,* published by Space & Time in 1990, was a finalist for a Lambda Literary Award in the category Best Gay SF/Fantasy Novel, and he is currently the founding editor of the magazine *Science Fiction Age,* launched in 1992.

As always, we lead off *Best New Horror* with one of the most powerful stories in the volume. As the author explains: "'The Suicide Artist' comes out of my desire to wrestle with the question not only of 'What is a horror story?' but also the equally important questions '*Why* is a horror story?' and 'What is a horror story for?'

"I have always felt that a story must do more than merely pass the time. It must defend its very existence as well. It must justify itself, and the demands it makes on your time.

"When I read 'The Suicide Artist' aloud at conventions, the audience response is unlike that I receive for anything else I've ever written. Other stories of mine insist on getting mixed emotions out of a group. But no such dichotomies occur with this story. 'The Suicide Artist' receives a singularity of response such as I've never seen before. I dive into the performance, and within a few paragraphs I realise that the room has grown hushed, as if people had become too fearful to breathe. I have considered the audience reaction, and I think I have finally figured out why that happens. It is because they know that the voice of 'The Suicide Artist' is more than a narrator just speaking to some faceless listener. They know that the narrator is speaking to them. "And to you."

I LONG AGO DECIDED THAT NOTHING, *nothing* should Suit a person's life so much as the leaving of it, and the universe has supported me in this notion.

The use of the word "decided" is perhaps inaccurate here. I am very concerned with accuracy, for it is important to me that you understand my story, perceive the reason I am telling it to you, and absorb it with all its exacting nuances. So let me retract the word "decided" right now, and strive henceforth to be more precise in my prose. For can it ever be said that we "decide" to learn the lessons that life, in its hammerlock on our attention, endeavors to teach us?

I was not as old as you might think I would have needed to be to have first learned that central precept. I was at an age when life was still vague, and death itself seemed apocryphal.

Will you listen while I tell you of it? Of course you will. Forgive my disingenuousness in asking, when of your attention I have no doubts.

I was never a social animal. Whether I took that path by personal choice or molded by cosmic design I do not know, and at this point in my life it is far too late to invest much concern in the issue. So entering kindergarten was in itself something of a shock to me. I had never even been inside a nursery school, as mother intended to keep me as far from churches and synagogues for as long as possible, and it seemed as if the only nursery schools she could find were affiliated in some way with a religious institution of one kind or another. Kindergarten, therefore, was my first exposure to peer humanity en masse.

I did not like it. Did you honestly expect that I would?

The short, stout woman who squinted at me through thick glasses was not the only teacher I encountered there. My brother and sister five and six year olds, who were better teachers of knowledge than she, taught me everything I need to know about cruelty and intolerance, about prejudice and insult, about hatred and pride. The lessons were not ones I wished to absorb, but obviously, at that age, I had little control over my attendance. So I went, and I learned.

I did not like the other children very much. I do not understand those who, as children, *did* like other children. To me, they were the ones who with angelic demeanor would deliberately bump into me when I was eating my milk and cookies, who pinched me and punched me, who would share with me only under warning of some undisclosed parental threat, who would not let an accidental sin of mine, such as spilling fingerpaint or coming back from the bathroom with my fly open, go unobserved and unreported if passing it on to the teacher would create a greater entertainment, who turned faces of menace to me and faces of innocence to adults. So when some of the children began to disappear and the parents when gathered together started speaking only in muffled whispers, I did not mind. At the time, I did not understand what was happening. I only knew that to me, a world with one less bully in it was a relief.

During this period, parents were not as lackadaisical as they had once been about being there in the playground waiting for us when school let out. Their faces as they stood by the open gate, puffing on their cigarettes, were no longer calm and happy ones; even I could read the tension. Momma was always early, but then, Momma was early for everything. My childhood had been populated with mad dashes, as if out of fear that if we ever took it slow, life would get away from us. One day, Momma was not there. I watched as all the other kids vanished with their parents. I was eventually left alone in a darkening schoolyard.

You might have thought that there would have been at least one parent who, in his or her concern for the safety of his or her own child, might have spared one iota of that concern for me. I know, years afterward, that is what I thought. I have resigned myself to the fact that it was just another one of my life lessons.

I stood there solitary for about fifteen minutes, holding in my hands a lion mask we had made that day out of a paper plate. While I was staring into the lion's eyes, a man approached and told me that my Momma had asked him to drive me home.

Yes, I know. And it seemed strange even at the time, but then, grownups were grownups, and to be obeyed. I followed him a long way from the school to where he had parked, and then we drove through winding streets I had never seen. During our entire ride, he spoke only once, and then in a soft, breathy voice.

"Your shirt," he said. "It's so ... so white."

When we parked, it was in front of a house unfamiliar to me. He must have noticed a puzzled expression, for he quickly told me that my Momma would not be getting home until later, that she wished me to wait there with him. He took my hand with cold and sweaty fingers, and led me inside. When the door clicked shut behind me, I did not like the sound of it.

You can guess what happened now, can you not? You have heard stories that have begun like this before, are familiar with the overtones, can intuit the direction in which this little incident is heading. Can I not simply leave you to *imagine* the rest, if details are what you require? Do I need to go on? I would rather not, but I know you, so I guess I must, I guess I must.

When, in the center of the room, I turned around at the sound of the locking door, when I saw the man's face in its home base light, stripped of what must have been its previous strained pretense of innocence, I realized that what I had up until then been interpreting in his eyes as levity was really insanity, that what I had been mistaking as nervousness was really desire.

He moved towards me, and I began to fight. I had never been a fighter, though I had been given many opportunities to learn. In the schoolyard, in response to the boys who took great delight in tormenting me, I normally rolled into a ball and waited for them to tire. At that instance, in that house, I intuitively knew that would not suffice. I kicked and punched wildly, only occasionally connecting with flesh as he pulled at my clothing. Buttons popped and cloth tore as I protested, and he had me naked almost before I knew it. He let me go and backed away, the clothing bunched tightly in his hands. Gasping, my nose bloodied, I crawled slowly away from him into a far comer of the room.

"You shouldn't have done that," he said, staring down at a bloodstain on my shirt. "You shouldn't have put up such a fight. Why do they always put up such a fight? Look at it. You've . . . *soiled* it."

"I didn't mean to," I whimpered, able from the tone in which he'd spoken to tell the seriousness of my supposed crime. I looked around the room for a way out, and could see none. I was amazed that I had not earlier noticed the room's bizarre decor. Fear had been clouding my perception, I imagine. The room's only piece of furniture was a small cot, its rumpled sheets stained and yellowed. The door through which we had come was not visible, for it and all four walls of that room were hung with a crazy quilt of shirts and pants and shorts and socks, all small and childlike and delicate. Some were ripped to shreds, some clean but used, some covered with blood, some neat and fresh with creases still showing as if hardly worn at all. At the time I did not understand enough of the world to know what this odd collection might mean.

Now I know, but I try not to think about it.

The man, who I fear I must keep referring to as simply that, "the man," because his name I was never to learn, kept glancing from my clothing to me to my clothing again. His eyes would widen when they sought out the fabric, and I tried to imagine what it was he saw there in its folds. I could not even come close then to describing that look, but these days, I often wonder if it is the same gleam that others find in my eyes. He finally turned from me, muttering, as if I was not there. He sat down on the edge of his bed, and began to ramble in a slurred speech. I shivered and strained to hear each word he said.

"There is so much . . . evil in the world. So much. Only innocence can ward it off, protect me. I can feel it, yes, oh yes, I can feel it. The innocence has been . . . absorbed. This one is a good one. He will help me mend my shield. I can be safe again. I can be. I can be safe."

Repeating himself, he slumped back, and then began to snore. I listened to the ticking of a clock, and made myself count along with it until I had measured out sixty ten times, wanting to be sure that he was really asleep. Once I felt confident about his lack of consciousness, I searched for the door beneath the makeshift curtain, and having found it gently turned the knob. It of course would not open. Did you expect that my travail would end so easily? You know better, don't you? You would not have bothered coming along with me on my journey if that is what you'd calculated, would you? You desire, you need, you must have . . . *more,* mustn't you?

I tiptoed quietly through the house of this man who thought he knew the secret of how to hide from evil. (If he could ask me now, I would tell him what I have learned: that evil cannot hide from evil, or from good.) For all my youth, the inventory I took on my wide-eyed tour was not difficult to interpret. It was as if a gruesome Grimm's fairy tale had suddenly become real before me.

Pots and pans of a slowly simmering stew bubbling on the kitchen burners.

The walls a badly patched tent, sewn together of children's clothes.

In the basement, which I descended into most trepidatiously, deep trenches filled with bones. I prayed they were those of neighborhood cats and dogs, but knew they were not.

I returned upstairs and surveyed the sleeping man. Unconscious as he was, he did present an appearance of innocence, did seem as innocent as he hoped was the cloth which his obsession told him would protect him from whatever unknown evil was his demon. The flesh of his face hung calmly, peacefully, unmolded by his mania, and I could almost believe the man belied his environment. But then I looked down to see my clothing within his slack fingers.

I grasped hold of my collar, and started slowly to pull my shirt from those fingers. If the man's digits jerked or tightened, I would stop my efforts, but as soon as he relaxed again, I would begin once more to pull. I stared at his trembling eyelids while I worked, wondering what dreams raced through his mind. After a span of time that to me seemed longer than my life had been up until then, at last it was in my hands.

I calmly watched him breath (oh how amazed I was at my own calmness), and at that very special moment when, chest concave and mouth wide, he reached for his next breath, I as quickly as I could shoved the fabric into his open mouth and pinched his nostrils closed. His eyes immediately bulged wide, and as he looked at me, I knew he was looking *into me.* I knew what he saw there, and I was afraid of it. I jumped atop him and wrapped my spindly legs about his chest, and amazed myself by holding on tightly as he bucked and tried to knock me from his chest, me, a six year old. Where did my strength come from to be able to steal the life from a grown man, and a lunatic at that? I do not know.

I never know.

Once I was sure that he was dead, I pulled my shirt from his mouth, and the rest of my clothing from his hands. I took them to the bathroom sink, the grout of which was red from the man's madness. There, I carefully washed my clothes. In the kitchen, I found an old iron with which to dry them as I had sometime seen my Momma do.

Momma. As I dressed I thought of Momma, and wondered how it was that she had failed to meet me at our appointed time. She had never failed me before. I hurriedly rummaged through the man's pockets, and found a key, with which I made my escape. I did not take the time to lock the door behind me. I had to get home quickly, to tell Momma ... I was not sure what.

It took many long hours of wandering before I found a street that was familiar to me. I then walked slowly home in a dark that I had never before seen alone. Even after what I had endured, maybe *because* of what I had endured, I took my time, almost blinded by the beauty of the night sky. As I turned the corner onto my street, I saw a police car parked in front of my house, its light flashing soundlessly. I well recall thinking that the lights flashed for me, for my absence. I was wrong.

I have perfect recall for so much else, yet I cannot remember how I reacted when they told me that Momma was dead. I can remember the moment before I learned of that death, and the moment after, but of the moment itself . . .

She died, as I understand it, as she lived, always racing. She had been rushing towards me as if by a pull of gravity, probably after having grown impatient behind a slow moving driver, or perhaps after having been frustrated even earlier behind a long line at the supermarket, and so zoomed forward at the sight of an amber light. She had not deviated from her usual style, only this time she was hit by another car jumping at the first trace of green. One of my great losses is that I do not know what I would have told Momma had we been reunited that night, had I returned home from my detour to discover her sitting pale and worried in our living room. I never had the chance. My father and the other relatives were too lost in their grief to notice anything other than my reappearance itself. They did not act as if anything unusual could have occurred during the absence that prefaced it. They never questioned me about anything that might have happened; perhaps they lacked the imagination.

Momma would have questioned me.

And so it is that up until this day I have told no one about what that dying man saw in my eyes–that (are you ready?) I *enjoyed* his death. Even then, even before my newfound discovery turned to well worn habit, it seemed . . . *apt.* I knew that he deserved his end and his end came in a way which made artistic sense of his life, such as it was, transforming chaos into poetry. And to discover that my mother had been taken from this world with that same sense of correctness, of artistry, of flair, well. . . that taught me a lesson.

I learned how death should be.

And that was a good thing, too, because there seemed to be so much of it.

I haven't yet told you about the rest of my family, and I'm sure you're probably wondering about them. (No? How sad. Yet how typical of you, to be so self-centered. I should have expected it.) I'll have you know that Momma's death affected not just me. It affected the entire family. Dad, oh how Dad did change. And Kate. It affected Kate.

Kate was my older sister by four years, which meant that she was almost ten when Momma died. Once we were down to a familial trinity, the whole chemistry of our house changed. At first, Kate tried to be Momma for both of us, but it didn't work for long. She would cook for us, and play with me, and when Dad would come home from work and sit wet-eyed before the flickering television set, silent to both of us, she would bring him a drink, and massage his temples. She so wanted to make his pain go away. She never seemed to act with as much tenderness to me, but I guess she figured I was too young to have any true pain.

The more she became like Momma to my father, the less she could be a Momma to me.

There came a time when I was awakened by Kate crying late at night. The wall between our rooms was not sufficient to contain her sobbing. My first thought was one of surprise, for Kate had always been a stoic, never one to give in to outward displays of emotion. She hadn't even cried at Momma's funeral. My next thought was fear. For if *Kate* was crying, something was terribly wrong. (Notice that I had not yet learned of the healthy, curative power of tears. I now know that I should have rejoiced at my sister's tears; they were the first sign of true recovery in our home in months.) I slipped from my room into hers quietly.

I had learned to move quietly through the house. I'd *had* to learn that; my survival depended on it. If I became an actual presence in the home, my father would sense me and look up and remember his pain, and I did not want to be the cause of that pain, both because of the way it would make him feel, and the way causing it would make *me* feel. (Guilt is another one of the lessons life teaches us young. It is one I have spent a lifetime, however, trying to forget.) I entered the room without my sister noticing.

She was curled up on one side, facing away from me. Her sheet was wrapped around her, and the moonlight made her bare shoulders gleam with perspiration. Her crying, as I stopped and watched her, grew very quiet. Now and then her body would tremble. Her pajamas were in a pile with her blankets in a far comer of the room. The sheet which enfolded her had been gathered and stuffed between her legs, and the panda bears were stained red. She moaned, and I crept over and lightly placed a hand on her arm to comfort her.

She screamed and spun, flinging me from her. Her eyes were full of hate and fear. As I was babbling apologies, the light clicked on. I covered my eyes with my hands, and squinted through the cracks between my fingers. Dad stood beside me, a towel wrapped around his waist, the dark hair on his chest damp, as if fresh from a shower. I looked from Dad to Kate and back again.

"Go to your room," Dad whispered. I turned to Kate. She nodded.

I went back to my room.

Do I have to make it any plainer? You are an adult, I was a child, do I have to decode it for you? Well, I will not. I refuse.

I grow tired of the explicitness you demand. Can't I just tell you that not long thereafter my father died, and leave it at that? I am a doer, a man of action, not one of your foul storytellers. Can't I just slip ahead past all of this . . . *horror,* and make my point?

No, you will not let me. And I guess ... I guess that if I am to make you see whereof I speak, that part deserves to be told.

Having gone back to my room, I did not simply go to sleep that night. I snuck past my sister's closed door and went back to the house where death had first shown me its bulging face. Though weeks had passed, the door was unlocked, as I had left it. That no one had been there since me I could tell before I entered the room, for the rotting body announced its presence to me before I ever saw it. The man still lay on the bed, his flesh puffy and foul-smelling.

It took me hours, but I ripped down the clothing that lined the living room walls. Neatness scored no points for my purpose. I carried the fabric to the basement and used the swatches to make bundles of the bones. The stew, which had long since congealed in its pots, I took to the bathroom and poured down the drain. In an upstairs bedroom, I found a display cabinet filled with a variety of trinkets: bracelets, some jacks and balls, baseball cards, barrettes, some rolled comic books, a necklace locket with a picture of a dog, a pair of broken glasses. I added these things to my packages. Throughout the night I walked back and forth to our house, secreting what I'd brought with me in our basement.

My task completed, I peered in once more upon my sister. She slept, but from the noises that she made, I could tell her sleep was not a peaceful one.

I punched three buttons on the phone, and whispered briefly to the man who answered.

I tucked into my bed, content.

Later, as the sun was beginning to rise, I was awakened by a loud knock on the door. Out the window I could see a police car parked out front. One policeman was already at our front door while a second moved around towards the back. I stayed in my room, listening to what transpired, acting as an uninvolved audience as my father's voice grew very loud and then quiet again, before seeing him walk off between the two policemen.

I was not to be left alone with him again before his death.

I met with him once in a small room with a large guard, and he seemed very confused, unsure why it was what had happened to him had happened. The guard kept his eyes fixed on my Dad's hands during the entire visit. Dad felt that for him to be there in prison meant there was no justice in the world. I left him with comforting words, but little else. I wonder whether Dad had that look of confusion on him still when he was stabbed to death in the showers by an embezzler bereft with grief who had lost a child to cancer just before coming into custody.

My sister and I were split up between family members, and never spoke about any of the things that had happened. I guess I can understand why she would feel that way. I don't like having to speak of any of it to you.

But you insist, don't you?

You'd have me tell you about all the deaths that followed, about the boy in grade school who would beat me up daily and take my lunch money, about the cigarette executive who pimped for the coffin nails that killed an uncle, about. . .

Never mind. You'd have me tell you about all of them, and the ends they met, each and every one, in extreme and nauseating detail.

But no.

I'd rather talk about you. You, who sit there reading these words, you who *delight* in the reading of these words, when you know as well as I, if you'd only admit the truth about yourself, that there is something oh so wrong with your liking of them.

I know you as well as I know myself.

You are reading these words in a magazine. On its cover is some putrid illustration of a man being tortured, or eaten by monsters, or having rotting flesh fall off his face. Maybe a woman is being raped. Maybe a child is being threatened. Perhaps the picture is crudely drawn. Perhaps it is not.

Maybe you are not holding a flimsy magazine, maybe it is a sturdy book, a handsomely bound volume with gold lettering embossed across its spine.

It does not matter. You have been reading my words, and you have actually, may God forgive you, been *enjoying* them. You have read the other stories before mine, both at this time and for years before, and you have smiled at the most horrible of things.

I have lived these things. This is not a story to me. I must continue living with them forever. If I could trade my life for another's, I would pay any price. And yet you find in yourself the ability to think it is fun to visit with me. You actually consider this a way of having a good time.

You go to movies of this type, with people in pain and buckets of blood. You read novels with rats gnawing still pulsing flesh. You read comic books, rife with mass-produced nightmares.

You discuss these books, these movies, with your friends, as casually as discussing a lunch order. You are the deadly market which creates these horrible demons. Just as illegal narcotics would not be grown if there were no addicts to purchase them, so it is that no miseries would be nurtured in the lonely dark if you were not there to be an audience for them.

And what an enthralled audience you are.

So enthralled, in fact, that as you read these words, you will not hear me creeping up behind you, coming to direct you to your most poetic of ends. Of all the fiends I have known, and I have had the misfortune to know many, there has been none who has so enjoyed the agony of others as have you. For you I have a special plan. I will not tell you of it. It must be a surprise.

Do you think you feel my breath hot on your neck even now, even though I am not yet there? Good. That is how I want it to be, until I come for you. You shall have no peace ever again as you read your morbid fantasies, for you will constantly be thinking, "Is that him yet? Is it time?" The sensation of my breath on your neck will be a constant companion. And when the anticipatory tingle you presently feel is replaced by warm reality, and you start to turn, but do not turn quickly enough, you will realize that yes, everything I have told you is true, your death is right, it is just, this is your correct and proper end.

You disagree? You think your final thoughts when I shortly come for you will be different ones? I don't see how you will possibly be able to deny the aptness of it all. Do you know why?

For you have had the stomach to travel with me so that we find ourselves still together at the end of this tale.

I look forward to meeting you in the flesh.
Soon.

THE MEDUSA

THOMAS LIGOTTI

"THE MOST STARTLING and unexpected discovery since Clive Barker" is how *The Washington Post* described the fiction of Thomas Ligotti. A regular toiler in the small presses for many years, he has recently been turning up in such anthologies as *The Best Horror from Fantasy Tales, Prime Evil, Fine Frights, A Whisper of Blood, The Year's Best Fantasy and Horror* and the previous two volumes of *Best New Horror.*

He has been a featured author in *Weird Tales,* and his recent short fiction has been collected in *Songs of a Dead Dreamer* and *Grimscribe: His Lives and Works.* "The Medusa" is yet another example of Ligotti's oblique and haunting prose . . .

I

BEFORE LEAVING HIS ROOM FOR THE first time in nobody knows how long, Lucian Dregler transcribed a few stray thoughts into his notebook.

> The sinister, the terrible never deceive: the state in which they leave us is always one of enlightenment. And only this condition of vicious insight enables us a full grasp of the world, *all* things considered, just as a frigid melancholy grants us full possession of ourselves.
>
> We may hide from horror only in the heart of horror. Could I be so unique among dreamers, having courted the Medusa—my first and oldest companion—to the exclusion of all others? Would I have her respond to this sweet talk?

Relieved to have these fragments safely on the page rather than in some precarious mental notebook, where they were likely to become smudged or completely effaced, Dregler slipped into a relatively old overcoat, locked the door of his room behind him, and exited down innumerable staircases at the back of his apartment building. A winding series of seldomly travelled streets was his established route to a certain place he now and then frequented, though for time's sake—in order to *waste* it, that is—he chose even more uncommon and chaotic avenues. He was meeting an acquaintance he had not seen in quite a while.

The place was very dark, though no more than in past memory, and much more populated than it first appeared to Dregler's eyes. He paused at the doorway, slowly but unsystematically removing his gloves, while his vision, still exceptional, worked with the faint halos of illumination offered by lamps of tarnished metal, which were spaced so widely along the walls that the light of one lamp seemed barely to link up and propagate that of its neighbour. Gradually, then, the darkness sifted away, revealing the shapes beneath it: a beaming forehead with the glitter of wire-rimmed eyeglasses below, cigarette-holding and beringed fingers lying asleep on a table, shoes of shining leather which ticked lightly against Dregler's own as he now passed cautiously through the room. At the back stood a column of stairs coiling up to another level, which was more an appended platform, a little brow of balcony or a puny pulpit, than what one might call a sub-section of the establishment proper. This level was caged in at its brink with a railing constructed of the same rather wiry and fragile material as the stairway, giving this area the appearance of a makeshift scaffolding. Rather slowly, Dregler ascended the stairs.

"Good evening, Joseph," Dregler said to the man seated at the table beside an unusually tall and narrow window. Joseph Gleer stared for a moment at the old gloves Dregler had tossed onto the table.

"You still have those same old gloves," he replied to the greeting, then lifted his gaze, grinning: "And that overcoat!"

Gleer stood up and the two men shook hands. Then they both sat down and Gleer, indicating the empty glass between them on the table, asked Dregler if he still drank brandy. Dregler nodded, and Gleer said "Coming up" before leaning over the rail a little way and holding out two fingers in view of someone in the shadows below.

"Is this just a sentimental symposium, Joseph?" inquired the now uncoated Dregler.

"In part. Wait until we've got our drinks, so you can properly congratulate me." Dregler nodded again, scanning Gleer's face without any observable upsurge in curiosity. A former colleague from Dregler's teaching days, Gleer had always possessed an open zest for minor intrigues, academic or otherwise, and an addiction to the details of ritual and protocol, anything preformulated and with precedent. He also had a liking for petty secrets, as long as he was among those privy to them. For instance, in discussions—no matter if the subject was philosophy or old films—Gleer took an obvious delight in revealing, usually at some advanced stage of the dispute, that he had quite knowingly supported some treacherously absurd school of thought. His perversity confessed, he would then assist, and even surpass, his opponent in demolishing what was left of his old position, supposedly for the greater glory of disinterested intellects everywhere. But at the same time, Dregler saw perfectly well what Gleer was up to. And though it was not always easy to play into Gleer's hands, it was this secret counter-knowledge that provided Dregler's sole amusement in these mental contests, for

> Nothing that asks for your arguments is worth arguing, just as nothing that solicits your belief is worth believing. The real and the unreal lovingly cohabit *in our terror,* the only "sphere" that matters.

Perhaps secretiveness, then, was the basis of the two men's relationship, a flawed secretiveness in Gleer's case, a consummate one in Dregler's.

Now here he was, Gleer. keeping Dregler in so-called suspense. His eyes, Dregler's, were aimed at the tall narrow window, beyond which were the bare upper branches of an elm that twisted with spectral movements under one of the floodlights fixed high upon the outside walls. But every few moments Dregler glanced at Gleer, whose babylike features were so remarkably unchanged: the cupid's bow lips, the cookie-dough cheeks, the tiny grey eyes now almost buried within the flesh of a face too often screwed up with laughter.

A woman with two glasses on a cork-bottomed tray was standing over the table. While Gleer paid for the drinks, Dregler lifted his and held it in the position of a lazy salute. The woman who had brought the drinks looked briefly and without expression at toastmaster Dregler. Then she went away and Dregler, with false ignorance, said: "To your upcoming or recently passed event, whatever it may be or have been."

"I hope it will be for life this time, thank you, Lucian."

"What is this, *quintus?*"

"*Quartus,* if you don't mind."

"Of course, my memory is as bad as my powers of observation. Actually I was looking for something shining on your finger, when I should have seen the shine of your eyes. No ring, though, from the bride?"

Gleer reached into his open shirt and pulled out a length of neck-chain, dangling at the end of which was a tiny rose-coloured diamond in a plain silver setting.

"Modem innovations," he said neutrally, replacing the chain and stone. "The moderns must have them, I suppose, but marriage is still marriage."

"Here's to the Middle Ages," Dregler said with unashamed weariness.

"And the middle-aged," refrained Gleer.

The men sat in silence for some moments. Dregler's eyes moved once more around that shadowy loft, where a few tables shared the light of a single lamp. Most of its dim glow backfired onto the wall, revealing the concentric coils of the wood's knotty surface. Taking a calm sip of his drink, Dregler waited.

"Lucian," Gleer finally began in a voice so quiet that it was nearly inaudible.

"I'm listening," Dregler assured him.

"I didn't ask you here just to commemorate my marriage. It's been almost a year, you know. Not that that would make any difference to you."

Dregler said nothing, encouraging Gleer with receptive silence.

"Since that time," Gleer continued, "my wife and I have both taken leaves from the university and have been traveling, mostly in Europe and the Mediterranean. We've just returned a few days ago. Would you like another drink? You went through that one rather quickly."

"No, thank you. Please go on," Dregler requested very politely.

After drinking the last of his brandy, Gleer continued. "Lucian, I've never understood your fascination with what you call the Medusa. I'm not sure I care to, though I've never told you that. But through no deliberate efforts of my own, let me emphasize, I think I can further your, I guess you could say, pursuit. You are still interested in the matter, aren't you?"

"Yes, but I'm too poor to affort Peloponnesian jaunts like the one you and your wife have just returned from. Was that what you had in mind?"

"Not at all. You needn't even leave town, which is the strange part, the real beauty of it. It's very complicated how I know what I know. Wait a second. Here, take this."

Gleer now produced an object he had earlier stowed away somewhere in the darkness, laying it on the table. Dregler stared at the book. It was bound in a rust-coloured cloth and the gold lettering across its spine was flaking away. From what Dregler could make out of the remaining fragments of the letters, the title of the book seemed to be: *Electro-Dynamics for the Beginner.*

"What is this supposed to be?" he asked Gleer.

"Only a kind of passport, meaningless in itself. This is going to sound ridiculous–how I know it!–but you want to bring the book to this establishment," said Gleer, placing a business card upon the book's front cover, "and ask the owner how much he'll give you for it. I know you go to these shops all the time. Are you familiar with it?"

"Only vaguely," replied Dregler.

The establishment in question, as the business card read, was *Brother's Books: Dealers in Rare and Antiquarian Books, Libraries and Collections Purchased, Large Stock of Esoteric Sciences and Civil War, No Appointment Needed, Member of Manhattan Society of Philosophical Bookdealers, Benjamin Brothers, Founder and Owner.*

"I'm told that the proprietor of this place knows you by your writings," said Gleer, adding in an ambiguous monotone: "He thinks you're a real philosopher."

Dregler gazed at length at Gleer, his long fingers abstractedly fiddling with the little card. "Are you telling me that the Medusa is supposed to be a book?" he said.

Gleer stared down at the table-top and then looked up. "I'm not telling you anything I do not know for certain, which is not a great deal. As far as I know, it could still be anything you can imagine, and perhaps already have. Of course you can take this imperfect information however you like, as I'm sure you will. If you want to know more than I do, then pay a visit to this bookstore."

"Who told you to tell me this?" Dregler calmly asked.

"You can't ask that, Lucian. Everything falls apart if you do."

"Very well," said Dregler, pulling out his wallet and inserting the business card into it. He stood up and began putting on his coat. "Is that all, then? I don't mean to be rude but– "

"Why should you be any different from the usual? But one more thing I should tell you. Please sit down. Now listen to me. We've known each other a long time, Lucian. And I know how much this means to you. So whatever happens, or doesn't happen, I don't want you to hold me responsible. I've only done what I thought you yourself would want me to do. Well, tell me if I was right."

Dregler stood up again and tucked the book under his arm. "Yes, I suppose. But I'm sure we'll be seeing each other. Good night, Joseph."

"One more drink," offered Gleer.

"No, good night," answered Dregler.

As he started away from the table, Dregler, to his embarrassment, nearly rapped his head against a massive wooden beam which hung hazardously low in the darkness. He glanced back to see if Gleer had noticed this clumsy mishap. And after merely a single drink! But Gleer was looking the other way, gazing out the window at the tangled tendrils of the elm and the livid complexion cast upon it by the floodlights fixed high upon the outside wall.

For some time Dregler thoughtlessly observed the wind-blown trees outside before turning away to stretch out on his bed, which was a few steps from the window of his room. Beside him now was a copy of his first book. *Meditations on the Medusa.* He picked it up and read piecemeal from its pages.

The worshipants of the Medusa, including those who clog pages with "insights" and interpretations such as these, are the most hideous citizens of this earth—and the most numerous. But how many of them *know* themselves as such? Conceivably there may be an inner cult of the Medusa, but then again: who could dwell on the existence of such beings for the length of time necessary to round them up for execution?

It is possible that only the dead are not in league with the Medusa. We, on the other hand, are her allies—but always against ourselves. How does one become her *companion* . . . and live?

We are never in danger of beholding the Medusa. For that to happen she needs our consent. But a far greater disaster awaits those who know the Medusa to be gazing at them and long to reciprocate in kind. What better definition of a marked man: one who "has eyes" for the Medusa, whose eyes have a will and a fate of their own.

Ah, to be a thing without eyes. What a break to be *born* a stone!

Dregler closed the book and then replaced it on one of the shelves across the room. On that overcrowded shelf, leather and cloth pressing against cloth and leather, was a fat notebook stuffed with loose pages. Dregler brought this back to the bed with him and began rummaging through it. Over the years the folder had grown enormously, beginning as a few random memoranda—clippings, photographs, miscellaneous references which Dregler copied out by hand—and expanding into a storehouse of infernal serendipity, a testament of terrible coincidence. And the subject of every entry, major and minor, of this inadvertent encyclopedia was the Medusa herself.

Some of the documents fell into a section marked "Facetious," including a comic book (which Dregler picked off a drugstore rack) that featured the Medusa as a benevolent superheroine who used her hideous powers only on equally hideous foes in a world without beauty. Others belonged under the heading of "Irrelevant," where was placed a three-inch strip from a decades-old sports page lauding the winning season of "Mr *(sic)* Medusa". There was also a meager division of the notebook which had no official designation, but which Dregler could not help regarding as items of "True Horror." Prominent among these was a feature article from a British scandal sheet: a photoless chronicle of a man's year-long suspicion that his wife was periodically possessed by the serpent-headed demon, a senseless little guignol which terminated with the wife's decapitation while she lay sleeping one night and the subsequent incarceration of a madman.

One of the least creditable subclasses of the notebook consisted of pseudo-data taken from the less legitimate propogators of mankind's knowledge: renegade "scientific" journals, occult-anthropology newsletters, and publications of various Centers of sundry "mythic" studies. Contributions to the notebook from periodicals such as *The Excentaur,* a back issue of which Dregler stumbled across in none other than Brother's Books, were collectively categorized as "Medusa and Medusans: Sightings and Material Explanations." An early number of this publication included an article which attributed the birth of the Medusa, and of all life on Earth, to one of many extraterrestrial visitors, for whom this planet has been a sort of truckstop or comfort station en route to other locales in other galactic systems.

All such enlightening finds Dregler relished with a surly joy, especially those proclamations from the high priests of the human mind and soul, who invariably relegated the Medusa to a psychic underworld where she serves as the image par excellence of romantic panic. But unique among the curiosities he cherished was an outburst of prose whose author seemed to follow in Dregler's own footsteps: a man *after his own heart.* "Can we be delivered," this writer rhetorically queried, "from the 'life force' as symbolized by Medusa? Can this energy, if such a thing exists, be put to death, crushed? Can we, in the arena of our being, come stomping out–gladiator-like–net and trident in hand, and, poking and swooping, pricking and swishing, *torment* this soulless and hideous demon into an excruciating madness, and, finally, annihilate it to the thumbs-down delight of our nerves and to our soul's deafening applause?" Unfortunately, however, these words were written in the meanest spirit of sarcasm by a critic who parodically reviewed Dregler's own *Meditations on the Medusa* when it first appeared twenty years earlier.

But Dregler never sought out reviews of his books, and the curious thing, the amazing thing, was that this item, like all the other bulletins and ponderings on the Medusa, had merely fallen into his hands unbidden. (In a dentist's office, of all places.) Though he had read widely in the lore of and commentary on the Medusa, none of the material in his rather haphazard notebook was attained through the normal channels of research. None of it was gained in an official manner, none of it foreseen. In the fewest words, it was all a gift of unforeseen circumstances, strictly unofficial matter.

But what did this prove, exactly, that he continued to be offered these pieces to his puzzle? It proved nothing, exactly or otherwise, and was merely a side-effect of his preoccupation with a single subject. Naturally he would be alert to its intermittent cameos on the stage of daily routine. This was normal. But although these "finds" proved nothing, rationally, they always did suggest more to Dregler's imagination than to his reason, especially when he pored over the collective contents of these archives devoted to his oldest companion.

It was, in fact, a reference to this kind of imagination for which he was now searching as he lay on his bed. And there it was, a paragraph he had once copied in the library from a little yellow book entitled *Things Near and Far.* "There is nothing in the nature of things," the quotation ran, "to prevent a man from seeing a dragon or a griffin, a gorgon or a unicorn. Nobody as a matter of fact has seen a woman whose hair consisted of snakes, nor a horse from whose forehead a horn projected; though very early man probably did see dragons—known to science as pterodactyls—and monsters more improbable than griffins. At any rate, none of these zoological fancies violates the fundamental laws of the intellect; the monsters of heraldry and mythology do not exist, but there is no reason in the nature of things nor in the laws of the mind why they should not exist."

It was therefore in line with the nature of things that Dregler suspended all judgements until he could pay a visit to a certain bookstore.

II

And it was late the following afternoon, emerging from daylong doubts and procrastinations, that Dregler entered a little slot-like shop squeezed between a grey building and a brown one. Nearly within arm's reach of each other, the opposing walls of the shop were solid with books. The higher shelves were all but unreachable except by means of a very tall ladder, and the highest shelves were apparently not intended for access. Back numbers of old magazines—*Blackwoods, The Spectator,* the *London* and *American Mercurys*—were stacked in plump, orderless piles by the front window, their pulpy covers dying in the sunlight. Missing pages from forgotten novels were stuck forever to a patch of floor or curled up in corners. Dregler noted page two hundred and two of *The Second Staircase* at his feet, and he couldn't help feeling a sardonic sympathy for the anonymous pair of eyes confronting an unexpected dead end in the narrative of that old mystery. Then again, he wondered, how many thousands of these volumes had already been browsed for the last time. This included, of course, the one he held in his own hand and for which he now succumbed to a brief and absurd sense of protectiveness. Dregler blamed his friend Gleer for this subtle aspect of what he suspected was a farce of far larger and cruder design.

Sitting behind a low counter in the telescopic distance of the rear of the store, a small and flabby man with wire-rimmed glasses was watching him. When Dregler approached the counter and lay the book upon it, the man—Benjamin Brothers—hopped alertly to his feet.

"Help you?" he asked. The bright tone of his voice was the formal and familiar greeting of an old servant.

Dregler nodded, vaguely recognizing the little man from a previous visit to his store some years ago. He adjusted the book on the counter, simply to draw attention to it, and said: "I don't suppose it was worth my trouble to bring this sort of thing here."

The man smiled politely. "You're correct in that, sir. Old texts like that, worth practically nothing to no one. Now down there in my basement," he said, gesturing toward a narrow doorway, "I've got literally thousands of things like that. Other things too, you know. The *Bookseller's Trade* called it 'Benny's Treasurehouse'. But maybe you're just interested in selling books today."

"Well, it seems that as long as I'm here . . ."

"Help yourself, Dr Dregler," the man said warmly as Dregler started toward the stairway. Hearing his name, Dregler paused and nodded back at the bookdealer; then he proceeded down the stairs.

Dregler now recalled the basement of this store, along with the three lengthy flights of stairs needed to reach its unusual depths. The narrow street-level above was no more than a messy little closet in comparison to the expansive disorder down below: a cavern of clutter, all heaps and mounds, with bulging tiers of bookshelves laid out according to no easily observable scheme. It was a universe constructed solely of the softly jagged brickwork of books. But if the Medusa was a book, how would he ever find it in this chaos? And if it was not, what other definite form could he expect to encounter of a phenomenon which he had avoided precisely defining all these years, one whose most nearly exact emblem was a hideous woman with a head of serpents?

For some time he merely wandered around the crooked aisles and deep niches of the basement. Every so often he took down some book whose appearance caught his interest, unwedging it from an indistinct mass of battered spines and rescuing it before years rooted to the same spot caused its words to mingle with others among the ceaseless volumes of "Benny's Treasurehouse", fusing them all into a bonded babble of senseless, unseen pages. Opening the book, he leaned a threadbare shoulder against the towering, filthy stacks. And after spending very little time in the cloistered desolation of that basement, Dregler found himself yawning openly and scratching himself unconsciously, as if he were secluded in some personal sanctum.

But suddenly he became aware of this assumption of privacy which had instilled itself in him, and the feeling instantly perished, perhaps because he suspected its deception. Now his sense of a secure isolation was replaced, at all levels of creaturely response, by its opposite. For hadn't he written that "personal well-being serves solely to excavate within your soul a chasm which waits to be filled by a landslide of dread, an empty mould whose peculiar dimensions will one day manufacture the shapes of your *unique* terror."

Whether or not it was the case, Dregler felt that he was no longer, or perhaps never had been, alone in the chaotic treasurehouse. But he continued acting as if he were, omitting only the yawns and the scratchings. Long ago he had discovered that a mild flush of panic was a condition capable, in certain strange and unknown ways, of *seasoning one's* more tedious moments. So he did not immediately attempt to discourage this probably delusory sensation. However, like any state dependent upon the play of delicate and unfathomable forces, Dregler's mood or intuition was subject to unexpected metamorphoses.

And when Dregler's mood or intuition passed into a new phase, his surroundings followed close behind: both he and the treasurehouse simultaneously crossed the boundary which divides playful panics from those of a more lethal nature. But this is not to say that one kind of apprehension was more excusable than the other; they were equally opposed to the likings of logic. ("Regarding dread, intensity in itself is no assurance of validity.") So it meant nothing, necessarily, that the twisting aisles of books appeared to be tightening around the suspicious bibliophile, that the shelves now looked more conspicuously over-swollen with their soft and musty stock, that faint shufflings and shadows seemed to be frolicking like a fugue through the dust and dimness of the underground treasurehouse. Could he, as he turned the next corner, be led to see that which should not be seen?

The next corner, as it happened, was the kind one enters rather than turns—a cul-de-sac of bookshelves forming three walls which nearly reached the rafters of the ceiling. Dregler found himself facing the rear wall like a bad schoolboy in punishment. He gazed up and down its height as if contemplating whether or not it was real, pondering if one could simply pass through it once one had conquered the illusion of its solidity. Just as he was about to turn and abandon this nook, something lightly brushed against his left shoulder. With involuntary suddenness he pivoted in this direction, only to feel the same airy caress now squarely across his back. Continuing counterclockwise, he executed one full revolution until he was standing and staring at someone who was standing and staring, back at him from the exact spot where he, a mere moment before, had been standing.

The woman's high-heeled boots put her face at the same level as his, while her turban-like hat made her appear somewhat taller. It was fastened on the right side, Dregler's left, with a metal clasp studded with watery pink stones. From beneath her hat a few strands of straw-coloured hair sprouted onto a triangle of unwrinkled forehead.

Then a pair of tinted eyeglasses, then a pair of unlipsticked lips, and finally a high-collared coat which descended as a dark, elegant cylinder down to her boots. She calmly withdrew a pad of paper from one of her pockets, tore off the top page, and presented it to Dregler.

"Sorry if I startled you," it said.

After reading the note, Dregler looked up at the woman and saw that she was gently chopping her hand against her neck, but only a few times and merely to indicate some vocal disability. Laryngitis? wondered Dregler, or something chronic. He examined the note once again and observed the name, address, and telephone number of a company that serviced furnaces and air-conditioners. This, of course, told him nothing.

The woman then tore off a second pre-written message from the pad and pressed it into Dregler's already paper-filled palm smiling at him very deliberately as she did so. (How he wanted to see what her eyes were doing!) She shook his hand a little before taking away hers and making a silent, scentless exit. So what was that reek Dregler detected in the air when he stared down at the note, which simply read: "Regarding M."

And below this word-and-a-half message was an address, and below that was a specified time on the following day. The handwriting was nicely formed, the most attractive Dregler had ever seen.

In light of the past few days, Dregler almost expected to find still another note waiting for him when he returned home. It was folded in half and stuffed underneath the door to his apartment. "Dear Lucian," it began, "just when you think things have reached their limit of ridiculousness, they become more ridiculous still. In brief–we've been had! Both of us. And by my wife, no less, along with a friend of hers. (A blond-haired anthropology prof whom I think you may know, or know of; at any rate she knows you, or at least your writings, maybe both.) I'll explain the whole thing when we meet, which I'm afraid won't be until my wife and I get back from another jaunt. (Eyeing some more islands, this time in the Pacific.)

"I was hoping that you would be skeptical enough not to go to the bookstore, but after finding you not at home I feared the worst. Hope you didn't have your hopes up, which I don't think has ever happened to you anyway. No harm done, in any case. The girls explained to me that it was a quasi-scientific hoax they were perpetrating, a recondite practical joke. If you think you were taken in, you can't imagine how I was. You can't believe how real and serious they made the whole ruse seem to me. But if you got as far as the bookstore, you know by now that the punch line to the joke was a pretty weak one. The whole point, as I was told, was merely to stir your interest just enough to get you to perform some mildly ridiculous act. I'm curious to know how Mr B. Bros. reacted when the distinguished author of *Meditations on the Medusa* and other ruminative volumes presented him with a hopelessly worthless old textbook.

"Seriously, I hope it caused you no embarrassment, and both of us, all *three* of us, apologize for wasting your time. See you soon, tanned and pacified by a South Sea Eden. And we have plans for making the whole thing up to you, that's a promise." The note was signed, of course, by Joseph Gleer.

But Gleer's confession, though it was evident to Dregler that he himself believed it, was no more convincing than his "lead" on a Bookstore Medusa. Because this lead, which Dregler had not credited for a moment, led further than Gleer, who no longer credited it, had knowledge of. So it seemed that while his friend had now been placated by a false illumination, Dregler was left to suffer alone the effects of a true state of unknowing. And whoever was behind this hoax, be it a true one or a false, knew the minds of both men very well.

Dregler took all the notes he had received that day, paper-clipped them together, and put them into a new section of his massive scrap-book. He tentatively labelled this section: "Personal Confrontations with the Medusa, Either Real or Apparent."

III

The address given to Dregler the day before was not too far for him to walk, restive peripatetic that he was. But for some reason he felt rather fatigued that morning; so he hired a taxi to speed him across a drizzle-darkened city. Settling into the spacious dilapidation of the taxi's back seat, he took note of a few things. Why, he wondered, were the driver's glasses, which every so often filled the rear-view mirror, even darker than the day? Did she make a practice of thus "admiring" all her passengers? And was this back-seat debris—the "L"-shaped cigarette butt on the door's armrest, the black apple core on the floor—supposed to serve as objects of *their* admiration? Dregler questioned a dozen other things about this routine ride, this drenched day, and the city outside where umbrellas multiplied like mushrooms in the greyness; and he was now satisfied with his lack of a sense of well-being. Earlier he was concerned that his flow of responses that day would not be those of a man who was possibly about to confront the Medusa. He was apprehensive that he might look on this ride and its destination with lively excitement or as an adventure of some kind; in brief, he feared that his attitude would prove, to a certain extent, to be one of insanity. To be sane, he held, was either to be sedated by melancholy or activated by hysteria, two responses which are "always and equally warranted for those of *sound* insight." All others were irrational, merely symptoms of imaginations left idle, of memories out of work. And above these mundane responses, the only elevation allowable, the only valid transcendence, was a sardonic one: a bliss that annihilated the visible universe with jeers of dark joy, a *mindful* ecstasy. Anything else in the way of "mysticism" was a sign of deviation or distraction, and a heresy to the obvious.

The taxi turned onto a block of wetted brownstones, stopping before a tiny streetside lawn overhung by the skeletal branches of two baby birch trees. Dregler paid the driver, who expressed no gratitude whatever for the tip, and walked quickly through the drizzle toward a golden-bricked building with black numbers—two-o-two—above a black door with a brass knob and knocker. Reviewing the information on the crumpled piece of paper he took from his pocket, Dregler pressed the glowing bell-button. There was no one else in sight along the street, its trees and pavement fragrantly damp.

The door opened and Dregler stepped swiftly inside. A shabbily dressed man of indefinite age closed the door behind him, then asked in a cordially nondescript voice: "Dregler?" He nodded in reply. After a few reactionless moments the man moved past Dregler, waving once for him to follow down the ground-floor hallway. They stopped at a door that was directly beneath the main stairway leading to the upper floors. "In here," said the man, placing his hand upon the doorknob. Dregler noticed the ring, its rosewater stone and silver band, and the disjunction between the man's otherwise dour appearance and this comparatively striking piece of jewelry. The man pushed open the door and, without entering the room, flipped a light-switch on the inside wall.

To all appearances it was an ordinary storeroom cluttered with a variety of objects. "Make yourself comfortable," the man said as he indicated to Dregler the way into the room. "Leave whenever you like, just close the door behind you."

Dregler gave a quick look around the room. "Isn't there anything else," he asked meekly, as if he were the stupidest student of the class. "This is it, then?" he persisted in a quieter, more dignified voice.

"This is it," the man echoed softly. Then he slowly closed the door, and from inside Dregler could hear the footsteps walking back down the hallway and up the staircase above the room.

The room was an average understairs niche, and its ceiling tapered downward into a smooth slant where angular steps ascended upward on the other side. Elsewhere its outline was obscure, confused by huge bedsheets shaped like lamps or tables or small horses; heaps of rocking chairs and baby-chairs and other items of broken furniture; bandaged hoses that drooped like dead pythons from hooks on the walls; animal cages whose doors hung open on a single hinge; old paint cans and pale tarps speckled like an egg; and a dusty light fixture that cast a grey haze over everything.

Somehow there was not a variety of smells imperfectly mingled in the room, each telling the tale of its origin, but only a single smell pieced like a puzzle out of many: its complete image was dark as the shadows in a cave and writhing in a dozen directions over curving walls. Dregler gazed around the room, picked up some small object and immediately set it down again because his hands were trembling. He found himself a solid carton of something to sit on, kept his eyes open, and waited.

Afterward he couldn't remember how long he had stayed in the room, though he did manage to store up every nuance of the eventless vigil for later use in his voluntary and involuntary dreams. (They were compiled into that increasingly useful section marked "Personal Confrontations with the Medusa", a section that was fleshing itself out as a zone swirling with red shapes and a hundred hissing voices.) Dregler recalled vividly, however, that he left the room in a state of panic after catching a glimpse of himself in an old mirror that had a hairline fracture slithering up its center. On his way out he lost his breath when he felt himself being pulled back into the room. But it was only a loose thread from his overcoat that had gotten caught in the door. It finally snapped cleanly off and he was free to go, his heart livened with dread.

And he never let on to his friends what a success that afternoon had been for him, not that he could have explained it to them in any practical way even if he desired to. As promised, they did make up for any inconvenience or embarrassment Dregler might have suffered as a result of, in Gleer's words, the "bookstore incident". The three of them held a party in Dregler's honor, and he finally met Gleer's new wife and her accomplice in the "hoax". (It became apparent to Dregler that no one, least of all himself, would admit it had gone further than that.) Dregler was left alone with this woman for only a brief time, and in the corner of a crowded room. While each of them knew of the other's work, this seemed to be the first time they had personally met. Nonetheless, they both confessed to a feeling of their prior acquaintance without being able, or willing, to substantiate its origins. And although plenty of mutually known parties were established, they failed to find any direct link between the two of them.

"Maybe you were a student of mine," Dregler suggested.

She smiled and said: "Thank you, Lucian, but I'm not as young as you seem to think."

Then she was jostled from behind ("Whoops," said a tipsy academic), and something she had been fiddling with in her hand ended up in Dregler's drink. It turned the clear bubbling beverage into a glassful of liquid rose-light.

"I'm so sorry. Let me get you another," she said, and then disappeared into the crowd.

Dregler fished the earring out of the glass and stole away with it before she had a chance to return with a fresh drink. Later in his room he placed it in a small box, which he labelled: "Treasures of the Medusa."

But there was nothing he could prove and he knew it.

IV

It was not many years later that Dregler was out on one of his now famous walks around the city. Since the bookstore incident, he had added several new titles to his works, and these had somehow gained him the faithful and fascinated audience of readers that had previously eluded him. Prior to his "discovery" he had been accorded only a distant interest in critical and popular circles alike, but now every little habit of his, not the least of all his daily meanderings, had been turned by commentators into "typifying traits" and "defining quirks". "Dregler's walks," stated one article, "are a constitutional of the modern mind, urban journeys by a tortured Ulysses *sans* Ithaca." Another article offered this back-cover superlative: "the most baroque inheritor of Existentialism's obsessions."

But whatever fatuosities they may have inspired, his recent books—*A Bouquet of Worms, Banquet for Spiders,* and *New Meditations on the Medusa*—had enabled him to "grip the minds of a dying generation and pass on to them his pain". These words were written, rather uncharacteristically, by Joseph Gleer in a highly favourable review of *New Meditations* for a philosophical quarterly. He probably thought they might revive his friendship with his old colleague, but Dregler never acknowledged Gleer's effort, nor the repeated invitations to join his wife and him for some get-together or other. What else could Dregler do? Whether Gleer knew it or not, he was now one of them. And so was Dregler, though his saving virtue was an awareness of this disturbing fact. And this was part of his pain.

"We can only live by leaving our 'soul' in the hands of the Medusa," Dregler wrote in *New Meditations*. "Whether she is an angel or a gargoyle is not the point. Each merely allows us a gruesome diversion from some ultimate catastrophe which would turn us to stone; each is a mask hiding the *worst* visage, a medicine that numbs the mind. And the Medusa will see to it that we are protected, sealing our eyelids closed with the gluey spittle of her snakes, while their bodies elongate and slither past our lips to devour us *from the inside.* This is what we must never witness, except in the imagination, where it is a charming sight. And in the word, no less than in the mind, the Medusa fascinates much more than she appalls, and haunts us just *this side* of petrification. On the other side is the unthinkable, the unheard-of, that-which-should-not-be: hence, the Real. This is what throttles our souls with a hundred fingers–somewhere, perhaps in that dim room which caused us to forget ourselves, that place where we left ourselves behind amid shadows and strange sounds–while our minds and words toy, like playful, stupid pets, with *diversions* of an immeasurable disaster. The tragedy is that we must steer so close in order to avoid this hazard. *We may hide from horror only in the heart of horror."*

Now Dregler had reached the outermost point of his daily walk, the point at which he usually turned and made his way back to his apartment, that *other* room. He gazed at the black door with the brass knob and knocker, glancing away to the street's porchlights and lofty bay windows which were glowing like mad in the late dusk. From bluish streetlights hung downward domes: inverted halos or open eyes. Then, for the first time in the history of these excursions, a light rain began to sprinkle down, nothing very troublesome. But in the next moment Dregler had already sought shelter in the welcoming brownstone.

He soon came to stand before the door of the room, keeping his hands deep in the pockets of his overcoat and away from temptation. Nothing had changed, he noticed, nothing at all. The door had not been opened by anyone since he had last closed it behind him on that hectic day years ago. And there was the proof, as he knew, somehow, it would be: that long thread from his coat still dangled from where it had been caught between door and frame. Now there was no question about what he would do.

It was to be a quick peek through a hand-wide crack, but enough to risk disillusionment and the dispersal of all the charming traumas he had articulated in his brain and books, scattering them like those peculiar shadows he supposed lingered in that room. And the voices, would he hear that hissing which heralded her presence as much as the flitting red shapes? He kept his eyes fixed upon his hand on the doorknob as it nudged open the door. So the first thing he saw was the way it, his hand, took on a rosy dawn-like glow, then a deeper twilight crimson as it was bathed more directly by the odd illumination within the room.

There was no need to reach in and flick the lightswitch just inside. He could see quite enough as his vision, still exceptional, was further aided by the way a certain cracked mirror was positioned, giving his eyes a reflected entrance into the dim depths of the room. And in the depths of the mirror? A split-image, something fractured by a thread-like chasm that oozed up a viscous red glow. There was a man in the mirror; no, not a man but a mannikin, or a frozen figure of some kind. It was naked and rigid, leaning against a wall of clutter, its arms outstretching and reaching behind, as if trying to break a backwards fall. Its head was also thrown back, almost broken-necked; its eyes were pressed shut into a pair of well-sealed creases, two ocular wrinkles which had taken the place of the sockets themselves. And its mouth gaped so widely with a soundless scream that all wrinkles had been smoothed away from that part of the old face.

He barely recognized this face, this naked and paralyzed form which he had all but forgotten, except as a lurid figure of speech he once used to describe the uncanny condition of his soul. But it was no longer a charming image of the imagination. Reflection had given it charm, made it acceptable to sanity, just as reflection had made those snakes, and the one who wore them, picturesque and not petrifying. But no amount of reflection could have conceived seeing the thing itself, nor the state of being stone.

The serpents were moving now, coiling themselves about the ankles and wrists, the neck; stealthily entering the screaming man's mouth and prying at his eyes. Deep in the mirror opened another pair of eyes the color of wine-mixed water, and through a dark tangled mass they glared. The eyes met his, but not in a mirror. And the mouth was screaming, but made no sound. Finally, he was reunited, in the worst possible way, with the thing within the room.

Stiff inside of stone now, he heard himself think. *Where is the world, my words?* No longer any world, any words, there would only be that narrow room and himself and the oldest companion of his soul. Nothing other than that would exist for him, could exist, nor, in fact, had ever existed. In its own rose-tinted heart, his horror had at last found him.

THE DEPARTED

CLIVE BARKER

SINCE THE PUBLICATION of his ground-breaking sextet of *Books of Blood* collections (1984-5), Clive Barker has produced very little short fiction, prefering to concentrate on such novels as *The Damnation Game, Weaveworld, The Hellhound Heart, Cabal, The Great and Secret Show, Imajica, The Thief of Always* and *Everville.*

However, he did find time to contribute "Lost Souls" to *Time Out,* "Coming to Grief to *Good Housekeeping,* and "On Amen's Shore" to *Demons and Deviants.* The atmospheric ghost story published here originally appeared under the title "Hermione and the Moon" in the *New York Times* the day before Hallowe'en 1992, and it was reprinted the following day under its present title in Britain's *The Guardian Weekend* magazine.

More recently, Barker was executive producer on the movies *Hellraiser III: Hell on Earth* (1992), *Candyman* (1992, based on his story "The Forbidden"), and a feature-length animated adaptation of his bestselling Young Adult novel *The Thief of Always.*

Eclipse is continuing the series of handsome graphic novels based on his stories, he has created the concepts for a "Barkerverse" of new titles from Marvel Comics *(Hyperkind, Hokum and Hex, Ecktokid* and *Saint Sinner),* and New York's Bess Cutler Gallery mounted an extensive exhibition of his paintings and drawings in 1993. There have also been a number of recent stage productions based on his fiction.

With all the above and more happening, perhaps it is not so surprising that Barker rarely gets the rime nowadays to write short stories. But he hasn't turned his back on them, or on the macabre, as the following proves . . .

IT WAS NOT ONLY PAINTERS WHO were connoisseurs of light, Hermione had come to learn in the three days since her death; so too were those obliged to shun it. She was a member of that fretful clan now–a phantom in the world of flesh–and if she hoped to linger here for long she would have to avoid the sun's gift as scrupulously as a celibate avoided sin, and for much the same reason. It tainted, corrupted, and finally drove the soul into the embrace of extinction.

She wasn't so unhappy to be dead; life had been no bowl of cherries. She had failed at love, failed at marriage, failed at friendship, failed at motherhood. That last stung the sharpest. If she could have plunged back into life to change one thing she would have left the broken romances in pieces and gone to her six-year-old son Finn to say: trust your dreams, and take the world lightly, for it means nothing, even in the losing. She had shared these ruminations with one person only. His name was Rice; an ethereal nomad like herself who had died wasted and crazed from the plague but was now in death returned to corpulence and wit. Together they had spent that third day behind the blinds of his shunned apartment, listening to the babble of the street and exchanging tit-bits. Towards evening, conversation turned to the subject of light.

"I don't see why the sun hurts us and the moon doesn't," Hermione reasoned. "The moon's reflected sunlight, isn't it?"

"Don't be so logical," Rice replied, "or so damn serious."

"And the stars are little suns. Why doesn't starlight hurt us?"

"I never liked looking at the stars," Rice replied. "They always made me feel lonely. Especially towards the end. I'd look up and see all that empty immensity and ..." He caught himself in mid-sentence. "Damn you, woman, listen to me! We're going to have to get out of here and party."

She drifted to the window.

"Down there?" she said.

"Down there."

"Will they see us?"

"Not if we go naked."

She glanced round at him. He was starting to unbutton his shirt.

"I can see you perfectly well," she told him.

"But you're dead, darling. The living have a lot more trouble." He tugged off his shirt and joined her at the window. "Shall we dare the dusk?" he asked her, and without waiting for a reply, raised the blind. There was just enough power in the light to give them both a pleasant buzz.

"I could get addicted to this," Hermione said, taking off her dress and letting the remnants of the day graze her breasts and belly.

"Now you're talking," said Rice. "Shall we take the air?"

All Hallows' Eve was a day away, a night away, and every shop along Main Street carried some sign of the season. A flight of paper witches here; a cardboard skeleton there.

"Contemptible," Rice remarked as they passed a nest of rubber bats. "We should protest."

"It's just a little fun," Hermione said.

"It's our holiday, darling. The Feast of the Dead. I feel like . . . like Jesus at a Sunday sermon. How dare they simplify me this way?" He slammed his phantom fists against the glass. It shook, and the remote din of his blow reached the ears of a passing family, all of whom looked towards the rattling window, saw nothing, and—trusting their eyes—moved on down the street.

Hermione gazed after them.

"I want to go and see Finn," she said.

"Not wise," Rice replied.

"Screw wise," she said. "I want to see him."

Rice already knew better than to attempt persuasion, so up the hill they went, towards her sister Elaine's house, where she assumed the boy had lodged since her passing.

"There's something you should know," Rice said as they climbed. "About being dead."

"Go on."

"It's difficult to explain. But it's no accident we feel safe under the moon. We're like the moon. Reflecting the light of something living; something that loves us. Does that make any sense?"

"Not much."

"Then it's probably the truth."

She stopped her ascent and turned to him. "Is this meant as a warning of some kind?" she asked.

"Would it matter if it were?"

"Not much."

He grinned. "I was the same. A warning was always an invitation."

"End of discussion."

There were lamps burning in every room of Elaine's house, as if to keep the night and all it concealed at bay.

How sad, Hermione thought, to live in fear of shadows. But then didn't the day now hold as many terrors for her as night did for Elaine? Finally, it seemed, after 31 years of troubled sisterhood, the mirrors they had always held up to each other—

fogged until this moment—were clear. Regret touched her, that she had not better known this lonely woman whom she had so resented for her lack of empathy.

"Stay here," she told Rice. "I want to see them on my own."

Rice shook his head. "I'm not missing this," he replied, and followed her up the path, then across the lawn towards the dining room window.

From inside came not two voices but three: a woman, a boy, and a man whose timbre was so recognisable it stopped Hermione in her invisible tracks.

"Thomas," she said.

"Your ex?" Rice murmured.

She nodded. "I hadn't expected ..."

"You'd have preferred him not to come and mourn you?"

"That doesn't sound like mourning to me," she replied.

Nor did it. The closer to the window they trod, the more merriment they heard. Thomas was cracking jokes, and Finn and Elaine were lapping up his performance.

"He's such a clown!" Hermione said. "Just listen to him."

They had reached the sill now, and peered in. It was worse than she'd expected. Them had Finn on his knee, his arms wrapped around the child. He was whispering something in the boy's ear, and as he did so a grin appeared on Finn's face.

Hermione could not remember ever being seized by such contrary feelings. She was as glad not to find her sweet Finn weeping—tears did not belong on that guileless face. But did he have to be quite so content; quite so forgetful of her passing? And as to Them the clown, how could he so quickly have found his way back into his son's affections, having been an absentee father for five years? What bribes had he used to win back Finn's favour, master of empty promises that he was?

"Can we go trick-or-treating tomorrow night?" the boy was asking.

"Sure we can, partner," Thomas replied. "We'll get you a mask and a cape and . . ."

"You too," Finn replied. "You have to come too."

"Anything you want. . ."

"Son of a bitch," Hermione said.

". . . from now on ..."

"He never even wrote to the boy while I was alive."

". . . anything you want."

"Maybe he's feeling guilty," Rice suggested.

"Guilty?" she hissed, clawing at the glass, longing to have her fingers at Thomas's lying throat. "He doesn't know the meaning of the word."

Her voice had risen in pitch and volume, and Elaine—who had always been so insensitive to nuance—seemed to hear its echo. She rose from the table, turning her troubled gaze towards the window.

"Come away," Rice said, taking hold of Hermione's arm. "Or this is going to end badly."

"I don't care," she said.

Her sister was crossing to the window now, and Thomas was sliding Finn off his knee, rising as he did so, a question on his lips.

"There's somebody . . . watching us," Elaine murmured. There was fear in her voice.

Thomas came to her side; slipped his arm around her waist.

Hermione expelled what she thought was a shuddering sigh, but at the sound of it the window shattered, a hail of glass driving man, woman and child back from the sill.

"Away!" Rice demanded, and this time she conceded; went with him, across the lawn, out into the street, through the benighted town and finally home to the cold apartment where she could weep out the rage and frustration she felt.

Her tears had not dried by dawn; nor even by noon. She wept for too many reasons, and for nothing at all. For Finn, for Thomas, for the fear in her sister's eyes; and for the terrible absence of sense in everything. At last, however, her unhappiness found a salve.

"I want to touch him one last time," she told Rice.

"Finn?"

"Of course Finn."

"You'll scare the bejeezus out of him."

"He'll never know it's me."

She had a plan. If she was invisible when naked, then she would clothe every part of herself, and put on a mask, and find him in the streets, playing trick-or-treat. She would smooth his fine hair with her palm, or lay her fingers on his lips, then be gone, forever, out of the twin states of living death and Idaho.

"I'm warning you," she told Rice, "you shouldn't come."

"Thanks for the invitation," he replied a little ruefully. "I accept."

His clothes had been boxed and awaited removal. They untaped the boxes, and dressed in motley. The cardboard they tore up and shaped into crude masks—horns for her, elfin ears for him. By the time they were ready for the streets All Hallows' Eve had settled on the town.

It was Hermione who led the way back towards Elaine's house, but she set a leisurely pace. Inevitable meetings did not have to be hurried to; and she was quite certain she would encounter Finn if she simply let instinct lead her.

There were children at every comer, dressed for the business of the night. Ghouls, zombies and fiends every one; freed to be cruel by mask and darkness, as she was freed to be loving, one last time, and then away.

"Here he comes," she heard Rice say, but she'd already recognised Finn's jaunty step.

"You distract Thom," she told Rice.

"My pleasure," came the reply, and the revenant was away from her side in an instant. Thom saw him coming, and sensed something awry. He reached to snatch hold of Finn, but Rice pitched himself against the solid body, his ether forceful enough to throw Thom to the ground.

He let out a ripe curse, and rising the next instant, snatched hold of his assailant. He might have landed a blow but that he caught sight of Hermione as she closed on Finn, and instead turned and snatched at her mask.

It came away in his hands, and the sight of her face drew from him a shout of horror. He retreated a step; then another.

"Jesus . . . Jesus ..." he said.

She advanced upon him, Rice's warning ringing in her head.

"What do you see?" she demanded.

By way of reply he heaved up his dinner in the gutter.

"He sees decay," Rice said. "He sees rot."

"Mow?"

She heard Finn's voice behind her; felt his little hand tug at her sleeve. "Mom, is that you?"

Now it was she who let out a cry of distress; she who trembled.

"Mom?" he said again.

She wanted so much to turn; to touch his hair, his cheek; to kiss him goodbye. But Thom had seen rot in her. Perhaps the child would see the same, or worse.

"Turn round," he begged.

"I . . . can't . . . Finn."

"Please."

And before she could stop herself, she was turning, her hands dropping from her face.

The boy squinted. Then he smiled.

"You're so *bright,*" he said.

"I am?"

She seemed to see her radiance in his eyes; touching his cheeks, his lips, his brow as lovingly as any hand. So this was what it felt like to be a moon, she thought; to reflect a living light. It was a fine condition.

"Finn . . .?"

Thom was summoning the boy to his side. "He's frightened of you," Finn explained. "I know. I'd better go." The boy nodded gravely.

"Will you explain to him?" she asked Finn. "Tell him what you saw?"

Again, the boy nodded. "I won't forget," he said.

That was all she needed; more than all. She left him with his father, and Rice led her away, through darkened alleyways and empty parking lots to the edge of town. They discarded their costumes as they went. By the time they reached the freeway, they were once more naked and invisible.

"Maybe we'll wander awhile," Rice suggested. "Go down south."

"Sure," she replied. "Why not?"

"Key West for Christmas. New Orleans for Mardi Gras. And maybe next year we'll come back here. See how things are going."

She shook her head. "Finn belongs to Thom now," she said. "He belongs to life."

"And who do we belong to?" Rice asked, a little sadly. She looked up. "You know damn well," she said, and pointed to the moon.

HOW TO GET AHEAD IN NEW YORK

POPPY Z. BRITE

POPPY Z. BRITE first appeared in these pages back in 1991 with her story "His Mouth Will Taste of Wormwood". Since then she has become one of the new rising stars of horror fiction, with the publication of two novels, Lost *Souls* and *Drawing Blood,* and the collection *Swamp Foetus.*

She has lived all over the American South and recently returned to her birthplace of New Orleans to live. When she was a child, her father used to take her around the voodoo shops in the French Quarter, and she wrote her first horror story, "The Attack of the Mud Monster," while still in second grade. Brite started submitting her stories to magazines at the age of 12, and sold her first story to *The Horror Show* when she was 18. She has worked as a candy maker, gourmet cook, mouse caretaker, artist's model and stripper, and she appeared nude in a 1992 short *Sim John S,* directed by Athens GA artist Jim Herbert, who also directs the REM videos. She is currently looking forward to seeing an autopsy.

"How to Get Ahead in New York" is part of the further adventures of her characters Steve and Ghost, who also appear in the story "Angels" (1987) and her debut novel

Lost Souls. "'How to Get Ahead' takes place the spring after *Lost Souls,*" explains the author, "as the guys are preparing to take off on an extended cross-country road trip and band tour (which should provide lots of other tales).

"I've only been in the Port Authority Bus Terminal once and never intend to go back, but I did get a story out of it. I wasn't attacked by homeless people, but the lady with cocoons in her hair was real."

She adds, "The thing with the heads didn't happen to me (hell, I would've bought one), but it did happen to someone I know, right there on St Mark's Place. Actually, I love New York. I hope that's evident in the story."

We'll leave it up to the reader to decide . . .

CONSIDER THIS SCENE :

Four a.m. in the Port Authority bus terminal, New York City. The Port Authority is a bad place at the best of times, a place where Lovecraft's wrong geometry might well hold sway. The master of purple prose maintained that the human mind could be driven mad by contemplation of angles subtly skewed, of other planes where the three comers of a triangle might add up to less than a hundred and eighty degrees, or to more.

Such is the Port Authority: even in the bustle of midday, comers do not appear to meet up quite right; corridors seem to slope from one end to the other. Even in full daylight, the Port Authority terminal is a bad place. At five a.m. it is wholly soulless.

Consider two young men just off a Greyhound from North Carolina. They were not brothers, but they might be thought brothers, although they looked nothing alike: it was suggested in the way the taller one, crow-black hair shoved messily behind his ears, kept close to his fairhaired companion as if protecting him. It was implied in the way they looked around the empty terminal and then glanced at each other, exchanging bad impressions without saying a word. They were not brothers, but they had known each other since childhood, and neither had ever been to New York before.

The corridor was flooded with dead fluorescent light. They had seen an EXIT sign pointing this way, but the corridor ended in a steel door marked NO ADMITTANCE. Should anyone find this message ambiguous, a heavy chain had been looped through the door handle and snapped shut with a padlock as large as a good-sized fist.

The fair boy turned around in a complete circle, lifted his head and flared his nostrils. His pale blue eyes slipped halfway shut, the lids fluttering. His friend watched him warily. After a minute he came out of it, shook himself a little, still nervous. "I don't like it here, Steve. I can't find my way anywhere."

Steve didn't like it either, wished they could have avoided the terminal altogether. They'd planned to drive up, but Steve's old T-bird had developed an alarming engine knock which threatened to become a death rattle if not dealt with kindly. The trip was all planned; they were booked to play at a club in the East Village—but they also meant to embark on a cross-country road trip next month. Steve left the car with his mechanic, telling him to fix it or scrap the motherfucker, Steve didn't care which. Ghost stood by half-smiling, listening to this exchange. Then, while Steve was still hitching, he had walked up the street to the Farmers' Hardware store that doubled as Missing Mile's bus station and charged two round-trip tickets to his credit card. He hated using that card, hated the feel of the thing in his pocket, but this surely counted as an emergency. That same night they were New York bound.

"It's just the damn *bus station,*" Steve said. "You ever know a town that could be judged by its bus station?" But as usual, there was no use arguing with Ghost's intuition. The place set Steve's teeth on edge too.

Ghost hitched his backpack up on his shoulder. They turned away from the padlocked door and tried to retrace their steps, but every corridor seemed to lead further into the bowels of the place. The soft sound of Ghost's sneakers and the sharp clatter of Steve's bootheels echoed back at them: *shush-clop, shush-clop.* Through Ghost's thin T-shirt Steve saw the sharp winglike jut of his shoulderblades, the shadowed knobs of his spine. The strap of the backpack pulled Ghost's shirt askew; his pale hair straggled silkily over his bare, sweaty neck. Steve carried only a guitar case, the instrument inside padded with a spare shirt and a few extra pairs of socks.

They came to another dead end, then to the motionless hulk of an escalator with a chain strung across its railings. A KEEP OUT sign hung from the chain, swinging lazily as if someone had given it a push and then ducked out of sight just before Steve and Ghost came around the corner. Steve began to feel like a stupid hick, to feel like the place was playing tricks on them. *Came to the Big City and couldn't even find our way out of the bus station. We ought to sit down right here and wait for the next bus headed south, and when it comes, we ought to hop on it and go right back home. Fuck New York, fuck the big club date. I don't like it here either.*

But that was stupid. The city was out there somewhere, and it had to get better than this.

Port Authority, Ghost decided, was about the worst place he had ever been in. Everything about it looked wrong, smelled wrong, leaned wrong. There were patterns on the floor made by the grime of a thousand soles; there was a bloody handprint on the tile wall. Looking at it, Ghost tried to close off his mind: he didn't want to know how it had gotten there. He managed to block out all but a faint impression of dirty knuckles plowing into a soft toothless mouth.

All at once the corridors shook and shuddered. The floor vibrated beneath his feet, throwing Ghost off balance. He had no way of knowing that this loss of equilibrium was caused by the subways constantly passing through; it made him feel as if the place were trying to digest him.

How did you ever get here? he thought. *How did you get from the green mountains, from the kudzu traintracks and the lazy hot summers, all the way to this city that could chew you up and spit you out like a*

wad of gum that's lost its flavor? How did you get to this place where you can never belong?

Immersed in his thoughts, he had let Steve get a little ahead of him. He looked up an instant before the apparition of death reeled around the comer; he heard Steve's curse, the sharp *"Fuckl"* that was nearly a gag, as the apparition lurched into Steve.

Steve's arms shot out reflexively, found the man's shoulders and shoved him away. The bum fell back against the wall, leaving a long wet smear on the tiles. His ragged suit jacket and the wattles of his throat were webbed with pale stringy vomit that dripped off his chin and made small foul splatters on the floor. His skin was grey, flaccid. It made Ghost think of a pumpkin that had sat too long in his grandmother's cellar once, waiting for Halloween; when he'd poked it, his finger had punched through the rind and sunk into the soft rotten meat. This man's skin looked as if it would rupture just as easily. One of his eyes was filmed over with a creamy yellowish cataract. The other eye listed toward the ceiling, watered and seemed about to spill over, then managed to track. When the eye met his, Ghost felt ice tingle along his spine. There was no one home behind that eye.

A wasted claw of a hand came up clutching a Styrofoam cup in which a few coins rattled. Veins stood out on the back of the hand. In the dead light they were as stark and clear as a map of the man's ruined soul. "Spare change for my li'l girl," he muttered. His voice caught in his throat, then dragged itself out slow as a bad recording. "My li'l girl's sick. Gotta catch the mornin' bus to Jersey."

Ghost looked at Steve. The understanding passed clearly between them: *bullshit.* There was no little girl in Jersey, there was nothing waiting for this man except the love at the bottom of a bottle. But the reality of him staggering through the desolate corridors in his vomit-caked coat, with his lone empty eye–that was worse than any sob story. Steve pulled out his wallet; Ghost dug through the pockets of his army jacket. They came up with a dollar each and stuffed the bills into the broken Styrofoam cup.

The bum threw his head back and a weird hooting sound came from his cracked lips. It was not quite a word, not quite a whistle. It reverberated off the tiles and ceilings.

And then the walls and the corridors of the Port Authority seemed to split wide open, and the legions of the hopeless spilled forth.

The bums were everywhere at once, coming from every direction, their eyes fixed on Steve's wallet and Ghost's open hands and the crisp bills poking out of the cup. Most of them had their own jingling cups; they shoved them at Steve, at Ghost, and their eyes implored. Their voices rose in a hundred meaningless pleas: *cuppa coffee. . . sick baby . . . hungry, mister, I'm hungry.* In the end the voices only meant one thing. *Give me. You who have, when I have none–give me.*

They kept coming. There seemed to be no end to them. Their hands reached for the money and grasped it. A persistent young brother grabbed a handful of Steve's hair and wouldn't let go until Steve reared back and punched him full in the face. He got a fistful of snot and ropy saliva for his trouble. As the boy fell away, Steve saw angry red holes in the pale flesh of his outstretched palms: needle marks. *He was my age,* Steve thought wildly; something in the eyes made him think the kid might have been even younger than twenty-four. *But he was already worn out enough to shoot up in the palms of his hands.*

Steve found himself flashing on *Dawn of the Dead,* a movie that had terrified him when he was a kid. He'd seen it again a couple of years ago and been surprised by how funny it really was: Romero's allegory of zombies roaming a modem mega-mall had escaped him at twelve. But now the original kid-terror flooded back. This was how it would be when the zombies ate you. They weren't very smart or quick, but there were a *lot* of them, and they would just keep coming and coming until you couldn't fight them any more.

Filth-caked nails scraped his flesh. The wallet was torn out of his grasp and dumped on the floor. Steve saw dirty hands shuffling through the trivia of his life. His driver's license. Ticket stubs from concerts he'd seen. A tattered review of Lost Souls?, his and Ghost's band, that had been written up in a Raleigh newspaper. Rage exploded like a crimson rocket in his brain. He had *worked* to get that money; he had *worked* to have a life, not see it trickle away from him like vomit on a dirty bus-station floor.

He hefted the guitar case—none of them seemed interested in that—and swung it in a wild arc. It connected with flesh, filthy hair, bone. Steve winced as he heard the jangling protest of the strings. He'd hit the first bum in his vomit-caked jacket, the only one they had willingly given money. *Try that for a handout, motherfucker.* The bum fell to his knees, clutching the back of his skull. Even the blood welling up between his fingers had an unhealthy look, like the watery blood at the bottom of a meat tray. It spattered the dirty floor in large uneven drops.

Ghost was grappling for his backpack. An old woman with skin like spoiled hamburger pulled at one shoulderstrap. The buttons of her flannel shirt had popped open and her shrivelled breasts tumbled out. The nipples were long and leathery as the stems of mushrooms. Her hair was a uniform grayish-yellow mat overlaid with a layer of white gauze which seemed to thicken, to form dense little balls, in several spots. Networks of delicate threads led away from these; dark shapes moved sluggishly within them. *Cocoons,* he realized sickly. *She has cocoons in her hair.*

He grabbed the woman by the shoulders and shoved her away. Ghost's notebooks were in that backpack—the lyrics to every song they had written. Ghost's eyes met Steve's, pale blue gone darker with panic.

Then, for no discernible reason, the creeps began to lift their heads and scent the air. A silent alarm seemed to pass among them. One by one they shrank away, sidled along the walls and disappeared like wraiths into the maze of corridors. The money in their Styrofoam cups rustled and jingled. Steve thought of cockroaches scuttling for cover when the kitchen light snaps on. In less than a minute they were all gone.

Steve and Ghost stared at each other, sweating, catching their breaths. Ghost held up a shaky hand. The cocoon lady's nails had left a long, shallow scratch along the back of it, from his knuckles to the bony knob of his wrist. A moment later they heard heavy, measured footsteps approaching. They edged closer together but did not otherwise react; this was surely the soul of the city itself coming to claim them.

The cop came around the comer all hard-edged and polished and gleaming, stopped at the sight of them, saw Steve's wallet and its contents scattered on the floor, frowned. His face was broad, Italian-looking, freshly shaved but the beard beneath the skin already showing faintly blue-black. "Help you with something?" he asked, his voice sharp with suspicion.

Steve drew in a long trembling breath and Ghost spoke quickly, before Steve could. Cussing cops was never a good idea, no matter where you were. "I think we got a little lost," he said. "Could you tell us how to get out of here?"

He was relieved when the cop pointed them in the right direction and Steve bent and scooped up his wallet, then stalked off without a word. Ghost's brain still ached from the long bus ride and the attack of the homeless people—or the people who lived, perhaps, in Port Authority. Worse than their grasping hands had been the touch of their minds upon his, as many-legged and hungry as mosquitoes. Their raw pain, the stink of their dead dreams. On top of that he hadn't needed Steve to get himself arrested. But Ghost was used to being the occasional peacemaker between Steve and almost everyone they knew. Steve bristled and Ghost calmed; that was just the way things were.

The sky was already brightening when they came out of the bus terminal. The city soared around them, bathed in a clear lavender light. The first building Ghost saw was an old stone church; the second was a four-storey sex emporium, its neon shimmering pale pink in the dawn. Steve leaned back against the glass doors and began to laugh.

"Good morning, Hell's Kitchen," he said.

Washington Square Park was in full regalia, though it was still early afternoon.

There were street musicians of every stripe, rappers clicking fast fingers and rattling heavy gold chains, old hippies with battered guitars and homemade pan pipes and permanent stoned smirks, young hippies singing solemn folk lyrics *a capella,* even a Dixieland brass band near the great stone arch. There was the savory mustard-chili tang of hot dogs, the harsh smoulder of city exhaust, the woodsy smell of ganja burning. There were homeboys and Rasta men and hairy-chested drag queens, slumming yuppies and street freaks. There were the folks for whom every day was Hallowe'en, faces painted pale, lips slashed crimson or black, ears and wrists decorated with silver crucifixes, skulls, charms of death and hoodoo. They huddled into their dark clothes, plucked at their dyed, teased, tortured hair, cut their black-rimmed eyes at passersby. There were punks in leather; there were drug dealers chanting the charms of their wares *(clean crystal. . . sweetest smoke in the city . . . goooood ice, goooood blow).* There were cops on the beat, cops looking the other way.

And, of course, there were two white boys from North Carolina whose feet had just this morning touched New York City asphalt for the first time.

They had drunk vile coffee from a stand in Times Square, then walked around for a while. They kept losing track of the Empire State Building, which was the only landmark they recognized. The tranquil light of early morning soon gave way to the hustle and shove of the day. The air came alive with shouts, blaring horns, the constant low thrum of the city-machine.

Eventually—as soon as they could stand to go below street level again—they descended into the subway at Penn Station and didn't get out again until the Washington Square stop. At that point Ghost swore he would never enter a transit station or board any subway in New York City or anywhere else, ever again. It wasn't the crowds; since Port Authority the only panhandlers they'd seen had been shaking discreet cups or quietly noodling on saxophones. No one else had bothered them. It was the merciless white light in the stations and the bleak garbage-strewn deadliness of the tracks and the great clattering ratcheting roar of the trains. It was hurtling through sections of tunnel where the tracks split in two at the last heartstopping second before you smashed into solid stone. It was the abandoned tunnels that split off like dead universes. The very idea of the trains worming along beneath the city, in their honeycombed burrows, seemed horribly organic.

But topside, he was fine. Ghost found himself liking the stew of sounds and smells that comprised the city, and the colorful variety of the minds that brushed his, and the carnival of Washington Square. Steve stopped to watch the Dixieland band, and Ghost listened to the dipping, soaring brass for several minutes too.

But in his peripheral vision a man was rooting in a garbage can. He tried not to look, but couldn't help himself as the man pulled out a whole dripping chilidog, brushed flies away, and bit into it.

The man was old and white, with long gray dreadlocks and mummified hands and the universal costume of the drifter, army jacket, baggy pants, Salvation Army shirt that just missed being a rag: an ensemble ready to fade into the background at a moment's notice. The chilidog was a carnage of ketchup and pickle relish and flaccid meat, the bun limp, sponge-soggy. The man's face registered more pleasure than distaste. The dog might taste awful, but there was still warm sun on his shoulders and a half-full bottle in his pocket and a goddamn huge party going on right here, right now. His eyes were curiously clear, almost childlike.

But it was garbage, *he was eating* garbage. The wire trashcan was crammed with ripening refuse. A redolent juice seeped out at the bottom, a distillation of every disgusting fluid in the can, moonshine for bluebottle flies. Ghost felt his mind stretching, trying to accommodate something he had never had to think closely about before. There were poor people in Missing Mile, sure. Most of the old men who played checkers outside the Farmers Hardware store were on some kind of government or military pension. Lots of people got food stamps. But were there people eating out of garbage cans? Were there people so desperate that they would band together and attack you for the change in your pocket?

You bet there are. They're everywhere. Your life has been just sheltered enough, just sanitized enough, that you didn't see them. But you can't get away from it here . . . this city chews up its young and spits them back in your face.

Ghost looked up, startled. He wasn't sure what had just happened; it felt as if the world, for an instant, had split and then reconverged. As if someone had had the exact same thought as him, at the exact same time.

He saw a young black man leaning on the low concrete wall nearby, also watching the old drifter. The young man was handsome, trendily barbered, dressed in casual but expensive-looking sport clothes. He wore gold-rimmed glasses with little round lenses, carried a radio Walkman in his breast pocket and a copy of Spy tucked under his arm. In his face as he watched the old man chewing was an ineffable sadness, not quite sympathy, not quite pity.

The hearts that would swell with rage back home–if you could call them hearts–to see a black man looking upon a white man with anything resembling pity . . .

(Get outta that garbage, boy)

The man shifted on the wall and looked straight at Ghost, warm mocha eyes meeting startled pale blue. And suddenly Ghost knew many things about this man. He was from a tiny town in south Georgia–Ghost didn't get the name–and his family had been crushingly poor. Not trash-eating poor . . . but there had been a man in the town who *was.* Ancient and alone, black as midnight, brains pickled by half a century of rotgut wine. He was no town hobo of the sort people laughed at but looked out for; he had no colorful nickname, no family, no history. He was a smelly old wino who pissed his pants, and most of the whites in town, if they were aware of him at all, called him Hey Boy. As in Hey, Boy, *get outta that garbage.* As in Hey, *Boy, I'm talkin' to you.* As in *Hey, Boy, get off my property before I blow your nigger guts to Hell.*

And this young man, as a hungry scrawny child in this stagnant backwater of a town, had seen that happen.

Ghost saw the blood exploding through the air, smelled flame and cordite, redneck sweat and the raw sewage odor of Hey Boy's ruptured, blasted guts. He felt the giddy terror of a child hiding—where?—he couldn't get it—viewing death up close for the first time, afraid its twin black barrels would swing his way next. He could not move, could not look away from the young man's calm brown eyes, until Steve touched his shoulder. "Somebody just gave me directions to the club. It's real near here. You want to go check it out?"

Ghost glanced back over his shoulder as they left the park. The young man was no longer looking at him, and Ghost felt no urge to speak. They had already had the most intimate contact possible; of what use were words?

They crossed a wide traffic-filled avenue and turned east. Ghost wasn't sure just where the Village began, but the streets seemed to be getting narrower, the window displays more fabulous, the crowds decidedly funkier. People wore silver studs in their noses, delicate hoops through their lips and eyebrows. A boy in a black fishnet shirt had both nipples pierced, with a filigree chain connecting the rings. There were shaved and painted scalps, long snaky braids, leather jackets jangling with zippers and buckles, flowing hippie dresses of gossamer and gauze. The streets of the East Village by day seemed a shrine to mutant fashion.

Steve pulled a joint from his sock, lit up, took a deep drag and passed it to Ghost. Ghost grabbed the burning cigarette and cupped it gingerly between his palms, trying to hide it, expecting a big cop hand to fall on his shoulder at any second. "Are you crazy?"

Steve shook his head, then blew out a giant plume of smoke. "It's cool. Terry said you could smoke right on the street up here, as long as you're discreet. He gave me this as a going-away present."

Terry owned the record store where Steve worked, and was the best-travelled and most worldly of their crowd; also the biggest stoner, so he ought to know. But Ghost could not stretch his definition of *discreet to* include walking down one of the busiest streets in New York City with a cloud of pot smoke trailing behind. Still ... He looked thoughtfully at the joint in his hand, then brought it up to his lips and took a cautious toke. The spicy green flavor filled his throat, swirled through his lungs and his brain. New York probably imported every exotic strain of reefer from every country in the world, but Southern homegrown had to beat them all.

A few blocks later the crowds thinned out. The streets here felt older, greyer, somehow more soothing. More like a place where you could actually live. There were little groceries on every block with wooden stands of flowers and produce in front. Ghost smelled ginger and ripe tomatoes, the subtle cool scent of ice, the tang of fresh greens and herbs. Sage, basil, onions, thyme, sweet rosemary and soapy-smelling coriander. As long as he could smell herbs he was happy.

New York, Steve decided, was a city bent upon providing its citizens with plenty of food and information. In other parts of the city there had been hot dog carte everywhere, pizza parlors and cappuccino shops, restaurants serving food from Thailand, Mongolia, Latino-China, and everywhere else in the world; newsstands on every comer carried hundreds of papers, magazines, and often a wide selection of hardcore pom. There were radios and TVs blaring, headlines shrieking. In the first part of the Village Steve had seen more restaurants, comics shops, and several intriguing bookstores he planned to check out later. Here you had the little groceries, though not quite so many restaurants. For information, there were the street vendors.

Steve had started noticing them a while back, though he'd been too busy noticing everything else to pay much attention at first. But here they were more frequent and less obscured by the flow of the crowd. They set up tables or spread out army blankets, then arranged the stuff they wanted to sell and sat down to wait until somebody bought it. There were tables of ratty paperbacks, boxes of old magazines, tie-dyed T-shirts and ugly nylon buttpacks, cheap watches and household appliances laid out on the sidewalk like the leftovers from somebody's yard sale.

But as they walked farther, the wares started to get a little strange. At first it was just stuff that no one could possibly want, like a box of broken crayon-ends or a shampoo bottle filled with sand. Then they passed a man selling what looked like medical equipment: bedpans in a dusty row, unidentifiable tubes and pouches, some jar-shaped humps covered with a tattered army blanket. In the center of his display was a single artificial leg that had once been painted a fleshy pink. Now the paint was chipped, the limb's surface webbed with a thousand tiny, grimy cracks. The toeless foot was flat and squared-off, little more than a block of wood. At the top was a nightmarish jumble of straps and braces meant, Steve supposed, to hold the leg onto a body. He could not imagine walking around on such a thing every day.

"Where is this club?" Ghost asked nervously.

"Well... I know we're near it." Steve stopped at the comer, shoved sweaty hair out of his face, and looked around hoping the place would appear. "The guy who gave me directions said it would be hard to find in the daytime. We're supposed to look for an unlit neon sign that says *Beware.*"

"Great."

"WHAT PLACE YEZ LOOKIN' FOR?" boomed a voice behind them. It took Steve several seconds to realize that the vendor had spoken and was now motioning them over.

"Yez look like gentlemen in search of the unusual," the vendor told them before they could say anything about clubs or directions. He was a white man of indeterminate age, dishwater-brown hair thin on top but straggling halfway down his back in an untidy braid. His eyes were hidden behind black wraparound shades, his grin as sharp and sudden as a razor. Steve noticed a strange ring on the second finger of the guy's right hand: a bird skull cast in silver, some species with huge hollow eyesockets and a long, tapering, lethal-looking beak that jutted out over the knuckle. It was lovely, but it also looked like a good tool for putting an eye out or ventilating a throat.

"Well, right now we're looking for this club - "

"Something UNUSUAL," the vendor overrode. "A collector's item maybe." His hand hovered over his wares, straightened tubes and straps, caressed the artificial leg. "Something yez don't see every day." His face went immobile, then split back into that sharp crazy grin. "Or rather–something yez DO see every day, but most of the time yez can't take the fuckers HOME WITH YA!"

His hand twitched back the army blanket covering the jar-shaped humps. A small cloud of dust rose into the air. Sunlight winked on polished glass. Steve cussed, took two steps back, then came forward again and bent to look.

Ghost, who had never in his life felt so far from home, burst into tears.

The man had six big glass jars arranged in two neat rows, sealed at the tops and filled with what could only be formaldehyde. Inside each jar, suspended in the murky liquid, was a large, pale, bloated shape: an undeniably real human head. The necks appeared to have been surgically severed. Ghost could see layers of tissue within the stumps as precisely delineated as the circles of wood inside a tree trunk. One head was tilted far enough to the side to show a neat peg of bone poking from the meat of the neck. Several had shaved scalps; one had dark hair that floated and trailed like seaweed. Parts of faces were pressed flat against the glass: an ear, a swollen nostril, a rubbery lip pulled askew. Blood-suffused eyeballs protruded from their sockets like pickled hard-boiled eggs.

"How much do you want for them?" Steve asked. Ghost sobbed harder.

The grin seemed to throw off light, it was so wide and dazzling. "Two apiece. Ten for all six of 'em."

"Ten *dollars?*"

"Hey, I'm in a hurry, I gotta unload these puppies today, yez think this is *legal* or somethin'?"

As if on cue, sirens rose out of the general distant cacophony, approaching fast. A pair of police cars rounded the comer and came shrieking up the block. Revolving blue light flickered across the lenses of the black wraparound shades. The grin disappeared. Without even a *good day to yez* the vendor scooped up the artificial leg and took off down the street. One car roared after him. The other slammed to a halt at the curb where Steve and Ghost still stood staring stupidly at the heads. "You weren't really going to buy one, were you?" Ghost whispered.

"Course not." Steve snorted. "I don't have any money anyway, remember? The bums got it all. I'm lucky to have an I.D. to show this cop." He dug out his wallet and flipped it open. "We're just a couple of hicks from North Carolina, Officer. We lay no claim to these jars or their contents."

Minds like butterflies preserved in brine, trapped under thick glass . . . It seemed that their friendly vendor, a gentleman whose given name was Robyn Moorhead but who was known variously as Robyn Hood, Moorhead Robbins, and (aptly enough) "More Head," had robbed a medical transport truck en route from Beth Israel Hospital to the Mutter Medical Museum in Philadelphia while it was stopped at a gas station. The truck's door had not latched properly, and More Head and an unidentified girlfriend had simply climbed in and cleaned it out. He had already sold several items before Steve and Ghost came along. The artificial leg, though, was his own. He used it for display purposes only, to call attention to whatever shady wares he sold; it was a valuable antique and not for sale; he carried it everywhere.

No, Ghost told himself. *You did* not *feel their minds beating against the jars like dying insects. You did not feel the raw bum of formaldehyde against your eyeballs, the dead taste of it in your mouth; you did not feel the subtle breakdown of the molecular dream that was your brain. They were not alive. You could not feel them.*

"I gotta know," said the cop as he finished writing up their statement. "How much did he want for 'em?" Steve told him, and the cop shrugged, then sighed. He was a decent sort and the affair seemed to have put him in a philosophical mood. "Man, even'f I was a crook, even'f I was tryna sell yuman heads, I'd't least be askin' more'n ten bucks. Kinda devalues the sanctity a'yuman life, y'know?"

Jewelled wings, beating themselves to powder against thick glass . . .

They had overshot the club by five blocks. The cops pointed them in the right direction and ten minutes later they were descending below street level again, past the unlit neon sign that said not *Beware* but *Be Aware,* though Ghost guessed it amounted to the same thing, and into the club. The poster they had sent was plastered everywhere: TONIGHT–LOST SOULS? They were too tired to consider doing a soundcheck yet, but it was just the two of them, Steve's guitar and Ghost's voice, and they didn't really need one. At any rate they wouldn't be going on rill midnight. Right now they needed sleep. One of the bartenders was out of town and had left them the keys to her apartment, which was just upstairs.

Too tired for the stairs, they rode the ancient, terrifying elevator up seven stories. Steve had bummed two beers at the bar. He guzzled most of one as they rode up. "New York is pretty interesting," he said.

"No shit."

Steve snorted into his beer. And then at once they were both laughing, losing it in a rickety box suspended from an antique cable in a building that was taller than any building in Missing Mile but small by the standards of this magical, morbid, million-storied city. They fell against each other and howled and slapped high-five. They were young and the one had a voice like gravelly gold and the other could play guitar with a diamond-hard edge born of sex and voodoo and despair, and it was all part of the Great Adventure.

They staggered out at the top still giggling, fumbled with three unfamiliar locks, and let themselves into the apartment. The place was decorated all in black: black walls, black lace dripping from the ceiling, black paint over the windows, black silk sheets on a huge futon that covered the floor. The effect was soothing, like being cradled in the womb of night. Their laughter wound down.

Steve stood his guitar case in a comer, gulped the second beer after Ghost refused it, and stretched his tired bones out on the futon. Ghost toed his sneakers off and lay down beside him. It was absolutely dark and, for the first time since Port Authority, nearly quiet. How strange to think that the whole teeming city was still out there, just beyond the walls of the building. Suddenly Ghost felt disoriented in the little pocket of blackness, as if the compass he always carried in his head had deserted him.

He shifted on the mattress so that his shoulder touched Steve's arm, so that he could feel Steve's familiar warmth all along the left side of his body. Steve heaved a great deep sigh like a sleeping hound. Ghost thought of all the highways, all the back roads, all the train tracks and green paths that led back home, and he did not feel so far away.

And there was music, there was always music to carry him wherever he wanted to go. Soon the distant thrum of the city and the tales it wanted to tell him faded completely, and the gouge of Steve's bony elbow in his side lulled him to sleep.

UNDER THE PYLON

GRAHAM JOYCE

GRAHAM JOYCE was born in 1954. After attending teacher training college in Derby, he won the George Fraser Poetry Award while taking an MA at Leicester University. He had a variety of jobs—fitter's mate, kitchen porter, bingo-caller, holiday camp attendant, fruit picker, supply teacher—before becoming a development officer for the National Association of Youth Clubs.

He quit in 1988 and went to live on the Greek island of Lesbos to concentrate on his writing. His first novel, *Dreamside,* was published to critical acclaim by Pan Books in 1991. Since then, two more books have appeared from Headline, *Dark Sister* and *House of Lost Dreams.* Although his stories have been published in *Dark Voices 5: The Pan Book of Horror, In Dreams, Darklands 2* and *Interzone,* he has hardly been prolific in this area. It's quality not quantity that we may expect from him, as "Under the Pylon" shows.

AFTER SCHOOL OR DURING THE LONG summer holidays we used to meet down by the electricity pylon. Though we never went there when the weather was wet because obviously there was no cover. Apart from that the wet power lines would vibrate and hum and throb and it would be ... well, I'm not saying I was scared but it would give you a bad feeling.

Wet or dry, we'd all been told not to play under the pylon. Our folks had lectured us time and again to keep away; and an Electricity Board disc fixed about nine feet up on the thing spelled out DANGER in red and white lettering. Two lightning shocks either side of the word set it in zigzag speech marks.

"Danger!"

I imagined the voice of the pylon would sound like a robot's speech-box from a science-fiction film, because that's what the pylon looked like, a colossal robot. Four skeletal steel legs straddled the ground, tapering up to a pointed head nudging the clouds. The struts bearing the massive power cables reached over like arms, adding a note of severity and anthropomorphism to the thing. Like someone standing with their hands on their hips. The power cables themselves drooped slightly until picked up by the next giant robot in the field beyond, and then to the next. Marching into the infinite distance, an army of obstinate robots.

But the pylon was situated on a large patch of waste ground between the houses, and when it came down to it, there was nowhere else for us kids to go. It was a green and overgrown little escape-hatch from suburbia. It smelled of wild grass and giant stalks of cow parsley, and of nettles and foxgloves and dumped housebricks. You could bash down a section to make a lair hidden from everything but the butterflies. Anyway, it wasn't the danger of electricity giving rise to any nervousness under the pylon. It was something else. Old Mrs Nantwich called it a shadow.

Joy Astley was eleven, and already wearing lipstick and make-up you could have peeled off like a mask. Her parents had big mouths and were always bawling. "The Nantwiches," she said airily, "could only afford to buy this house because it's under the pylon. No one wants a house under the pylon."

"Why not?" said Clive Mann. It was all he ever said. Clive had a metal brace across his teeth, and even though he was odd and stared at things a lot, people mostly bothered to answer him. "Why?"

"Because you don't," said Joy, "that's why."

Tania Brown was in my class at school (she used to pronounce her name Tarnia because of the sunshine jokes) and agreed with Joy. Kev Duffy burped and said, "Crap!" It was Kev's word for the month. He would use it repeatedly up until the end of August. Joy just looked at Kev and wiggled her head from side to side, as if that somehow answered his remark.

The Nantwiches Joy was being so snobbish about were retired barge people. Why anyone would want to rub two pennies together I've never understood, but they were always described as looking as though they couldn't accomplish this dubious feat; and then in the same breath people would always add "yet they're the people who have got it". I doubted it somehow. They'd lived a hard life transporting coal on the barges, and it showed. Their faces had more channels and ruts and canals than the waterways of the Grand Union.

"They're illiterate," Joy always pointed out whenever they were mentioned. And then she'd add, "Can't read or write."

The Nantwiches' house did indeed stand under the shadow of the giant pylon. Mr Nantwich was one of those old guys with a red face and white hair, forever forking over the earth in his backyard. Their garden backed up to the pylon. A creosoted wooden fence closed off one side of the square defined by the structure's four legs. One day when I was there alone old Mrs Nantwich had scared me by popping her head over the fence and saying, "You don't wanna play there."

Her face looked as old as a church gate. Fine white bristles sprouted from her chin. Her hair was always drawn back under a headscarf, and she wore spectacles with plastic frames and lenses like magnifying glasses. They made her eyes huge.

"Why?" I'd croaked.

She threw her head back slowly and pointed her chin towards the top of the pylon. Then she looked at me and did it again.

"There's a *shadow* orf of it."

I felt embarrassed as she stared, waiting for me to say something. "What do you mean?"

Before she answered, another head popped alongside her own. It was her daughter Olive. Olive looked as old as her mother. She had wild, iron-grey hair. Her teeth were terribly blackened and crooked. The thing about Olive was she never uttered a word. She hadn't spoken, according to my mother, since a man had "jumped out at her from behind a bush". I didn't see how that could make someone dumb for the rest of their life, but then I didn't understand what my mother meant by that deceptively careful phrase either.

"Wasn't me," said Mrs Nantwich a little fiercely, "as decided to come 'ere." And then her head disappeared back behind the fence, leaving Olive to stare beadily at me as if I'd done something wrong. Then her head too popped out of sight.

I looked up at the wires and they seemed to hum with spiteful merriment.

Another day I came across Clive Mann, crouched under the pylon, and listening. At that time, the three sides of the pylon had been closed off. We'd found some rusty corrugated sheeting to lean against one end, and a few lengths of torn curtain to screen off another. The third side, running up to the Nantwiches' creosoted fence, was shielded by an impenetrable jungle of five-foot-high stinging nettles.

It had been raining, and the curtains sagged badly. I ducked through the gap between them to find Clive crouched and staring directly up into the tower of the pylon. He said nothing. "What are you doing?"

"You can hear," he said. "You can hear what they're saying."

I looked up and listened. The lines always made an eerie hissing after rain, but there was no other sound.

"Hear what?"

"No! The people. On the telephones. Mrs Astley is talking to the landlord of the Dog and Trumpet. He's knocking her off."

I looked up again and listened. I knew he wasn't joking because Clive had no sense of humour. He just stared at things. I was about to protest that the cables were power lines, not telephone wires, when the curtains parted and Joy Astley came in.

"What are you two doing?"

We didn't answer.

"My Dad says these curtains and things have got to come down," said Joy.

"Why?"

"He says he doesn't like the idea."

"What's it got to do with him?"

"He thinks," Joy said, closing her eyes, "things go on here."

"You mean he's worried about what his angelic daughter gets up to," I said.

Joy turned around, nicked up her skirt and wiggled her bottom at us. It was a gesture too familiar to be of any interest. At least that day she was wearing panties.

I had to pass by the Dog and Trumpet as I walked home later that afternoon. I noticed Mrs Astley going in by the back door, which was odd because the pub was closed in the afternoon. But I thought little of it at the time.

Just as we were accustomed to Joy flashing her bottom at us, so were we well inured to the vague parental unease about us playing under the pylon. None of our parents ever defined the exact nature of their anxieties. They would mention things about *electricity* and *generators,* but these didn't add up to much more than old Mrs Nantwich's dark mutterings about a *shadow.* I got my physics and my science all mixed up as usual, and managed to infect the rest of the group with my store of misapprehensions.

"Radiation," I announced. "The reason they're scared is because if there was an accidental power surge feedback . . ." (I was improvising like mad) ". . . then we'd all get *radiated.*"

Radiated. It was a great word. Radiated. It got everyone going.

"There was a woman in the newspaper," said Joy. "Her microwave oven went wrong and she was *radiated.* Her bones all turned to jelly."

Tania could cap that. "There was one on television. A woman. She gave birth to a cow with two heads. After being *radiated.*" The girls were always better at horror stories.

Kev Duffy said, "Crap!" Then he looked up into the pyramid of the tower and said, "What's the chances of it happening?"

"Eighteen hundred to one," I said. With that talent for tossing out utterly bogus statistics I should have gone on to become a politician.

Then they were all looking up, and in the silence you could hear the abacus beads whizzing and clacking in their brains. Joy's parents needn't have worried. Not much went on behind the pylon screens of which they could disapprove. Well, that's not entirely true, since one or two efforts were made seriously to misbehave, but they never amounted to much. Communal cigarettes were sucked down to their filters, bottles of cider were shared round. Clive and I once tried sniffing Airfix but it made us sick as dogs and we were never attracted to the idea again. We once persuaded Joy to take off her clothes for a dare, which she did; but then she immediately put them back on again, so it all seemed a bit pointless and no more erotic than the episode of solvent abuse.

It was the last summer holiday before we were due to be dispatched to what we all called the Big Schools. It all depended on which side of the waste ground you lived. Joy and Kev were to go to President Kennedy, where you didn't have to wear a school uniform; Clive and I were off to Cardinal Wiseman, where you did. It all seemed so unfair. Tania was being sent to some snooty private school where they wore straw hats in the summer. She hated the idea, but her father was what my old man called one of the nobs.

Once, Tania and I were on our own under the pylon. Tania had long blond hair, and was pretty in a willowy sort of way. Her green eyes always seemed wide open with amazement at the things we'd talk about or at what we'd get up to. She spoke quietly in her rather posh accent, and for some reason she always seemed desperately grateful that we didn't exclude her from our activities.

Out of the blue she asked me if I'd ever kissed a girl.

"Loads," I lied. "Why?"

"I've never kissed anyone. And now I'm going to a girls' school I'll probably never get the chance."

We sat on an old door elevated from the grass by a few housebricks. I looked away. The seconds thrummed by. I imagined I heard the wires overhead going *chock chock chock.*

"Would you like to?" she said softly.

"Like to what?"

"To kiss me?"

I shrugged. "If you want." My muscles went as stiff as the board on which we perched.

She moved closer, put her head at an angle and closed her eyes. I looked at her thin lips, leaned over and rested my mouth against hers. We stayed like that for some time, stock-still. The power lines overhead vibrated with noisy impatience. Eventually she opened her eyes and pulled back, blinking at me and licking her lips. I realised my hands were clenched to the side of the board as if it had been a magic carpet hurtling across the sky.

So Tania and I were "going out". Our kissing improved slightly, and we got a lot of ribbing from the others, but beyond that, nothing had changed. Because 1 was going out with Tania, Kev Duffy was considered to be "going out" with Joy, at least nominally; though to be fair to him, he was elected to this position only because Clive was beyond the pale. Kev resented this status as something of an imposition, though he did go along with the occasional bout of simulated kissing. But when Joy appeared one day sporting livid, gash-crimson lipstick and calling him "darling" at every turn, he got mad and smudged the stuff all round her face with the ball of his hand. The others pretended not to notice, but I could see she was hurt by it.

Another time I'd been reading something about hypnotism, and Joy decided she wanted to be hypnotised. I'd decided I had a talent for this, so I sat her on the grass inside the pylon while the other three watched. I did all that "you're feeling very relaxed" stuff and she went under easily; too easily. Then I didn't know what to ask her to do. There was no point asking her to take her clothes off, since she hardly needed prompting to do that.

"Get 'er to run around like a 'eadless chicken," was Kev's inspirational idea.

"Tell 'er to describe life on Jupiter," Clive said obscurely.

"Ask her to go back to a past life," said Tania.

That seemed the most intelligent suggestion, so I offered a few cliched phrases and took her back, back into the mists of time. I was about to ask her what she could see when I felt a thrum of energy. It distracted me for a moment, and I looked up into the apex of the pylon. There was nothing to see, but I remembered I'd felt it before. Once, when I'd first kissed Tania.

When I looked back, there were tears streaming down Joy's face. She was trembling and sobbing in silence.

"Bring her out of it," said Tania.

"Why?" Clive protested.

"Yer," said Kev. "Better stop it now."

I couldn't. I did all that finger clicking rubbish and barked various commands. But she just sat there shaking and sobbing. I was terrified. Tania took hold of her hands and, thankfully, after a while Joy just seemed to come out of it on her own. She was none the worse for the experience, and laughed it off; but she wouldn't tell us what she saw.

They all had a go. Kev wouldn't take it seriously, however, and insisted on staggering around like a stage drunk. Clive claimed to have gone under but we all agreed we couldn't tell the difference.

Finally it was Tania's turn. She was afraid, but Joy dared her. Tania made me promise not to make her experience a past life. I'd read enough about hypnotism to know you can't make people do anything they don't already want to do, but convincing folk of that is another thing. Tania had been frightened by what happened to Joy, so I had to swear on my grandmother's soul and hope to be struck by lightning and so on before she'd let me do it.

Tania went under with equal ease, a feat I've never been able to accomplish since.

"What are you going to get her to do?" Joy wanted to know.

"Pretend to ride a bike?" I suggested lamely.

"Crap," said Kev. "Tell her she's the sexiest woman in the world and she wants to make mad passionate love to you."

Naturally Joy thought this was a good idea, so I put it to Tania. She opened her eyes in a way that made me think she'd just been stringing us along. She smiled at me serenely and shook her head. Then there was a thrum of electrical activity from the wires overhead. I looked up and before I knew what was happening, Tania had jumped on me and locked her legs behind my back. I staggered and fell backwards on to the grass. Tania had her tongue halfway down my throat. I'd heard of French kissing, but it had never appealed. Joy and Kev were laughing and cheering her on.

Tania came up for air, and she was making a weird growling from the back of her throat. Then she power-kissed me again.

"This is great!" whooped Kev.

"Hey!" went Clive. "Hey!"

"Tiger tiger!" shouted Joy.

I was still pinned under Tania's knees when she sat up and stripped off her white T-shirt in one deft move.

"Bloody hell!" Kev couldn't believe it any more than I could. "This is brilliant!"

"Gerrem off!" screamed Joy.

Tania stood up quickly and hooked her thumbs inside the waist of her denims and her panties, slipping them off. Before I'd had time to blink she was naked. She was breathing hard. Then she was fumbling at my jeans.

"Bloody fucking hell!" Joy shouted. "Bloody fucking hell!"

The lines overhead thrummed again. Tania had twice my strength. I had this crazy idea she was drawing it from the pylon. She had my pants halfway down my legs.

Then everything was interrupted by a high-pitched screaming.

At first I thought it was Tania, but it was coming from behind her. The screaming brought Tania to her senses. It was Olive, the Nantwiches' deranged daughter. Her head had appeared over the fence and she was screaming and pointing at something. What she pointed at was my semi-erect penis; half-erect from Tania's brutal stimulation; half-flaccid from terror at her ferocious strength.

Olive continued to point and shriek. Then she was joined at the fence by Mrs Nantwich. "Filthy buggers," said the old woman. "Get on with yer! Filthy buggers!"

A third head appeared. Red-faced Mr Nantwich. He was just laughing. "Look at that!" he shouted. "Look at that!"

Tania wasn't laughing. She looked at me with disgust. "Bastard," she spat, climbing quickly back into her clothes. "Bastard!"

I ran after her. "You can't make anyone do what they don't want to," I tried. She shrugged me off tearfully. I let her go.

"Filthy buggers!" Mrs Nantwich muttered.

"You can't make anyone!" I screamed at her.

"Look at that!" laughed Joe Nantwich.

Olive was still shrieking. The power lines were still throbbing. Clive was trying to tell me something, but I wasn't listening. "It wasn't you," he was saying. He was pointing up at the pylon. "It were *that.*"

I never spoke another word to Tania, and she never came near the pylon again. I was terrified the story would get back to my folks. I didn't see why exactly, but I had the feeling I'd reap all the blame. But a few days later something happened which overshadowed the entire incident.

And it happened to Clive.

One afternoon he and I had been sharing a bottle of Woodpecker. He'd been *listening* again.

"Old man Astley's found out."

"Eh? How do you know?"

He looked up at the overhead wires. "She's been on the phone to the Dog and Trumpet."

He was always reporting what he'd "heard" on the wires. We all knew he was completely cracked, but it was best to ignore him. I changed the subject. I started regaling him with some nonsense I'd heard about a burglar's fingers bitten clean off by an Alsatian, when Clive took it into his head to start climbing the pylon. I didn't think it was a sensible thing to do but it was pointless saying anything.

"Not a good idea, that."

"Why?"

Climbing the pylon wasn't easy. The inspection ladder didn't start until a height of nine feet–obviously with schoolboys in mind–but that didn't stop Clive. He lifted the door we used as a bench and leaned it against the struts of one of the pylon's legs. Climbing on the struts, he pulled himself to the top of the door, and standing on its top edge he was able to haul himself up to the inspection ladder. He ascended a few rungs and seemed happy to hang there for a while. I got bored watching him.

It was late afternoon and the sky had gone a dark, cobalt shade of blue. I finished off the cider, unzipped my trousers and stuck my dick outside the curtains to empty my bladder. A kind of spasm shot through me before I'd finished, stronger even than those I'd felt before. I ignored it. "So the burglar," I was telling Clive, "knew the key was on a string inside the letter box. So when the owners came home they got into the hallway and found," I finished pissing, zipped up and turned to complete the story. But my words tailed off, "two fingers still holding the string . . ."

I looked up the inspection ladder to the top of the pylon. I looked at the grey metal struts. I looked everywhere. Clive had vanished.

"Clive?"

I checked all around. Then I went outside. I thought he might have jumped down, or fallen. He wasn't there. I went back inside. Then I went outside again.

Spots of rain started to appear. I looked up at the wires and they seemed to hum contentedly. I waited for a while until the rain came more heavily, and went home.

That night while I was lying in bed, I heard the telephone ring. I knew what time it was because I could hear the television signature blaring from the lounge. It was the end of the late night news. Then my mother came upstairs. Had I seen Clive? His mother had phoned. She was worried.

The next day I was interviewed by a policewoman. I explained we were playing under the pylon, I turned my back and he'd disappeared. She made a note and left.

A few days later the police were out like blackberries in September. Half the neighbourhood joined in the fine-toothcomb search of the waste ground and the nearby fields. They found nothing. Not a hair from his head.

While the searches went on, I started to have a recurring nightmare. I'd be back under the pylon, pissing and happily talking away to Clive. Only it wasn't urine coming out, it was painful fat blue and white sparks of electricity. I'd turn to Clive in surprise, who would be descending the inspection ladder wearing fluorescent blue overalls, his face out of view. And his entire body would be rippling with eels of electricity, gold sparks arcing wildly. Then slowly his head would begin to rotate towards me and I'd start screaming; but before I ever got to see his awful face I'd wake up.

We stopped playing under the pylon after that. No one had to say anything, we just stopped going there. I did go back once, to satisfy my own curiosity. The screens had been ripped away in the failed search, but the nettles bashed down by the police were already springing up again.

I looked up into the tower of the pylon, and although there was nothing to see, I felt a terrible sense of dread. Then a face appeared over the Nantwiches' fence. It was Olive. She'd seen me looking.

"Gone," she said. It was the only word I ever heard her say. "Gone."

Summer came to an end and we went off to our respective schools. I saw Tania once or twice in her straw boater, but she passed me with her nose in the air. Eventually she married a Tory MP. I often wonder if she's happy.

Inevitably Kev and I stopped hanging around together, but not before there was a murder in the district. The landlord of the Dog and Trumpet was stabbed to death. They never found who did it. Joy moved out of the area when her parents split up. She went to live with her mother.

Joy went on to become a rock and roll singer. A star. Well, not a star exactly, but I did once sec her on *Top of the Pops.* She had a kind of trade mark, turning her back on the cameras to wiggle her bottom. I felt pleased for her that she'd managed to put the habit to good use.

Just occasionally I bump into Kev in this pub or that but we never really know what to say to each other. After a while Kev always says, "Do you remember the time you hypnotised Tania Brown and . . ." and I always say "Yes" before he gets to the end of the story. Then we look at the floor for a while until one of us says, "Anyway, good to see you, all the best." It's that *anyway* that gets me.

Clive Mann is never mentioned.

Occasionally I make myself walk past the old place. A new group of kids has started playing there, including Kev Duffy's oldest girl. Yesterday as I passed by that way there were no children around because an Electricity Board operative was servicing the pylon. He was halfway up the inspection ladder, and he wore blue overalls exactly like Clive in my dream. It stopped me with a jolt. I had to stare, even though I could sense the man's irritation at being watched.

Then came that singular, familiar thrum of energy. The maintenance man let his arm drop and turned to face me, challenging me to go away. But I was transfixed. Because it was dive's face I saw in that man's body. He smiled at me, but tiny white sparks of electricity were leaking from his eyes like tears. Then he made to speak, but all I heard or saw was a fizz of electricity arcing across the metal brace on his teeth. Then he was the maintenance man again, meeting my desolate gaze with an expression of contempt.

I left hurriedly, and I resolved, after all, not to pass by the pylon again.

UNDER THE ICE

JOHN GORDON

JOHN GORDON lives with his wife in Norwich. Born in Jarrow-on-Tyne, he grew up in the Fens and during World War Two joined the Navy from school and served on minesweepers and destroyers. After the war he became a journalist and worked on papers in East Anglia and Plymouth.

His acclaimed books for Young Adults include the wonderful *Catch Your Death and Other Ghost Stories, The Ghost on the Hill, The Grasshopper, The House on the Brink, The Spitfire Grave and Other Stories, The Waterfall Box* and *The Burning Baby and Other Ghosts.* He has also written his autobiography, entitled *Ordinary Seaman.*

Gordon's journalistic background created the impetus for the atmospheric ghost story which follows, as the author explains:

"Working as a reporter in the Fens I found myself having to write about everything from the Crown Jewels of England, which King John is supposed to have lost in the marshes near Wisbech, to court cases, inquests, water diviners, and men who knew what it was like to skate for the prize of a leg of mutton to keep their families from hunger.

"There's a lot of water in the Fens, and I heard of one farmworker who, coming out of the pub on a Saturday night, would regularly fall into the dyke and flounder about calling out, 'I'm a swimmer! I'm a swimmer!' He did it one night in winter, nobody heard him, and they didn't find him until the thaw.

"'Under the Ice' started there . . ."

VERY FEW PEOPLE HAVE ACTUALLY SEEN a ghost. I have. But I wish I hadn't.

Rupert saw it long before I did, and I was the only person he ever told about it. I just wish he'd kept quiet, and then things might have turned out differently—at least I wouldn't have been there on that terrible day and I would never have seen what I did see. And I would never have known how unfair it was. There was no justice in it. None.

I have often thought I could have done something to stop it—but now I know that was impossible; I couldn't have done a thing. I'm only telling you this because I can't keep it to myself any longer.

I suppose you'd expect anybody who'd seen a ghost to tell everyone about it. Rupert was different. He kept things to himself. Quite a lot of people are like that, out in the flat fens. He had nobody much to talk to, so he got out of the habit, even with me, and I was always reckoned to be his best friend. He was a thin, gangly sort of boy, a bit taller than me, and he was tough in all sorts of ways you'd never guess just by looking at him.

I knew something was bothering him, but I didn't know what, although it had to be pretty important because one day, out of the blue, he asked me if I'd go home with him after school. It was a half holiday, in the middle of a bitter winter, and I didn't fancy cycling such a long way.

"It'll be dark before long," I said, trying to make an excuse.

"That doesn't matter," he said in a rush. "My father will take us, and we can go skating. There's no danger, the ice is rock hard . . . So that'll be all right, will it?"

"Hold your hosses," I said. This wasn't like Rupert at all, the quiet boy from far out of town. "What am I going to do with my bike?" I wasn't going to leave that in the cycle shed all night, not with some of the characters I knew hanging about. "And what about my tea–my mum'll be expecting me."

"I'll give you some tea," he said, just as if he owned the whole house, the bread and butter and everything. "Give your mum a ring–and you can put your bike in the boot." His father had a Volvo like a battle tank, so that was OK.

"Skates," I said. "I haven't got any." My lovely brother in the sixth form nicked everything that belonged to me. "William's screwed my skates on to his boots," I told Rupert, "so what's the use?"

"How big are your feet?" he said suddenly.

"Not as big as his."

"Same size as me." He plonked his foot down next to mine. "You can have my old fen runners."

"Gee," I said. "Thanks a million."

He went red. "Or you can have my Norwegians. I don't mind."

"Don't worry about it, Rupe." I was beginning to feel sorry for him; he seemed so eager for me to go with him that it would have been just like disappointing a little kid if I'd said no. So I said yes. You never do know what you're letting yourself in for.

He was in a fidget waiting for his father after school and he didn't calm down until we'd stowed the bike and were sitting side by side in the back seat. You could have told it was a farmer's car by the old fertilizer sacks in the boot, but even the back of his father's neck would have let you into the secret because it was brown and creased, and the trilby hat he wore was a mud colour through always being out in the sun and rain. I used to get on with his father quite well, chatting about this and that, but I hadn't seen him for some time, and now he was like Rupert—so quiet that after a while I began to feel as if he was some sort of servant in the front seat, just doing his job by driving us home. This made me so awkward that I kept silent, too.

Rupert practically ignored me. He sat back in his corner and gazed out of the window with his mind on something else while the heater blew warm air at us and I began to wish I was at home by the fire. If I'd had any sense I would have stopped feeling sorry for myself and would have remembered what it was that kept them so subdued. Everybody knew what had happened last summer, but that afternoon it just didn't come into my mind.

It had been freezing for a week so I was used to a nip in the air when I was cycling home, but when we got to where Rupert lived and stepped out of the car the cold was something else. In town it lay in chunks like massive ice cubes between the houses and you felt you could dodge some of it, but out here, where there were no streets and no street lights, the cold was a solid black mass that seemed to press even the birds to the ground.

"Don't know what there is to eat," said Rupert's father. "Bread and pull-it, I reckon." I couldn't tell if he smiled because he turned his head away, but I guessed he didn't bother. "The wife wasn't expecting anyone."

Nice welcome, I thought, but I was polite. "I don't mind, Mr Granger," I said. "I'm not very hungry."

"That's all right, then," and he left us, striding away over the crackling gravel to the farm out-buildings.

"I don't think I should've come," I said, but Rupert was already taking me past the frozen bushes to the back door.

He went ahead of me, and the instant the door opened his mother gave a little cry and called out "Who's there?" as if we were burglars. Even when Rupert told her it was just the two of us she kept peering over his shoulder to make sure exactly who was following him out of the shadows.

"It's only me," I said.

"Oh," she said, and some of the alarm went out of her eyes, but the worry remained. "David Maxey. What are you doing here?"

This time even Rupert could tell I wasn't being given a very warm welcome, and he was embarrassed. "He's hungry," he said.

"But you never said you were bringing anyone." She was quite bitchy with him. "You never told me."

I butted in. "I'm sorry, Mrs Granger," I said, and wished more strongly than ever to be somewhere else. "It's Rupert's fault. He wants me to go skating."

"Skating?" The idea seemed to confuse her.

"Mother." Rupert went close to her. "You know you don't like me to go skating on my own—so that's why I brought him. Two together are quite safe."

She was looking from one to the other of us, and I said, "If she cracks she bears, if she bends she breaks." It was something they said about the ice in the fens, where everybody was a skater and knew about such things. "It's very thick now, Mrs Granger, and it'll never bend an inch."

She didn't answer. Instead, she turned to the dresser and took down plates to set a new place for me. "I'm afraid there's not much," she said.

I'd always liked Rupert's mother. She'd never seemed as if she belonged out here, miles from anywhere, with no neighbours. It was partly the way she dressed I suppose, as if she was ready to leave the farm behind at that instant and take us both up to town for a good time. But now there wasn't a trace of make-up on her face, and the shadows around her eyes were genuine.

"I'll get the skates," said Rupert. "They're in the garage."

I didn't want him to leave me, but I made the best of it by trying to help his mother. There wasn't as much on the table as I was used to when I went there, and she apologized. "I haven't been able to get out to the shops in this weather," she said. It wasn't true; there hadn't been enough snow to make the roads dangerous, and I knew she had her own car.

"This is fine, Mrs Granger," I said. "I can hardly eat a thing."

At any other time she would have seen through the lie and laughed; now she just turned towards me, her face full of anxiety, and said, "Are you sure? Are you really sure?"

I'd always thought that, as mothers go, she was rather pretty, and I was so shocked at how pale and lined her face had become that I found I had no words, and I was very relieved when Rupert returned with the fen runners for me. The little skates, which were like the blades of table knives set in blocks of wood, were those he'd started with when he was younger. The boots were tight, but I managed to squeeze my feet into them.

Dusk was beginning to fall by the time we'd eaten and left the house. Mrs Granger stood at the door with her hands clenched in front of her as if she had to struggle not to reach out and hold us back.

"The ice is rock hard, Mrs Granger," I said, making a new attempt to stop her worrying. "We couldn't go through it even if we tried."

"Don't," she said, "please don't say things like that." She looked around the yard. "Rupert, why don't you get your father to go with you?"

But Rupert was already walking away and his father, who had not joined us at tea, was nowhere to be seen.

I'd always known that the farmhouse was lonely, but I'd never realized just how isolated it really was until I caught up with Rupert on the road outside. In summer, green trees and bushes and tall grass crowded around the house and disguised its loneliness but now the curtains of leaves had been stripped away, and the flat fields, the black furrows ridged with white, stretched away like the bare boards of an empty house.

"Cold," I said, and the blades of the skates that swung in our hands rattled like chattering teeth.

The proper road petered out just beyond the farmhouse and became a track that only tractors could use. There were no hedges out here, only ditches with thin crusts of ice where the water had seeped away beneath. I would have stopped to throw stones through the ice sheets except that Rupert was hurrying ahead, intent on getting somewhere—even though there seemed to be no place better than any other out here.

"It's getting dark early," he said. "It's all this cloud. You won't be able to see it soon."

"Sec what?" I asked, but he had run on as if he didn't want to answer.

We came to a gate across the track and beyond it a low bank stretched away to left and right like the rampart of an ancient fort. On the other side lay the waterway, except that now it was an iceway, reaching in a dead straight line to the black horizon.

"When there's a moon," said Rupert, "you can skate out of sight."

Our voices were so small in the vast space that I doubt if they reached the far bank of the wide channel, not that there was anybody in the whole of creation to hear us. An ice age had made the world a waste land, and we were alone in it.

"Where are you taking me?" I asked, because I'd guessed by now that he had something more than skating on his mind.

"Hurry up and get those runners on," he said, and he had laced up his Norwegians and was crabbing down the bank almost before I'd started. I heard his long blades strike the ice as I still struggled with my laces. "Wait for me," I called, because he was already gliding out from the bank.

"Hurry up. It's getting dark."

He was out in the middle of the channel when I reached the edge, caught the tip of one skate in a tussock of frozen grass and stumbled forward. I was sure I was going to get a wet foot in the seepage that is always at the margin, but my blades ran through the grass on solid ice. It was as hard as a marble floor from bank to bank. There was no risk of falling through;

none at all—but Rupert was leading me on to a danger that was much worse.

We skated, sawing the air with our arms and feeling it bite back at our cheeks and noses, but he, riding high on blades twice the length of mine, easily outpaced me, and I was so far behind that there must have been a hundred metres of ice between us when I saw him circling, waiting for me to catch up.

I was a breathless plodder following a racehorse, and I had lost patience with him so I deliberately dawdled, bending low from time to time, merely letting myself slide slowly along. It must have been infuriating for him, but he gave no sign of it, and continued to cut his slow circles as I drifted closer.

"We don't need a moon," I called. "You can still see for miles." The scatter of snow had made the banks white enough to catch all the thin light that came from the sky and we stood out like dark birds gliding low over frozen fields. But what food would birds find out here? What could they peck at? I was soon to find out.

"I'm flying!" I cried, and I leant forward and spread my arms wide. He had stopped and was waiting for me, and I wondered if I could reach him without pushing again, so I allowed myself to glide.

I was looking down, watching the little blades of the fen runners barely rocking as they skimmed forward, and I realized how smooth the ice was. It was a glassy pavement, polished, without cracks or blemishes, and it came as a shock to see that it was so clear I was actually looking through it. Even in this light I could see into the dark water below, where I knew the long weeds trailed in summer, and I gazed down into a giddy blackness.

My glide had been so successful that I was laughing as my skates came to rest almost at Rupert's feet, and I was just about to raise my head when I caught a glimpse of something beneath the ice. At first I thought it was a twist of weed, and I stooped to look closer. The shape became clear, and in that instant it reached inside me with a sick coldness that held me fixed to the spot. And then, horrified, not wanting to touch the ice anywhere near what I had seen, I eased myself backwards, still crouching, and stood up.

It was only then that I raised my eyes to Rupert.

There was a bridge behind him, in the distance. It was a single span where the track from the farm crossed the channel, and I remember it because it made a black shadow on a level with his shoulders and he seemed for an instant to have enormous arms that stretched from bank to bank. At that awful moment even he terrified me, and I was beginning to draw further back, when he spoke.

"So you can see it, too." The words were like frost on his lips.

I nodded. I saw it clearly. There was a drowned man under the ice.

I could see the folds of his trousers and a shoe twisted at an awkward angle. The sleeves of his jacket were rigid, but his fingers seemed to lie at ease in the ice, resting, as plump and white as the flesh of a plucked chicken. His head was turned away from us, so all we saw was hair and one ear.

I said something, but I can't remember what. All I knew was that we had to go for help even if it was too late–we had to let someone know. That object locked beneath us had to be freed. Words came from me, but Rupert did nothing. He stood quite still.

"Look again," he said.

I turned my eyes to the ice between us but I must have drifted too far back because now I could see nothing. I edged forward. The ice was black, and empty. I cast around, stooping to peer closer, but nothing showed itself.

"Where is it?" I said. The hideous thought came to my mind that a current still flowed under the ice and that the man was rolling slowly beneath our feet. "Where is it now?" I was beginning to panic, taking timid steps on my skates away from the spot as if the ice were about to open and take me down to join the corpse in its frozen coffin. "Where?" I said. "Where?"

"It's still there." His voice was so flat and calm it made me jerk my head up. "It's my uncle," he said.

He skated slowly forward. The extra height of his Norwegians made him tower over me, and once again I was afraid of him. His uncle! He had seen his uncle dead under the ice, and now he was gliding towards me without a sign of grief or even surprise on his face. I was backing clumsily away when he came level with me, and a thin smile appeared on his lips.

"You're not thinking of skating backwards all the way home, are you?" he said.

The fact that he could say something so ordinary, and smile as he spoke, jolted me out of my panic. I even managed to shrug. "How can it be your uncle?" I began . . . and then I remembered. It all came flooding back to me, and at the same instant I knew why his mother was so haggard and his father so silent. The tragedy that had slipped from my mind was still strong within them.

"Oh," I said feebly, "your uncle."

And then my stomach turned over yet again, for his uncle had been dead many months, drowned out here in the fens.

"That was where it happened," Rupert said. "Last summer."

I was ashamed of myself for having forgotten, and for a moment this blotted everything else from my mind. "I'm sorry," I said. "I should have remembered."

"I was there when he was found." He began to move away. "That's how I know who it is in the ice."

So there really was a body there . . . but he was talking nonsense to say it was his uncle. "It can't be," I said. "It's just some old clothes."

"With fingers?"

"Well, it's another body." I didn't want to admit it. "Someone else. We've got to tell somebody. We've got to."

He said nothing. He moved away and I went with him. Our skates were silent and we drifted like ghosts through the bitter dusk. I twisted my head to look behind.

"There's nothing to see," he said. "Even if you go back you won't find it. It's gone."

"How do you know?"

He turned a gaunt face towards me, and once again he smiled. "Do you think I haven't tried?"

"But I saw it. If I can see it, so can somebody else. Have you tried to show anybody?"

Suddenly, as though we were racing, he lowered his head and stretched his legs in long, sweeping strokes that left me behind. I did not catch up with him until we reached the place where we had left our shoes. He was already crouching on the bank unlacing his boots. "Too late to go any further," he said. "Too dark."

We had just seen something impossible to explain, and that was ail he had to say.

"It was a ghost," I said, "wasn't it?" And when that had no effect on him, I added, "Or a shadow or something. Some sort of cracks and bubbles in the ice. The light might just catch them at times." He remained silent, but I wasn't going to leave it there. "You ought to tell somebody about it," I said. "Why not your mother?"

"She's got too much on her mind." He concentrated on his laces for a while, and then, speaking so low I could hardly hear him, he said, "She liked my uncle. She liked him a lot."

"Well, you've got to speak to your father–you've got to tell him."

"I can't." He shook his head without looking up. "I can't." His fingers ceased rumbling with his laces but his head remained bowed, and after a while I saw his shoulders tremble and I realized he was crying.

We were side by side in the frozen grass and Rupert had bent his head to his knees and was sobbing like a little child. I had never seen him in tears; and now that it had happened, I did not know what to do. I began unfastening my own skates, waiting until his sobbing subsided, trying to think of something to say, and failing. His grief was too deep for me to reach. Then, suddenly, he raised his head and was once again speaking clearly.

"He hated him," he said. "My father hated him. They used to be friends and then he hated him."

"But they were brothers."

"What difference does that make?" His voice was harsh. "He liked my mother! My uncle liked my mother, didn't he? A lot. Too much. I heard him say so, didn't I?"

He spat the words at me so fiercely I had to face up to him. "I don't know what you heard," I said.

"I heard everything!" He sucked in his cheeks and glared at me as though I was the most detestable creature on earth. "My father said he'd kill him if he didn't go away. Kill him!"

He stooped forward suddenly and hauled off his skates. "Now you can go home," he said. "Get lost!"

Neither of us said another word. I climbed the bank alone and got to his house ahead of him. I could see his mother and father through the kitchen window, but I didn't go in. I was in a hurry to get away from that place, so I found my bike and left.

The freeze got worse. Rupert and I saw each other at school and were still friends, but we never once mentioned what had happened. His outburst seemed to have shut the door on it, and there was a kind of haughtiness in him that made me see that he was so deeply ashamed of what he had told me he could never speak of it. I told myself that what I had seen in the ice was made by weeds frozen near the surface, and that it was Rupert's imagination because of the terrible time he'd been through that had somehow forced us both to see what he'd seen last summer when they found his uncle.

Then one day the sun shone. The clouds, that for weeks had ground their way towards the horizon as slowly as a glacier, showed gaps of blue, and the sun began to put its fingers through the thin crust of snow on gardens and gutters. Even Rupert smiled and said, "We shan't get much more skating this year, I reckon."

"Too bad," I replied, thinking that he wanted to shrug the whole business away for ever.

"So why don't you come over tomorrow before it's too late?" he asked.

He had taken me by surprise and I looked so sharply at him that he reddened and mumbled something, saying that there were bound to be other people around as it was a Saturday, so there was nothing to worry about. It was the nearest he'd come to mentioning what was on our minds, and I was a bit nettled that he thought I may have been afraid to go skating alone out there, so of course I said yes.

I even managed to get my skates from my brother, so I was properly equipped when I cycled out to see him. The sun was bright, but I had to push against a biting wind which kept the temperature so low that I knew the ice would still be in good condition. And Rupert was right about other people being there. You could never say the ice was crowded because there was so much of it, but there were skaters wherever you looked, and their tiny black figures were dotted away into the distance. An occasional speed man came slicing by, one arm behind his back and the other swinging, and we decided we would join these long-distance skimmers.

Without either of us saying a word we set out towards the distant bridge and this meant we had to go over the spot where the shadows had frightened us so badly. We did not ignore it, but neither did we linger. We circled once, gazing down, and I was certain of the exact spot because the ice there was clear even though its surface was now criss-crossed by blade strokes. The sunlight would have shown any dead man beneath the ice, but there was nothing. There was only darkness below, and when I looked up and caught Rupert's eye he grinned sheepishly and skated off at speed as if to put it behind him once and for all.

We could hear the squeals of girls and the shouts of boys long before we reached the little groups that were strung out over the ice, but we skimmed by until we were far out in the fens. The sun, although now a blazing red, had shed the last of its heat for the day and was beginning to bury itself in the horizon before we thought of turning back. We stretched out on the frozen grass for a few minutes to rest our ankles.

"It's good out here," said Rupert. He was panting and there was even some colour in his cheeks. "I'm glad you could come today."

We weren't in the habit of paying each other compliments, so I just mumbled that I, too, was enjoying myself. I expected the matter to end there, but Rupert had something on his mind; unfinished business.

"Sorry I was such an idiot last time," he said.

"That's OK." I didn't look at him.

"It's just that everything was getting on top of me–Mum and Dad not being very happy and all that. Things had just been getting worse and worse, ever since ..."

He seemed to want me to say it for him.

"I know what you mean," I said, but that wasn't good enough for him; he wanted it out in the open.

"Since my uncle drowned himself." He spoke very clearly, forcing me to look at him. "Drowned himself," he repeated. "I told you something stupid about my dad last time. It wasn't true."

"I know it wasn't." I had to agree with him. His father could never have done such a terrible thing as murder his brother, no matter what he might have said. "You were feeling pretty bad," I told Rupert. "And we'd just seen that thing in the ice."

"*Thought* we'd seen. It's not there now."

"And it wasn't there then," I insisted, backing him up. "It was just imagination. By both of us."

"Both of us." He nodded. He was glad he had a friend, and to know that between us we'd scattered all the shadows from his mind. "Right," he said, "I'll race you back."

It was no race. He had done much more skating than me and his ankles were stronger, so from time to time he had to wait for me to catch up. We had gone further out into the fen than I had realized and, with my slow progress, the sun had dipped below the horizon and had left only an afterglow before the bridge came in sight.

We were alone, the other skaters having long since climbed the banks and gone home, so when we came up to the bridge it was our voices alone that echoed beneath it.

"One at a rime," said Rupert. "The thaw has made it wet under there."

He went first. There was no suggestion of a crack as he went forward cautiously, but when I followed I could see that his weight had made a pulse of water spill from the edge, so I kept to the centre as he waited for me to come through.

I was concentrating so intensely on the ice beneath my skates that I almost ran into him and had to make a wide swerve to keep my balance. That was why I saw his father before he did. Mr Granger was at the top of the bank, looking down.

"Where have you been?" he called to Rupert. "Your mother was worried."

Rupert did not answer. He was leaning forward like a runner trying to get his breath, and I went up alongside him to taunt him. He did not even turn his head my way and I was stooping to look into his face when I saw that, although his mouth was open, he was not gasping for breath. He was in the grip of terror.

I did not wish to follow his gaze, but I was forced to turn my head and look down. It was there. I saw the frozen shoe and trouser leg, the stiff folds of the jacket and the fingers cased in ice. Even the hair on the back of the twisted head was visible.

Neither Rupert nor I moved. We were locked to that dreadful place. "What are you doing down there?" It was his father's voice from the bank. "It's time to go home."

I had my hand on Rupert's arm. I was beginning to pull him back, gently tugging at him, and my skates were making a faint rasping sound on the ice when it happened. The head began to turn. It was as though I had been scratching at the other side of a window pane and had aroused it. The head within the ice came round to face us. Yellow cheeks and an open mouth. And then the eyes, tight shut.

"What's happening?" Mr Granger's voice died and, as it did so, leaving the air empty of all sound, the eyelids lifted. A handspan of ice lay over them, but the eyelids slipped back like a flicker of moonlight, and a pair of dead eyes, grey and as pale as milk, stared up at us.

The cold air brushed the back of my neck as I jerked backwards, but Rupert did not stir. He remained where he was as the fingers came through the ice, and with them, the bulge of the head. It came up like a sleeper pushing back a sheet.

I heard Rupert's name shouted from the top of the bank, and his father came thudding and slithering towards him and snatched him away.

I had slid backwards and was beneath the bridge when the dead figure stood upright and came to collect them. Water ran from its sleeves and dripped from its pale, plump fingers, and its sodden shoes swished on the ice as it advanced. Without realizing it, I had backed even further away, out of the shelter of the bridge, so I was clear of what happened. I was a spectator . . . as Rupert should have been. But he was with his father.

I saw them enter the shadow of the dark arch together, and I saw Rupert slip and fall full length. His father stooped for him, but never got a chance to lift his son upright. The dripping figure came moving towards them and, in the black shadow under the bridge, embraced them both.

The impact of Rupert's fall had been too much for the ice. There was a soft, rending crack and a sheet the size of a table up-ended itself and in an instant, without a sound, the huddle of figures had gone. I flung myself forward, but the ice had slid back into place. I kicked it, but it was wedged. I put my full weight on its edge, and still it did not budge. I knelt and hammered on it, but Rupert was with his father on the other side of that door, and I never saw him again.

MIRROR MAN

STEVE RASNIC TEM

AS USUAL, it's been a prolific year for Steve Rasnic Tem, with short stories published in *MetaHorror, In Dreams, Narrow Houses, The Mammoth Book of Vampires, The Dedalus Book of Femmes Fatales, Gauntlet 3, Dark at Heart, Best New Horror 3,* and elsewhere.

He collaborated with his wife Melanie on the chapbook *Beautiful Strangers,* and contributed three new stories to the solo booklet, *Decoded Mirrors: 3 Tales After Lovecraft.*

"Mirror Man" comes from the latter and, as the publisher's blurb reveals: "The sources of horror in Steve Rasnic Tem's fiction are not monsters, but moments of revelation and self-discovery, when characters find their deepest doubts and fears reflected in the world around them . . . Through its powerful evocation of personal alienation, this triptych of 'tales after Lovecraft' reminds us that Lovecraft, in teaching us new ways to view our world, also taught us new ways in which to view ourselves."

By way of a coda to that insightful evaluation, the author explains that, "'Mirror Man' was the reason I did the *Decoded Mirrors* chapbook–I actually wrote it several years ago, liked it, but couldn't sell it anywhere (most everybody didn't like the Lovecraft angle in it). So when Necronomicon Press started up their chapbook line, a Lovecraftian trilogy seemed to be in order."

We are delighted to present Tem's disturbing story to a wider audience . . .

JEFF LIKED TO THINK OF THE white hairs in his ears as signs of maturity, although he suspected they were really the first outcroppings of old age. He hadn't even noticed them until they were a half-inch or more long; that bothered him. They were pale and looked slightly rubbery, like the hairs on some mutant onion. Once he knew they were there he spent hours examining himself for any new phenomena. Sometimes he would use Liz's magnified makeup mirror. He was convinced that his face was changing every day, but other than the somewhat dramatic ear-hairs he had found nothing to confirm this.

In the mirror, silvered fog turned to beads, then rivulets that bent his flesh and attempted to drag his face into the sink. He wondered if Susan would still love him if he were deformed. Adults *were* mutants—he could think of no better way to define the accretion of distortions as children grew into adults.

He remembered his embarrassment over his own father—the man's appearance, his views about race and nationality. During his teen years he had sought a theory to explain his father's condition—the brain parasite, the secret society, his father's hidden lizard face.

Some day Susan would find him hideously embarrassing. That was why he had to take her on this trip with him. The time when she was uncompromisingly proud of him was fast approaching an end.

Liz had stopped loving him years ago. There must have been a final day when she'd passed beyond her love for him into whatever indifference or resentment she felt now, but he'd been unable to pinpoint it. There was a kind of unspoken pact between them that they not speak of it, perhaps the ultimate in the series of unspoken pacts which had characterized their marriage. But it had been so obvious, so stupid and banal. He'd continued to love her even after that, in that youthful love-sick and inarticulate way he always had, until that too was gone one day, maybe the same lost day he'd first become the adult mutant, when he'd started growing hair in his ears.

An area of cleared mirror containing a section of his left jaw and earlobe fogged over again beneath his breath. His face had fractured in the mirror, broken out into a collage. Some of the layers of his face were as young as his first memories (his lost tricycle half-buried in a pile of coal behind the house, his mother's breath smelling like warm bread), and others were far older than he was. In fact some of the layers of the mirrored face, he was convinced, didn't even belong to him.

"Are we ever going, Daddy?" He saw Susan in one corner of the mirror, dolled up in her party dress, ready for the trip out. Liz had done up her hair in a mass of tight curls—it must have taken hours. "Well, are we?"

"Just give me a few more minutes, honey. I want to look good for the reunion, haven't seen some of these people in a very long time." He couldn't make himself turn around. The mirror was much safer. If he looked at his daughter directly he would want to hold her all the time, until that day she stopped breathing.

Sometimes she made him want to cry—out of some strange sadness because he was growing older every day or because he loved her so much or because he'd recently realized she was the only person in the world he really did love, and even there he wasn't sure he was very effective at it. As he'd grown older he seemed so frightened and suspicious, so inept at loving. So he contented himself with staring at her reflection, admiring the light she cast. "We'll be leaving real soon, honey. I promise."

Liz was waiting in the bedroom when he walked in. "She'll be bored to tears, Jeff. I really don't understand this."

Her shadow rippled across the wall as she paced the room. That flicker of grey reminded him of a small bird that had been trapped in the house one night. They couldn't quite see it, they were just aware of its grey wings beating and beating against the light's reflection on the glossy wallpaper. In the morning they had found torn feathers, spots of blood on the bed. He spoke to Liz's shadow as it moved across the wall. "None of my old classmates or teachers have ever met my daughter. I want to show her off. I have a right–I'm proud of her."

"Providence is a long way to drag an eleven-year-old. Just to stroke your vanity." Her shadow danced a graceful ballet across the wall. It was a terrible irony that adult mutants cast the delicate shadows of children.

He'd always believed that saying things more than once was pointless. And during the course of an unusually verbal marriage he'd said about everything possible. It was like looking in the mirror every day: if things did change it was too gradual to notice. But if he didn't say something, she'd embrace him with silence until he'd left the house. "I'm sorry," he said. "I don't think that's what I'm doing." The words cracked in his mouth from all the years of repetition. One day they'd degenerate into another, far more primitive language. Some sort of eldritch, decadent phrasing. If he didn't do something. If he was still capable.

There was the expected pause while she decided whether there was going to be an argument this morning. Jeff found himself holding his breath in anticipation of her decision, and that made him resentful. Some mornings that would be enough to make him say the little more which would guarantee an argument, but not today. Today he was going to take his beautiful daughter down to Rhode Island for that ten-year reunion. Everyone from the graduate school was going to know that he'd had it in him to have a family, a normal family like other people. With a beautiful daughter, a daughter who depended on him and who called him Daddy.

He heard the agitated beating of grey wings in his head, but he tried to ignore it, moving about the bedroom getting dressed as quickly as he could, waiting for Liz to say whatever she was going to say. He wanted to ask her what ties he should take, if his grey corduroy jacket with the elbow patches would take one more important wearing, but first he had to know if there was going to be an argument or not. If there was going to be an argument he thought he might never be able to ask such questions of her again.

He caught her reflection in the dresser mirror as she sat on the bed, staring at his half-full suitcase on the other end. She looked so unhappy he wanted to go over and sit beside her, take her in his arms, but then she would tell him all that he had done to make her feel the way she did, and that would start the argument he could not have this morning.

In the mirror he saw the silvering in her long black hair. He'd never noticed it before, looking at her every day, watching her eat breakfast before she left for the university. Again the mirror provided him with secret, arcane knowledge. But then she always wore her hair up for work, and she was usually in good humor–she actually enjoyed the work she was forced to do. Sadness brought out the silver in her hair. Not for the first time, Jeff realized how difficult he must be for her to live with.

"You used to be so impressive," she began softly. "You were the only person I'd ever met who early on decided what kind of person he was going to be, and then became that person. You used to make me feel so good about myself."

Her reflection stared at him, talked to him. Liz had learned where to look if she wanted to look into his eyes. Her image in the mirror was so clear, so direct, that Jeff thought he might be loving her again, if he had ever in fact stopped loving her. The room's reflection around her image looked vaguely warped, shimmering with distortion. The contrast between the room's distortion and Liz's clear image brought a tremor of anxiety into his hands struggling with the tie, and he wondered vaguely at the physics involved. There appeared to be dark pockets where the vertical lines of the room's image warped or broke. There appeared to be distant movement behind Liz where the reflected colors of the room bled. Liz's face was singular and unwavering, her eyes fixed on him, even as the rest of the world appeared chaotic with layers, the room about to dissolve around her, peel away revealing. . . what? He could see in the mirror that she was silently crying now. But if he didn't turn to look at her directly she was not crying at all. If she was sad only in his mirror, he had not made her sad at all. In the mirror her eyes begged him for the first time in years. Jeff looked away, embarrassed, and fumbled again with his tie, trying to imagine it tied.

"I'll . . . talk to you about it just as soon as we get back tomorrow. I promise."

"Okay, Jeff. Whatever. Whatever you say." When Jeff looked back up at the mirror she had left it. The lines of the room moved jaggedly, the furniture blending with increasing speed, as if the world of the mirror was being heated.

Susan was good in the car. It made him proud when Susan was good. "Am I going to meet your friends?" she asked.

"Old friends," he said.

"But are they still your friends?"

He didn't know what to say. He pretended to busy himself with the rearview mirror, adjusting it in order to view as much of the landscape behind him as possible. Early in their marriage Liz would kid him about his habit of fiddling with the mirror, as if something was following him. He had never laughed, and eventually she dropped the joke. "I don't know, honey," he said now. "Adults don't always know who their friends are, I guess. It's simpler at your age. Friendships get complicated when you're an adult. You get set in your ways, and then you forget how to make friends."

Liz nodded solemnly in his rear-view mirror. Jeff stared at the mirror until his wife's face vanished and Susan's reappeared. He adjusted the mirror both to expose the maximum amount of receding landscape and to see as much of Susan as he could, while limiting her view of his own mutating expressions. He had to keep an eye on her, he had to keep her safe—that was his responsibility as a father—and yet he didn't want her to feel that he was spying on her.

"Why won't you look at me, Daddy?" Obviously he had the mirror adjusted correctly. She hadn't asked the question in a long time.

He licked his lips. But he couldn't see himself in the mirror now, so he had to wonder if he was in fact licking his lips. "I'm driving, honey. I can't look at you and drive at the same time."

She nodded again. "That's why I can't sit in the front seat with you. That's the rule."

Every few months she seemed compelled to check out his expectations. He hated it when she called them rules. He preferred to think of them as guidelines which held reality in place. Mutants needed as many of these mini-strictures as they could generate, just to get through the day. Jeff didn't bother to tell Susan about all of them, thinking that if she knew them all it would hasten her evolution into mutancy. So he had always told her strictly on a need-to-know basis. "When you sit in the front seat, it distracts me, honey. And when that happens things aren't so safe any more. I guess you distract me because you're so pretty." He laughed but Susan did not laugh with him. "Driving is serious business," he continued. "Daddy has to concentrate."

"Someday I still want to sit in the front seat, Daddy."

"I know." And someday soon, he knew, she would no longer accept his interpretations of what was safe.

They passed through Attleboro on Highway 123 before connecting with 1-95 which would take them south out of Massachusetts and down into the heart of Providence. Jeff had taken the long way out of New Hampshire, avoiding Concord, Portsmouth, the entire Boston area. He hadn't exactly planned it that way. He drove as he always drove, allowing himself plenty of time, constantly referring to the map so he would have some vague idea where the roads led. Vague because maps lied—he'd discovered this a long time ago—taking you into all manner of locales not even hinted at by the pale colors and wandering veins etched into the paper.

He never chose the shortest route. You couldn't tell anyway because traffic and road conditions were never indicated, and the nature of the driving experience itself was beyond the scope of any map. He avoided the interstates as much as possible—he was scared of not seeing those hidden taints in the bypassed towns.

He preferred to feel his way through the landscape, watching not only the road but also the ambient architecture and the local residents, constantly checking his mirrors for the backward look that often revealed all—the secret faces, the unconscious expressions.

Then he would find the next road on the map, and, if the drive had been pleasant, he would choose routes which he sensed would somehow maintain the experience. But if the look of the buildings or the people or even the particular rake or curvature of the road disturbed him, he would search the map for the quickest, most likely release.

But the indigenous inhabitants were most important. They were the ones who built and maintained the buildings, who landscaped the environment. Even the most neutral of settings would reveal some sort of signature.

They stopped for gas in a small New England town which had somehow escaped the urban sprawl. Perhaps no one had ever noticed it was there. It was tucked away beneath one edge of the highway, a faded green sign hanging askew on rusted bolts pointing to a narrow exit lane. Jeff took the lane past a row of dilapidated houses to a one-pump station.

The boy appeared suddenly at the driver's side window. His dark skin was mottled by patches of pink and grey peeling away beneath his eyes, like poorly-applied makeup. His eyes were narrow and dark. The phrase *melting pot* came to mind. Jeff's father used to talk a great deal about a "melting pot" when Jeff was a child. The phrase had filled him with unease.

"Gas you?" The dark spaces of the boy's eyes betrayed no life. Jeff found himself grunting an affirmative. The boy nodded, replying with a series of expressions, gestures, even simple looks Jeff could not fully understand. It made him uncomfortable.

So perhaps he wasn't so different from his father at all, only marginally better-educated. Educated enough to feel the guilt.

In Jeffs mirror, Susan was layered in shadow and light, her deepset eyes unreadable. But he suspected she felt it, too. He'd always wanted to blame his own father for teaching him such profound unease. But he suspected it wasn't upbringing. Unease was bred in the womb.

He tipped the boy much too generously and hurried back to the main highway. He passed through several similar villages. He changed routes several times, and still the worn out houses and patchwork faces continued, the accumulation of them sloughing off his mirror into memory.

In Jeff's rearview mirror shadowed faces appeared in backwards perspective, layer after layer of them in grey doorways and open windows and behind polarized windshields. But what disturbed him more than the faces themselves were the eyes they held—as a bare setting might hold its jewel—too small to see and yet which themselves might see so much. Thousands of eyes glittering with dark color, moving slowly, scanning, telescoping, perhaps jittering a wild, drug-induced dance within the ravaged face within a ravaged hovel. The eyes his rearview mirror could not catch in the act.

He knew such things weren't safe to talk about. Early in his graduate history studies he had been interested in the writings of such American nativists as Madison Grant, Lothrop Stoddard, and H. P. Lovecraft. He'd wanted to know if they had had certain perceptions, and if perhaps they'd so misunderstood these perceptions that their rather bizarre racial theories had come about. He'd wanted to know what they saw when they looked into the mirror.

Regularly he checked on Susan in the mirror. She slept off and on, slumped against the right-hand door. Now and then she would wake up and gaze into the mirror with bewildered eyes, as if this were something she had never seen before, as if she had seen her adult self, her mutancy, her lone animal self. Then she would nod off again. Children were blessed with an expansive capacity for sleep, because the world was too complicated a place for them to take in all at once. Now and then she would wake again and look, and as it grew darker outside the car there came a time when Jeff could not see her eyes in the mirror, although he sensed their heat.

It was night by the time they'd reached the outskirts of Providence. But not the complete dark he would have experienced at home, surrounded by open fields and with the nearest streetlight miles away. This was the brown dark that surrounded large cities, diluted by chemical smoke and exotic lighting.

He'd always found driving at night to be disorienting. Each vehicle was a bubble of dim light, a marginally sufficient and self-contained ecosystem. You wandered up and down grey ribbons of highway you could barely see, seeking clues as to your route. It was a wonder any one of you reached your destination. Night driving seemed a matter of blind and ancient instinct, aided by appeals to the gods of luck.

He remembered being lost one time and driving with the window down, seeking some sort of guidance from the local smells: wet salt, cedar smoke, or a thick, treacly plasma that seemed to cling to his clothing. He'd read somewhere that smells often had a powerful impact on people's moods, especially the moods of children. He wondered how many sociopaths had grown up with stale, evil fragrances.

Now he rolled the window up tight, cursing himself for exposing Susan to the air of the highway. He searched for her in his rearview mirror, eventually finding her curled up against the right-hand door, the top half of her face eaten by shadow. "Susan?" She didn't move. He spoke it again, louder, and still no response. He felt her panicky, screamed name rising swiftly up his throat, but held it back. He should have been watching her all the time. Then she stirred in her sleep. He was relieved, and then suddenly a little irritated with her. He needed to have her alert and charming for his reunion. He pulled off the road and into a small convenience store on the northeast edge of the city.

The man behind the counter seemed too old for the long silver chain dangling from his left ear. His eyes were greasy.

He gazed past Jeff out the front window. "Your little girl sick?" he asked, with minimal movement of his lips.

For some reason the very idea that the clerk had noticed his daughter in the car, had used the words "your little girl," alarmed Jeff. He found himself searching the man's face for a lascivious wink or tongue across the lips. In the high chrome polish of the cash register, shelves, and counter trim, Jeff could feel a thousand fragments of the clerk's slick eyes, watching him, sliding closer.

Jeff turned and found himself looking at his daughter directly, without the protection of reflection. She sat like an elderly doll slumped with a heavy weight of medication, her forehead pressing the car window, staring at him. The red and yellow neon of the store's sign washed her face, made it seem thinner, the shadows darker. She was his beautiful doll, his Auschwitz doll. He turned and almost desperately his gaze latched on to the clerk's greasy eyes. "It's just the reflection from your sign. That damned garish neon. That's what makes her look so ill." He said it inviting argument, but there was none. The clerk cast his subhuman eyes down and waited for Jeff's order.

When he got into the car he handed the sack of food back to her without looking. He held his breath a beat, anticipating some sort of terrible breakage—the car windows, the store beyond, perhaps even the tight sheen of skin stretched over his skull, but after a moment a hand took the bag from him. "I couldn't remember what you liked." He forced a laugh and it sounded oddly falsetto. "So I bought enough for six ... six daughters, six little girls."

He was embarrassing himself. She said nothing in reply; he thought she must be terribly angry with him now. He was glad Liz wasn't there to point out how badly he was handling things. It was obviously much too trying a trip for a little girl. He had given her coffee and donuts, cupcakes and a nut bar and two colas in the bag, brands he had never heard of, Rhode Island brands he supposed. He thought she was too young for coffee but he couldn't remember. He couldn't remember any of the things she liked to eat. Suddenly he didn't know her at all. She had grown up much too fast and soon she would be dead. They all would be dead. Everyone had told him that all his life but he hadn't believed it until now.

She didn't say anything. But he thought he could hear her eating now. Not loudly, but slowly consuming everything he had given her. Good.

He didn't recognize any of the streets around Brown. They were all torn up, decades of asphalt pulled up like geologic strata, detours leading him around the gaping excavations floored with oily liquid to oddly-shaped parking spaces overlooked by black ruins. He thought he recognized the Rockefeller Library but he couldn't be sure. He finally pulled the car into what may or may not have been a parking space, opened Susan's door, and reached into the shadows there. Her hand caught his timidly. "We're late," he barked nervously, turning his head as he dragged her from the car and started racing up the steps. Her tread grew lighter the harder he pulled. He had a vision of his beautiful daughter entering the reception hand-in-hand with proud papa. He whispered back into the cool wind blowing off the damp pavement, "You're beautiful." He knew her shyness would not permit her to reply to that, and she didn't.

The night air in Providence seemed a far more substantial thing than he remembered, but it had been a very long time since he had done more than drive through the city during daylight hours. He supposed there was much more pollution these days, more dust from all the reconstruction. Shadows underwent a congealing process; black spaces solidified. At times it was like walking through veils. The air had a feeling of age, as in a room long kept shut. Try as he might, he couldn't imagine how as a student here he had ever tolerated such Lovecraftian gloom.

The printed sign on the door said that the City Works department had ruled this particular classroom building "unsafe." Another hastily-scrawled red note on blue paper—Professor Lawrence's old stationery?—explained that the reunion had been moved to the Biltmore hotel.

Rather than trying to maneuver those torn and reshuffled streets again, Jeff decided they would walk. He wouldn't worry about getting lost; everyone knew where the Biltmore was.

After several blocks he had to remove his coat. He could not believe the heat. His shirt stuck to his skin like layers of molt—he suspected it was ruined. Liz would be unhappy—she had given it to him last birthday, although it was the only present he could remember receiving. Perhaps an ugly tie from Susan with her child's taste. He vaguely remembered looking into the mirror and seeing a line of distortion hanging from his neck, squeezing it so tightly he couldn't breathe. Susan kept slipping from his grasp; he regripped her hand so tightly he was surprised when she didn't cry out. In the dark puddles spotting the pavement his reflection looked bodiless, his head screaming as it flew through the night air.

Store windows strangely refused to give up all of his reflection. In passing he would see a cheek and an eye, downward slash of a mouth, an outthrust leg, one hand trailing back, desperately clutching at a daughter who seemed to have lost her bright image in their flight across town. He tried to attribute the gaps in his own image and his daughter's complete absence to dust and grease on the glass.

Now and then he lost track of the Biltmore's direction in the tangle of disrupted streets and gutted buildings. He stopped and gave a dark passerby his best "lost" look—the man's shambling made it impossible to ask him directly. He wasn't surprised that the man ignored him. He tried this tack again and again, finally working up the courage to at least touch the shoulder of one or two. Some of those citizens obviously didn't take kindly to his touching them so—some looked as if they might have killed him had there been no witnesses. All his life, he had met people who seemed somehow too cold, too cruel to be human; they behaved in ways Jeff believed no human should behave.

A man turned suddenly and gestured awkwardly toward a narrow side street. Jeff was struck by the mouth, which seemed too wide, as if he had undergone one of those mouth surgeries movie stars had had, but in this case the incision had gone much too far. Jeff stared, but the man's eyes refused to blink, collecting more and more water which caught the dim light and magnified it, making them look heavy with ground glass. Jeff finally turned away.

The gathering at the Biltmore was sedate, and no one seemed to recognize him. The hotel itself was under reconstruction, tall scaffolding leaning precariously against the walls where workers in white coveralls labored overtime at replastering the cracked and stained surfaces. Or perhaps they themselves were applying the cracks and stains. Jeff drank until the workers and scaffolding disappeared, and then he had a vision of the hotel's more elegant future firmly in mind.

"Bill, is that you?" Someone clutched his shoulder, as if desperately seeking directions.

"No," Jeff replied to the staggering fat man in front of him. "Tonight I'm not me at all."

Now and then a stranger would smile and slap Jeff on the back, chant a few endearments and then leave again. Jeff thought that in another time and world they might have been his friends. Everyone had always liked him, but he had no talent for friendship.

Some time near midnight Jeff discovered Professor Lawrence chatting with some men and women Jeffs own age whom he vaguely remembered as having been in his classes in graduate school. He watched the elderly man for some time before he could muster enough courage to speak to him. He wore glasses still, but a different, squarer shape. His speech, his entire presentation seemed a bit more hesitant, his former students interrupting frequently to take command of the conversation and discuss their own researches.

"Professor Lawrence?" he said, pushing himself right up to the old man's glasses. "Jeff Reynolds. It's great to see you again!"

The old man nodded absently, then raised an eyebrow slightly. "Oh, I remember," he said, sounding tired. "You did some work on the nativists, as I recall. Most peculiar. Those old bigots. Most peculiar," he said again, as if describing Jeff himself, and Jeff watched as his reflected face in his imagined father's glasses turned dark, broad, lizard-like.

"Here," Jeff said suddenly, rocking forward and spilling his drink on Lawrence, who blanched and stepped back. "I have a *family* now! Me! A wife and a beautiful. . . beautiful daughter. Susan!" He called, looking around, and suddenly realizing in a panic he had no idea where she was. "Susan!" He tried to grab Lawrence's hands in both of his but Lawrence stumbled and jerked away from him. As if Jeffs touch might contaminate the old fraud. "Susan!" He stared at Lawrence in horror. "You have to believe me!" he cried. "You were important to me. I *do* have a daughter!" But the hotel shimmered so loudly Jeff had no idea if Professor Lawrence heard him at all.

After a few hours Jeff stopped calling out the name of his beautiful daughter, wondering–helpless not to–whether that was truly her name. If she was alive, if she even existed anymore, he felt she would find him. If only he could cover enough ground in time. The sky had lightened somewhat–dawn would be there soon–but as yet there were only night people out on the Providence streets.

He did not know what he could tell Elizabeth, if there was ever an Elizabeth to tell. He didn't think he would ever be able to tell her anything if he could not find Susan. The pale light falling between the buildings into the narrow streets had its own kind of solidity, as if there were a clear line between this light and what lay beyond and the ordinary morning this side of it. Like a curtain, or a sheet of glass. He stepped through.

In the expanding light Providence tried to reveal its secrets to him. Where store fronts had been torn open metal armature was revealed, a multitude of electrical cable and the complex network of plumbing added to and subtracted from so often over the years that he doubted anyone could trace it all. Posters had been rubbed away unevenly from the exterior walls of shops so that the portions of words remaining spelled out bizarre phrases which nonetheless seemed vaguely familiar to him. Ornate architectural decoration had been weathered so that even more ornate subsurfaces showed through. Disparate building styles had been jammed together to create new styles. The city appeared unfinished, and yet already renewing itself.

Two of the men with too-broad mouths rode huge street cleaning machines, running over the same spots again and again. From broken window panes fragments of many eyes reflected down. At the bronzed edges of buildings mishappen limbs attempted to stir from the reflective surfaces. In the finish of a shiny red car he saw his body beginning to warp and catch fire. In the polished tile of a pedestrian plaza he caught a glimpse of his true eyes. In the curve of a broken bottle he watched himself striking again and again at the child he loved so much, whom he could not find in all these mirrors.

"This is the way it begins," he thought, as world rubbed against, world, and his own skin grew veined and layered. "This is the way it ends," he thought, as stink and dark erupted from every crack in the pavement, every opening in the walls, and the raw edges of his reality. "This is simply one of those moments," he thought, when suddenly and just for the moment you forget that you are a human being in the company of human beings, and you find that you are capable of doing something truly terrible. Just for that moment there seems no reason not to do the worst thing you can think of. There seems to be no one to judge you, and for that moment you are incapable of guilt. A life is defined by the choices made during moments like these.

He found Susan's body somewhere between the world he had always dreamed he lived in and the dark impulses beyond. Her body had been taken apart beyond all hope of reassembly. In the dull mirror of her eye he could see the lizard he had become, and the goat, a lone member of that dark mysterious race that would forever corrupt the lives of the human animal.

NIGHT SHIFT SISTER

NICHOLAS ROYLE

1993 HAS BEEN a busy year for Nicholas Royle. Barrington Books published his first novel, *Counterparts,* as a limited edition paperback and New English Library released the first mass-market edition of his British Fantasy Award-winning anthology *Darklands,* with a second and possibly further volumes to follow.

Recent new stories have appeared in *The Mammoth Book of Zombies, Dark Voices 5: The Pan Book of Horror, In Dreams, The Sun Rises Red, Sugar Sleep* and *Sunk Island Review.*

Bump in the Night Books recently issued a chapbook of short stories by Royle and Michael Marshall Smith, and his fiction has been selected for five consecutive volumes of *The Year's Best Horror Stories,* all four volumes of *Best New Horror,* and his contribution to *Narrow Houses* was one of only two to be chosen from that anthology for *The Year's Best Fantasy and Horror: Sixth Annual Collection.*

No wonder *Fear* called him "Britain's most successful young writer of short horror fiction."

As the author explains, "'Night Shift Sister' was partly inspired by the video for the Siouxsie and the Banshee's single 'Kiss Them for Me'." It also brings together some of his other favourite things, such as maps, hidden realms/parallel worlds, and gasholders, and became the starting point for a new novel entitled *In the City*.

FIRST CARL FOUND THE MAP. It was a photocopy *of* a page taken from a book of street maps. He found it on the pavement outside the record shop one night when he'd worked later than usual sorting secondhand singles into categories. He knew that his customers would soon refile so many of them that his system would be ruined. That was partly why he liked doing it: to give the kids something to knock down. These days he rebelled only vicariously.

But there were patterns everywhere. Even in his own filing systems he discerned some arcane force at work. Something which came from above him and directed his hands as they lifted and turned and slotted. When the customers changed the system they did so according to some secret order not even they were aware of.

He left the shop late and became conscious while he was locking up of a fresh wind that carried a faint unpleasant odour reminiscent of domestic gas. For a moment he worried that there might be a leak in the shop but then it dispersed and he saw the map at his feet.

Studying the map as he walked to his old Escort parked a couple of streets away, Carl became confused. It looked like a detail of a city, presumably his own because of where he found it, but the streets were unnamed. They were obviously streets, and railway lines, too, and parks, ponds, canals and open spaces and closed spaces, but none of them were named so he couldn't say what locality it represented.

He unlocked the car door and got in. Dropping the map on the passenger seat he started the engine and pulled away from the kerb. At a red light he looked at himself in the rearview mirror and ran a hand through his long black hair which was perhaps in need of another bottle of dye and certainly a thorough wash. He also needed a shave. His dirty white leather jacket creaked comfortably and he reached down to take the packet of Camels out of his left boot and light one using the car lighter. The light went green, he turned right and the Escort bounced over the uneven road surface in the gathering darkness. Carl liked this time of day. Once he'd shut up shop his time was his own. He liked company but only of his own selection. Crowds weren't his scene. There was a radio in the car but he generally didn't switch it on. He welcomed quiet after spinning singles all day to keep the kids from getting bored.

He called in at the Cantonese takeaway and studied the map while he waited for his food. There were long straight drives and grids of narrow streets, and an area of streets which curved round and round like a game of solitaire where you have to get the ball to the middle. There was even a little circle at the centre.

When he reached the flat he took the map and his A to Z from the glove compartment, and his sweet and sour, and went upstairs. The flat was sparsely furnished but all the walls were shelved to house his enormous record collection. In the living room there was also a battered old sofa, a low sturdy table with an overflowing ashtray, and a pretty good TV and VCR. The white-painted ceiling was nicotine-stained.

He spent most of what remained of the evening going through the A to Z looking for a street layout that mirrored the one on his photocopied fragment, but without success.

It had occurred to him that the map could be of a different city, but then why was the original owner using it here? Carl decided whatever the map depicted was to be found here or nowhere.

The map's patterns attracted him but when frustration set in he lit a cigarette and slid a cassette into the VCR. A big fan of Siouxsie and the Banshees, Carl just couldn't get enough of the latest single. He played it several times a day at the shop and at home he watched the video over and over again. It helped him relax. And just looking at the way she moved made him feel less lonely, which was often a problem since Christine had fucked off to Paris without even leaving him a phone number. Or saying goodbye for that matter. All she'd said was something about him being a worthless drifter with less sense than her little sister. It had seemed harsh to him.

Sometimes he got so miserable he felt like crying. Nearly thirty, he had nothing apart from a scummy record shop, a decrepit Ford Escort, four or five thousand records and a few videos. His only company was Siouxsie Sioux. On video. Christine had left a hole in his life and, rather than try to fill it with someone else, he preferred to slip out through it and find something new.

Most of his old friends were married and couldn't come out because "it's such short notice and we couldn't get anyone to sit". The only one of his old friends who was still single was Baz and all he ever offered Carl was a fix. Things weren't that bad, he always thought to himself. Seeing Baz sometimes had the effect of cheering him up because he realised there was still a lot further to fall. He was determined to hang on. Maybe when the car dropped dead and he could no longer afford the spiralling rent on the shop. Maybe then he'd turn to Baz.

Carl took another cigarette from the pack on the table and reached for his matches because like a dickhead he'd left his lighter at the shop. But the box was very light. He shook it. Empty.

"Shit."

Kitchen.

Carl switched on one of the electric rings on the hob and waited for it to heat up. When it was bright orange he swept his hair away from his face and bent down to light the cigarette. He didn't turn the ring off but watched it becoming brighter and hotter as he smoked. He flinched as he remembered pressing the flat of his hand down on one of his mother's electric rings when it was on. He'd been trying to climb on to a work surface and was using the cooker to lever his body up. As soon as he had felt the pain he had tried to withdraw his hand, but all his weight was on it, so he had screamed loud enough to pierce his mother's eardrums and she had looked round as he began to fall. He remembered her picking him up off the floor, trying to uncurl his hand. The rings had left dark brown marks on his skin and the smell made him sick.

He pulled on his cigarette. The scars had healed quite quickly but he had been left with a fear of the cooker. When he had bought his flat he had wanted gas but there wasn't any, so he intended to get a cooker with a modern ceramic hob, but Christine bought him a moving-in present: a nice old-fashioned electric cooker with rings just like his mother's.

He stared hard at the orange spiral, mesmerised by it. It wasn't just a bad memory. The shape meant something to him. It both attracted and repelled him without him knowing why.

Carl took the photocopied map to bed with him and fell asleep clutching it.

Carl became obsessed with the map and discovering the place it was based on. He thought about it constantly while serving customers and sorting through boxes of old singles people brought in to sell. He was bored with their mewling complaints and saw the map as an escape route.

An original '76 punk with bad teeth said he wanted £25 for The Skids' "Into the Valley" on white vinyl and £30 for the "Wide Open" EP, twelve-inch on red. Carl suggested wearily he'd do better to advertise in the music papers. He'd already got two copies of one and three of the other in the shop and no one seemed to want to buy them.

"What about Roxy Music 'Viva!' on Island? Forty quid."

"I've got three in stock."

"Not on Island," the punk argued. "It's rare."

"It's rare but I've got three of them."

Two French students asked if he'd got anything by Michel Petrucciani. Carl directed them to the jazz shop a couple of blocks away, then began to wonder if the map was of Paris and he was supposed to use it to find Christine. He discounted this quickly, feeling certain that he was the last person Christine wanted to see. To lift his spirits he stuck "Kiss Them for Me" on the turntable. He took the map out of the back pocket of his jeans and lit a cigarette. Out of the corner of his eye he noticed two young girls playing peek-a-boo with him from behind the soundtracks section. Did they know anything about it? Was it a deliberate plant?

He stepped forward to the till to serve a boy buying a clutch of house singles and when he looked up again the girls had gone. When he gave it some thought, he realised a great many people passed through his shop, trailing their lives and their secrets. Did some of what they carried get left behind? When he shut the shop at night the atmosphere always seemed a little bit richer. The secondhand records contained so many memories, different memories for different people, but each record would reek of the particular recollections of its previous owners. Had he bought the Skids' singles off the punk, he would have taken part of the punk into his shop to stay after the doors were locked. Perhaps that was why he had said no.

He lit another cigarette and held the map up to the light to see if that revealed any clues. It didn't. So he slipped his cigarettes down his boot, locked up and drove home.

The Hat was quiet. When the downstairs tenant was in, Carl's life felt like a film with a soundtrack. A heavy metal soundtrack. Which meant you knew it was a crap film. He slung his leather jacket on a chair in the kitchen and took a bottle of Peroni beer from the fridge. He was running low. There were only six boxes left. Lighting a Camel he wandered into the moonlit living room and trailed his finger along rows of singles. He filed them alphabetically by artist. Hundreds had been bought new, but most were second-hand. He thought about what had occurred to him in the shop and wondered if he would be able to sense someone else's memories by playing their single.

He turned his attention to the shelf that held twelve-inch singles and took down "IV Songs" by In Camera. He switched everything on and played the first track. Spidery guitar, deliberately flat vocals, a spiny bass line and chattering cymbals. But no atmosphere. It was a depressing record but only because of the music. He took it off and looked at the words scratched into the runout groove. "Thanks Ilona." Inscribed on to the original acetate by the cutting engineer at his lathe, these messages fascinated Carl because they were like dues to a whole world of secrets and relationships behind the record. He put back the In Camera single and crossed the room to the C section of his LPs and proudly took out Elvis Costello's "This Year's Model". Inscribed on the runout groove was "Special Pressing No. 003. Ring Moira on 434 3232 For Your Special Prize." He had bought the record the day it came out and, noticing the inscription, found a phone box and dialled the number, winning free tickets to a Costello concert. The message had been intended to appear on the first 500 copies, but it overran by about 20,000 and a lot of people got very pissed off. But it was a good gig and now the record felt like a trophy.

He slid the LP back in its sleeve and went and lit another Camel from the electric ring because he'd forgotten his lighter again. The orange spiral burned into his brain and he reflected on how pathetic it was to be going through his record collection trawling for memories, his own and other people's.

He dragged on the cigarette and blew smoke rings. He watched them uncoil and re-form, a series of loops and twists. From his back pocket he took out the map and traced its streets with his eye. He shut his eyes and ran his fingers over the paper to see if that would yield anything. But all he felt were the slight ridges of toner from the photocopier.

He pressed play on the Siouxsie video and lit another cigarette from the stub of the old one. When it finished he rewound and played it again. While he was aware of how they could ensnare and reduce life to a series of repeats, Carl found some comfort at times of stress in following routines and resorting to icons. He fancied Siouxsie like mad and loved the song but he was still restless. Prowling down the shelves into the hallway he came across his huge collection of white labels. At the shop he bought a lot of white label promos in blank sleeves from collectors and if there were any he wanted to keep he just took them home. It was all the same money, whether it was at the shop or at home. Many of the promo copies in his collection had the artist's name scrawled across the white label in felt tip, but some were blank and these he liked best because if there were no distinguishing marks he could forget who the record was by and playing it was always a surprise.

He fell asleep on the sofa and woke with a start when his cigarette burned right down and stung his finger. He sucked it as he drew his legs off the table and stood up. In the bathroom he ran his finger under the cold tap and examined it under the light over the mirror. There was a tiny patch where the whorls of his fingerprint had been smoothed over. He stared fascinated at the pattern of parallel lines. On the third finger of his right hand the lines seemed to fan out in a spiral from a central point, like hair growing from the crown. But Carl realised that when you'd got down to examining your own fingerprints it was time to say goodnight.

He played a random selection of singles at the shop and listened with one ear to the lyrics. He looked carefully at the records he had bought during the morning in case their titles revealed anything. But there was nothing. He knew he could make something up out of all the material at his fingertips, but he would know he'd invented it. If a genuine message were to stand out from the dross he'd know it because he'd feel it. By the end of the day he felt saturated by voices and longed for silence. The roads were refreshingly empty. His tyres hissed on wet tarmac and he cruised with the radio off. The red lights in the distance became a cascade of reflections in the puddles as he knocked the gear lever into neutral and coasted down to meet them. He rolled into position behind a girl in a Mini who like him was waiting for the lights to change. She had shoulder-length black hair like Siouxsie Sioux and was bobbing up and down on her seat and moving from side to side, tapping her fingers on the steering wheel and banging the dash.

What was she listening to?

Carl suddenly felt his stomach twist as he realised that whatever music the girl was listening to was a due. If only he could hear it he would share a secret with her and perhaps he'd know the way to drive to the streets on the map. Maybe she'd let him follow her. He wound his window down but her window was up and he couldn't hear anything. She bounced on her seat and the little car moved like a cocoon when she did. He couldn't pull alongside because there was only one lane.

The lights changed and she was off. He jerked into first and followed, reaching across to switch on the radio to see if she was listening to a station he could tune into. The gap between the two cars lengthened as he slewed across the dial, stopping to catch fragments of music. But there was nothing that spoke to him as clearly as the girl's movements. It must have been a tape. She was a long way ahead now. He jumped a red light to keep her in sight but she turned into a side street and although he followed suit she had vanished into a warren of crescents he barely knew.

He was smoking and reading a thriller in bed when the front door rattled in its frame. With a clear view of the door from his bed, Carl looked up and put his book down beside him. When the door opened he wasn't altogether surprised to see the girl from the car. Her black hair framed a face that was Siouxsie's, except that it wasn't. Because it was Christine's. She was like a composite of both of them. The only two women in his life, both now very much on the fringes of it, synthesised into this one girl.

She walked in and turned past his doorway to enter the living room. He noticed as he got out of bed to follow her that she was carrying a long knife in the back pocket of her jeans, the same pocket he kept his map in. He felt in his own pocket and was relieved to find it still there. The girl went over to Carl's stereo equipment and slipped a single from inside her denim jacket on to the turntable. She stood back and Carl came forward to see what she'd brought him. A white label disc spun at 45 and the needle cut into it. He looked up but the girl had gone. He whirled round and ran to the door but it was shut and there was no sound in the stairwell. He bent over the record player again and saw that as the needle travelled round the groove towards the centre it left a fine spiral of blood in its wake.

Carl jumped and woke up. His cigarette had burnt a hole in the duvet cover. He smothered it quickly with a pillow, but there was no need: the cigarette was cold. He shivered and felt sick. Brushing the curtain behind his head to one side he looked down into the street for a Mini, but there was only his Escort and one or two other familiar cars.

He stomped out of his bedroom and checked the front door—undisturbed—and the stereo. There was no record on the turntable and no blood but the power was on. He never left the power on. Groaning, he flicked the switch and went to make as much and as many different uses of the bathroom as his body would let him.

In bed once more he tossed and turned but sleep eluded him. *Got to get up, got to get up,* he thought over and over. He pulled on a pair of boxer shorts and went through to the living room. A cigarette and the Siouxsie video. They had a placebo effect but he was neither completely relaxed nor did he feel sleepy. Yet his body was exhausted. At dawn he was thinking of taking the car for a run down to the crescent where he'd lost the girl in her Mini when he finally fell asleep in front of the TV.

Driving to the shop a couple of hours later he felt like a jigsaw that had been put together wrongly. Someone had tried to force pieces into each other and they held but only just. He had a craving for pure orange juice but made do with a cigarette instead. He pushed in the dashboard lighter and waited for it to pop out. He withdrew it and brought it up to his mouth. While driving he looked down to align the end of the cigarette with the lighter and was shocked by the sight of the burning orange element. He lost his grip on the steering wheel and went the wrong way round a set of bollards. Feeling sick, he righted the car and coasted in to the kerb. He got out, threw the cigarette in the gutter and leaned against the bonnet for a few minutes. The shop would have to open late for once.

He kept seeing the image from his dream of the needle cutting into the record and drawing blood. He got back in the car and set off for the shop again. Every Mini turned his head. He'd never noticed them before but now it seemed like the city streets were full of them. He couldn't remember what colour the hybrid Siouxsie/Christine girl had been driving. It had, after all, been dark when he'd seen it.

During the hours of daylight he imagined it was parked up in one of the nameless streets on his map. Only by night, when there wasn't any, did she venture into the light of the real world.

Carl struggled to concentrate on the business of running the shop. The jigsaw feeling had faded but he still wasn't on top form. He chainsmoked and played randomly selected singles back to back all morning. Customers brought him boxes of records and he bought them all with the briefest examinations and without haggling over the amount he would pay for them. The shop seemed infested with Siouxsie clones but they were all years out of date, painted birds and scarecrows, their faces plastered with the Hallowe'en makeup Siouxsie herself now did without. Over the years, as the masks had been slowly stripped away she had become more and more beautiful to the point where her beauty was now a dangerous, provocative thing, like the music had always been.

Carl slipped 'Superstition' into the CD player and pressed repeat. The album played for the rest of the day.

In a stream of people offering him their old picture discs and limited edition gatefold sleeves a girl's hand pushed a white label single on to the counter. Carl gave a small cry and immediately looked up but the floor was crowded with customers. Out of the comer of his eye he saw the door close but it could have been anybody. Nevertheless, he squeezed under the counter and pushed through the crowd to the door. He craned his neck and looked in all directions but she had disappeared. There was no sign of a Mini parked nearby. His heart pounding, he re-entered the shop and returned to his place behind the counter.

Word must have got round that he was throwing money away today: it seemed as if the whole teenage population of the city had descended on his shop. "Whose is this?" he asked, holding up the white label. No one claimed it. "Is it yours?" he asked the next girl in the queue. She nodded. Someone behind her cackled like a hyena and he felt foolish, but for all he knew it could really have been hers and she'd been too shy to stick her hand up. The colour of the label could have prompted him to imagine someone who hadn't been there at all. He took the other stuff the girl clearly hadn't been expecting to sell, then lit a cigarette and put the white label underneath a stack of CDs to look at later.

It was with enormous relief that he locked the door and flipped the open/closed sign. He didn't need all this unrest. He stood and watched the rain through the glass as he lit a cigarette and put the lighter away in his jacket pocket. Cars squealed softly as they braked for the red light. Carl smoked nervously, unhappy about acknowledging his fear of the unknown girl and the white label she'd brought him. In the brightness of the afternoon it had been easier to rationalise. But in the shadowtime of dusk it seemed indisputable that his obsession was based on fact. He watched car headlamps dazzle and melt into wet reflections like silver waterfalls. Taking a deep drag that caused his head to spin he turned away from the window and went back to the counter. He felt like a bug in a killing jar. They could be watching him through the windows from across the street. They would want to see how he reacted when he listened to the white label. Well let them! He picked it up and slipped it out of its blank sleeve, holding it by the edges and angling it so that the light fell across it. There was nothing written on the label, but on the runout groove he made out the inscription "It's a gas." It meant nothing to him. It just seemed like the kind of throwaway remark that cutting engineers sometimes went in for.

He placed the record on the turntable with great care and positioned the needle before pressing release. It landed with that satisfying clunk he had heard a million times. It didn't matter how new a vinyl record was, you always heard something apart from the music, even if it was only the hiss of dust. He wondered what he would hear as the needle wound its way towards the music.

But none came. He checked the amp controls. Everything was on and the volume was turned up. He looked at the needle. It was a third of the- way into the record and still there was no sound.

He turned the volume higher and listened harder. He heard the usual rumble of ricks and bumps you got at the beginning and end of records. When it finished he reposirioned the needle and played it again. With the volume full up he fancied he could hear the needle itself scoring the groove a fraction deeper. He found himself becoming quite drawn to the sound. Without the distraction of music it was somehow purer, more elemental. He played the flip side and it was the same. The more he played it and the harder he listened, the more it sank into him. He noticed also that his forehead had begun to hurt where the skin stretched rightly across it. A sharp irritating pain like a paper cut.

Pain or no pain he was in thrall to the record. He loved its silence just as he soon came to need the sounds that *were* there to be heard if you listened hard enough. He played it again and again until he entered a state approaching rhapsody.

Towards midnight he locked up and walked to the car. The white label was in a padded envelope under his arm. He laid it carefully on the passenger seat and started the engine. He drove like an automaton, unblinking eyes sweeping the road ahead in search of the hybrid's car. He knew what she'd been dancing to and now he'd been there himself. In the shop. Listening to the record over and over again. The walls and ceiling had receded and he had felt himself at the centre of a huge spiral which descended upon him from the sky.

Waiting at a red light, rain lightly stippling the windscreen, Carl pressed in the cigarette lighter and reached into his boot. He stuck a cigarette between his lips. The lighter popped out and he withdrew it. He stared fixedly at the burning spiral for a few moments before sticking the third finger of his left hand inside the lighter and pressing the rip against the element. He didn't blink. Rain fell more heavily on the car, bearing a tinny tattoo on the roof. The light went green but he didn't move. The smell of burning flesh infused the air in the car.

Deep inside Carl, in a small part of him, a tiny scream caught like a flame in a tinderbox, then flickered and died.

He only pulled his finger away when he felt his nail grating unpleasantly against the metal coil.

His finger was black and cauterised. His face was blank. The light was red again. He replaced the cigarette lighter and waited for the light to change. When it did he shifted into first gear, wincing and moaning slightly as his burnt finger brushed against the passenger seat.

How long would it be before she appeared? He cruised slowly to give her enough rime, but there was no sign of her and soon he was pulling up outside the flat. Maybe she'd be waiting for him inside. He looked at his finger with a curious, childlike expression as he climbed the stairs. It still wasn't bleeding. He stuffed his hand in his back pocket to check on the map. It was still there. His mind dulled in response to the friction against his jeans.

The flat was empty but it didn't feel like his own any more. When he put the record on and turned the volume right up he felt a druggy mixture of euphoria and emptiness. His forehead itched. He wondered dully if Baz was involved. The inscription on the runout groove. "It's a gas." It was the kind of thing Baz would say. The girl couldn't have recorded, cut and pressed a record all on her own; she needed accomplices. Someone had to inhabit the streets on his map.

He looked at the thousands of records lining his walls. He'd wasted so much time searching for all that noise when all along the real music had been waiting for him just a few streets away.

In the kitchen he switched the ring on full and watched it get hot. He could still hear the music swirling around him, making of him its heart. But his forehead was hurting, like scratched sunburn. Maybe he could bum up the pain by lowering his forehead on to the ring. He bent over the cooker and was about to do it when he heard a car pull up outside.

It was her.

He left the kitchen without switching off the cooker and looked out of the living-room window. There was a black Mini parked in front of his Escort. He crossed to the door and as he looked back for a moment before closing the door he felt a tug. He realised this was his last chance. If he didn't turn back now he might never be able to. He looked at the photograph of Christine he still kept by the bed and felt a stab of regret. But as he sharpened his focus on the picture he saw that now she looked more like Siouxsie. And more like the candyman waiting outside in the car.

He left the door open and walked down the staircase. As he stepped into the street he felt a warm breeze and detected the faint odour of gas. The map was in his back pocket. He reached for the door handle on the Mini but the girl gunned the engine into life and moved forward several feet to dissuade him. He walked towards his own car and glanced in through the Mini's windows.

On the back seat lay a long knife.

He followed her in the Escort. She turned off his familiar route into the warren of semi-circular streets where he'd lost her for the first time. Despite his injured finger he kept pace with her. The road curved round to the right, then they turned right and curved some more. They seemed to be drawing in towards some hidden centre. He noticed a clocktower among a group of school buildings, but the clockface was devoid of hands. He accelerated and felt the road, once he'd passed the playground, twist round to the right. The streets were lined with bay-window semis. What suburban relapse could have occurred at the heart of this model landscape?

Carl fumbled the map from his back pocket and unfolded it. As he had vaguely remembered, there was a pocket of circular streets, effectively a spiral.

Take me back, take me back, he silently entreated the girl in the car ahead. But she took him on.

They turned right again and eventually the houses disappeared, giving way to waste ground, a procession of electricity pylons and an enormous gasholder.

The girl parked and started walking. Carl had to run to catch her up. They walked over ground dotted with sorrel and belladonna. He looked at the map. They were heading for the circle which lay at the centre of the curled maze of streets. The gasholder.

It reared up before them, a wonderful monster of overlapping curved metal plates. A telescopic spiral ready to expand or contract. It glowed in the moonlight and appeared to hover just above the ground like a ghostly carousel.

Carl followed the girl to the base of the gasholder. The long knife stuck out of the back pocket of her jeans. When she reached an opening she turned and looked back. The moon fell on her face which Carl now saw for the first time outside of his dream. She was, as he had dreamt, the perfect synthesis of Siouxsie and Christine. She had the most beautiful face he had ever seen. His stomach went into a slow dive. But it was love in a void and he felt his heart turn to stone. He would have wept but for the detail on her forehead which, though he caught only the briefest of glimpses, chilled him to the bone.

She turned and vanished inside the gasholder.

Carl followed because, no longer in control of his actions, there was nothing else he could do.

Inside the gargantuan chamber it was dark and Carl was forced to rely on other senses. He raised his arms to protect his face as he stepped forward. The overwhelming impression was of noise: of hundreds or thousands of slowly shuffling feet and in the highest reaches of the metal skin there resounded the magnified hiss and clicks and cannon booms of the white label. It threw its hooks into Carl immediately and he felt himself being drawn into a mass of swaying bodies. He visualised a charnel house of carcasses and raw heads and bloody bones.

There was something else he sensed but couldn't put a name to.

Carl succumbed to the silent music but the darkness awakened his fear and he felt pulled to bits. He pictured the girl's forehead and imagined all the flitting spellbound shapes around him to be similarly disfigured.

They pressed nearer and he was horrified to realise he felt close to them in mind as well as body. He imagined he could feel Christine's breath on his face and for a moment the gasholder almost became a place of paradise. But there was still the niggling feeling that something else was wrong but he didn't know what. Something around him that he should be aware of.

A cold object sliced his forehead and he felt a warm liquid run down into his eyes. Then the girl pressed harder with the knife but it was always a light, intimate touch, intended to brand rather than hurt.

Carl panicked. These weren't his people. It wasn't his celebration. He had never wanted oblivion, just a change. Something secret and new. Now he wanted his life back.

As far as he could tell, they were scared of the light.

He slipped his hand into the pocket of his leather jacket and closed his fingers round his cigarette lighter. He lifted it up to eye level and in the very same moment that he spun the wheel and created a dazzling, vivid snapshot of hundreds of raised foreheads marked by needle-fine spiral scars, he realised what the other thing was. A silly thing really.

The smell of gas.

THE LITTLE GREEN ONES

LES DANIELS

LES DANIELS was recently honoured as co-Writer Guest of Honour with Peter Straub at the 1993 World Horror Convention, held in Stamford, Connecticut.

His short fiction has been published in *Cutting Edge, Borderlands, Dark Voices 4* and *5, After the Darkness, The Mammoth Book of Vampires* and *The Mammoth Book of Zombies,* but he is perhaps best known for his series of novels about the vampire anti-hero Don Sebastian de Villanueva. They include *The Black Castle, The Silver Skull, Citizen Vampire, Yellow Fog, No Blood Spilled,* and the still forthcoming *White Demon.*

A long-time devotee of comic books, Daniels has contributed a chapter on vampire comics to *The Compleat Vampire's Companion,* is the author of the recent bestseller *Marvel:*

Five Fabulous Decades of the World's Greatest Comics, and he is currently working on a similar volume about the history of DC Comics.

The initial inspiration for the "The Little Green Ones" occurred when the author attended the 1988 World Fantasy Convention, held in West London. The child-like statues in the story can be found in the cemetery adjacent to the convention hotel, and we can attest to the fact that they are definitely as creepy as Daniels' chilling description . . .

HE NEVER KNEW WHO IT WAS that he followed into the cemetery, much less why. His mind was on something else entirely as he wandered down the leafy London street, and evidently he had fallen into step behind some stranger, for when he looked up he was just inside the gate. He felt as if he were teetering on the edge of a dream. Behind him was a modem street, and he knew that if he turned his head he would see a photocopy shop with a bright orange sign, but in front of him was a shady expanse of ancient trees and weathered stone.

"The Public Are Permitted to Walk in the Cemetery Daily," proclaimed a sign, as if it were the most natural thing in the world for people to stroll through rows of corpses for their pleasure, and in fact he saw figures in the distance, moving slowly through the autumn haze. He couldn't see their faces. He wondered what his friends in Phoenix would say if they saw him go inside himself; it certainly wasn't like him to be morbid, but somehow this spot aroused his curiosity. He felt that this was the real London, that the cars and television sets outside were only a facade hiding something much less modem. Even the cemetery, apparently Victorian, was only a few layers deeper into the layers of disguise that covered something almost sinister in the city, something unutterably old.

He didn't like that, and he wanted to go home.

He had come on business, but there wasn't much business: he wouldn't have been walking around if someone hadn't cancelled an appointment. He didn't even have a room at the convention hotel: some mix-up had shunted him off to a dingy, dark place where the elevator creaked and his room was a box just barely big enough to hold a bed. He was beginning to think he didn't even care if franchises for Cowboy Bob's

Bar-B-Q sprang up all over London or not. All that glass and plastic and concrete would be just another trick to fool the eye; the real London stretched out before him.

He stepped through the stone arch in the wall and went into the cemetery. It was quiet, and so big he couldn't see the end of it. Dead leaves littered the pathway, crunching unpleasantly under his feet, but there was still green in the trees overheard. He noticed a squirrel fleeing frantically from his intrusion, and scrambling up the side of a small mausoleum. The motion drew his eyes to the words "Devoted and Gentle Son", and to the pale stone face of a youth beside them. He looked to be about twenty, but his countenance was blackened in spots by time, especially around the eyes. The sculpture was giving way to some sort of rot, like the decay that long ago had turned the face inside the tomb to putrid fruit.

He felt the first hint of a shudder, looked away, and saw the children. There were two of them, standing on the other side of the path, and they were green.

He realized almost at once that they were statues, but somehow he was not reassured. Both of them, the girl and the boy, were staring at him with that disconcerting directness which only small children can summon; they appeared to be about seven, and they had been made lifesize. Except for their colour, which really was quite odd, they looked like figures from an antiquated textbook, a typical pair of typical children from several generations ago. The girl wore a dress that hung straight down from her shoulders to her knees; her shoes had little straps and there was a big bow in her short hair. The boy wore a sailor suit, complete with cap and kerchief; he had short pants and long stockings. They had their heads thrust forward, as if to increase the intensity of their gaze, and they had their arms behind their backs. They stood straight, almost at attention, yet time had tilted each one slightly away from the other, as if they might at any moment fall rigid to the ground. Their faces were earnestly expressionless.

He was only a few paces from the gate, yet in the presence of these little ones he felt terribly alone; he decided on the spot that he would not venture any further into the realm they seemed to guard. After all, he had no business in a graveyard anyway. Still, he stepped across the path to take a closer look at them. He couldn't quite resist the pull of these odd little figures, which seemed so commonplace and yet so horrible. Evidently someone's kids had died, and been commemorated in a fashion that was perhaps not in the best of taste, especially since the statues had turned green. He never would have contemplated such a thing if anything had happened to his two boys, who of course were safe at home, and certain to outlive him in any case. There was no connection with his family anyway; these really quite atrocious little figures were from another time and place.

The girl and boy stood watch over a slab of granite, conventionally grey and shaped somewhat like a coffin. There was an inscription on either side of it, and he discovered to his astonishment that the people buried here were a married couple who had died in middle age. She had given up the ghost in 1927, and he had followed her less than a year later. These were not the graves of children after all.

Then what was the significance of these little green ones who gazed at him so balefully, their loathsome, almost iridescent colour a match for the few leaves clinging to a turnorous old tree behind them? Why were they looking at him, and why was he looking back?

What weird sentiment had inspired these nasty little statues? Who had commissioned them? Was it some whimsical relative, or perhaps the grieving husband, who realized that his time was near and chose to commemorate their early days as childhood sweethearts? Had he killed himself to join her? Had he been hanged for killing her? And why were they so damned green?

It was a sickly, milky green, like lichen or moss, although it might have been oxidation if the things were made of metal. He could have found out easily enough, but he was damned if he was going to touch them. It was too easy to imagine them crumbling beneath his touch, held together by nothing but the strange stuff that encrusted them. Worse yet, his hand might sink into a mass of fungus. People thought green was the colour of life, but this was a festering life that fed on death. He hurried away from there, hardly taking time to notice another sign beside the gate: "Persons in Charge of Children Are Required to Control Them."

His nerves were shot, no doubt. The trip wasn't going well, and he hadn't been sleeping much: jet-lag. But it was this city, too, and the whole country, really. It was on the wrong side of the world. The gravity was wrong here, and so was the light. He longed to be back in God's country, where things stood new and clean against a desert sky, where nothing was old and nothing was green.

On his way back to the hotel, he had to wait for a hateful and ridiculous traffic signal. Instead of an honest and direct "WALK" or "DON'T WALK", the electric sign displayed a slumped red figure to keep pedestrians immobile, and a strutting, glowing green figure when it was time to march. He stared at something green taking its first step and felt his eyelids twitch.

He was bone weary, no doubt about that, and he would be expected to perform like a happy salesman at the reception that was only a few hours away. He stumbled into his hotel, made his way to his room, locked the door behind him and fell into his little bed. He told himself he was taking a nap. After all, your health is more important. The room grew dark around him while he lay like a man who had been poleaxed.

Half asleep in his overpriced coffin, he heard a quiet voice, something between a groan and a sigh. It was right there in the cramped confines of his room. He jerked upright like an old-fashioned mechanical toy and peered into the twilight. Was someone there? Or had he made that noise himself?

He got up, more drained than ever, and turned on the light. There was nothing to be seen, but the bathroom door was closed and he decided to leave it that way. He went out to the convention without bothering to shave or shower or change his clothes.

The party was noisier and stupider than he would have thought possible. He drank heavily and tried not to talk to anyone. A man got up on a table and took his pants down. The future of Cowboy Bob's Bar-B-Q was in his hands. Amazingly, nobody seemed to object. Even the English seemed crude and crass, oblivious to the verdant mysteries that slept beneath their soil. Christ, even Robin Hood had dressed in green. Was everybody blind?

He took a cab back to his hotel and wondered whether his wife was going to leave him. He was in London, but there wasn't even any goddam fog. He could see every landmark they passed, even Brompton Cemetery. The gates, thank God, were locked, and the little green ones safe inside—unless they'd been out for hours. Do you know where your children are tonight?

The cab dropped him off, and every building he could see around him was the work of men long dead. The sky was gigantic. Everyone was going to die, no matter what they did, and something small was going to come around the comer unless he got inside. Why was this happening to him? He hadn't done anything—he'd only looked.

He stood outside his room, so sure the little green ones were inside that he couldn't even bring himself to open the door. He thought about them for a long time, then said the hell with it and went inside, which was a reasonable plan since they didn't visit him until after he was asleep. It wasn't sleep, really, just the fitful snooze of the ageing and the afraid, but it was good enough until he saw the kids again, their arms locked behind their backs as if they were tied. They didn't reach out for him, and they didn't come toward him; instead they went into the bathroom and stood in the shower. They made no sound, but all at once the silence seemed shrill, as if someone had turned up the volume on an unplugged radio. The boy and the girl waited under the running water, their little faces bland and boring and reproachful, and the green that covered them dribbled away, filling the tub and overflowing on to the floor. It slopped toward him, while the children, washed free of it, gave forth a blistering white light that streamed into his eyes and woke him up.

It was sunlight, of course, and it was his last day in London. All he had to do was survive this, and he would be safe.

A phoney banquet at the big hotel. International food franchise folks, eat this. It couldn't have been worse. Everything was green.

He had walked past the cemetery on his way, and had peered in for long enough to see the kiddies still standing there, but he sensed that they were not through with him, and every course he ate confirmed it. Watercress soup. Avocado salad. Lamb with mint sauce, the green flecks swimming up through the innocuous oil. Green beans, potatoes sprinkled with parsley. Lime mousse for dessert, and mints wrapped in green foil. It was all rucking green, and he didn't eat much. Green Perrier bottles were all around him, but he was slugging back cheap Scotch.

He ran for the plane.

Whatever it was that there was dropped behind him as he soared into the sky, but not before he looked out of the window and saw the whole accursed island spread out below him. It was green, green from stem to stem, green for hundreds of miles in every direction, as far as the eye could see. An alien empire, drifting into insignificance. Christopher Robin's dead.

It was hard to shake them, of course. Their grave little features were engraved on each one of the peas in his plastic plate, and when the plane hit an air pocket he would see their small, sad faces.

They were gone, however, by the time he got to Phoenix, and Death was something that grew in the old world.

He told himself that, even when his wife showed up in a green rented car and asked him for a divorce. She had spent his money on green contact lenses, which transformed her eyes into something glassy, cold, and enigmatic. Maybe she was right, but how could fake and hate bring happiness? It was all nonsense, right up to the last moment, the land around him brown and clean and honest and American. The dead kids were a thousand, thousand miles away. There was nothing to remind him of them.

Dead was dead, and green was green, and that was the end of it.

Yet when his own children ran out to greet him at the door, he saw to his dismay that they were not alone.

THE DAY OF THE SHARKS

KATE WILHELM

KATE WILHELM was born in Louisville, Kentucky, and lives in Eugene, Oregon with her husband, noted writer and critic Damon Knight. *Locus* has described her novels as being "among the most immediate, trenchant commentaries on our world and our lives available today."

She received her first Nebula Award in 1968 for her story "The Planners", and her latest Nebula in 1988 for "Forever Yours, Anna". She has also been honoured with a Hugo Award (for her novel *Where Late the Sweet Birds Sang*), a Prix Apollo Award and a Jupiter Award. Her recent books include a fantasy novel, *Cambio Bay*, and a mystery entitled *Justice for Some*. "The Day of the Sharks" originally appeared in her landmark collection *And the Angels Sing*. Set during a seemingly idyllic Florida vacation, a faltering marriage takes a disturbingly nightmarish turn in the powerful narrative which follows . . .

HER TRANQUILIZER IS WEARING OFF, Gary thinks, when Veronica begins to tell him about it again. He stops listening almost immediately, and watches the road.

". . . that thin voice coming in my ears, hour after hour. You know, he doesn't dictate it like that. He pauses and goes out, has coffee, sees other patients, but day after day, having that box talk to me . . ."

The road is a glare, the sun straight ahead, centered in the dazzling whiteness of the concrete; the bay they are skirting is without a ripple, an endless mirror of eye-hurting brilliance. It will be beautiful when the sun is actually setting, he thinks, but now his eyes bum, and the damn air-conditioning in the rented car is malfunctioning, alternately shocking them with random cold blasts, or leaving them sweltering in the airless machine that smells of deodorizers and cleaning fluids.

". . . and they weren't people. Not after a while. They were gall bladders and thyroids and kidney stones. I began to wonder if there were any people even connected to them. You know? Free-floating kidney stones."

A flight of birds catches his attention; they just clear the water, almost touching the surface with their broad wings that look tattered, old, as if they have been at war, are flak-torn.

". . . system's supposed to help with the filing, for the computers, or something. Everything by number, not even parts of the anatomy any longer. Just numbers and prices. Case histories of numbers."

Her voice is getting high, tight, the way it does these days. Her posture has become rigid, her gaze fixed on a point straight ahead; she can stay this way for hours, unmoving, seeing what? He can't imagine what she sees. He grasps the steering wheel harder, wishes she would take another damn tranquilizer and be done with it. She will eventually. But she is afraid of them throughout the day until after dinner when it doesn't matter if she falls asleep. She took two at breakfast and dozed on the flight from Chicago to Tampa; it was a peaceful flight.

Ahead, a squat, ugly complex comes into view, black against the glaring sky, his next landmark. He slows to make the turn off the highway over a bridge onto a narrower road. Now, with the sun to his right, he can drive faster. The islands have nothing on them, a few palm trees, some dunes, scrub that looks like felled palm trees, more birds. Sea gulls, he thinks, with near triumph. At least he knows sea gulls. Six miles farther.

His thoughts turn to Bill Hendrix and his wife Shar. And then he is thinking only of Shar. For the first time after she and Bill moved down here she pleaded with him to come visit. He could fake a business trip. He could meet her in Tallahassee, or Miami, or somewhere. Then no more begging, no more anything, until the call from Bill. "If you're going to the Bahamas, hell, man, you've got to come for the weekend, at least. You can fly on from Tampa on Monday."

"We should have gone straight on to Grand Bahama," Veronica mumbles, facing the arrowlike road that seems to plunge into the blue water in the distance. A low dense clump of green rises on the left. The greenery expands, becomes pine trees, motionless in the still, late afternoon. "Turn again just after the pines," Bill's instructions went on. There is only one way to turn, left. They enter the subdivision under construction.

Unfinished houses are ugly, Gary thinks, obscenely ugly, naked, no illusions about them, the land around the buildings cluttered with junk that will be hidden away by the bulldozers, but there, always there. The landfill is dazzling white: sand, shells, the detritus dredged from the bay to create land, brought up long enough ago to have bleached to snow white.

"We should have gone straight on to Grand Bahama," Veronica says again, louder, still not looking at him.

"I told you, I have this business with Bill. We'll leave first thing Monday morning."

They wind through the subdivision, following instructions. A short causeway, to the end of the street, on to the point. There is Bill's house, with a yard fully landscaped, green and flowering. Gary's eyes narrow as he looks at it. The house is almost hidden from the street, but what shows is expensive, and the landscaping cost a fortune.

Bill said only three houses were finished, and that one is still vacant. The buyers will move in on the first of the month. They have not passed the other completed houses.

"I hardly even know them," Veronica says, not quite whining although a petulant tone has entered her voice. Gary doesn't know what that is supposed to mean. They were friends for more than five years. Gary wonders if she ever suspected Shar, if Bill ever did. He is almost certain no one did, but still, there is the possibility. Veronica knows there was someone. She always knows.

He parks in the driveway, but before they can get out of the car, they are suddenly chilled by a last effort of the air conditioner. He feels goose bumps rise; Veronica's skin takes on a bluish cast. Bill and Shar are coming out to meet them. She has a beautiful tan, the same dark gold all over her legs, her arms, her face. Her hair is blonder than it was before; she might have been a little thinner before, but otherwise she looks exactly the same. There is a sheen on her skin, as if she has been polished. She is tall and strong, a Viking type, she calls herself. Nothing willowy about her, nothing fat or slack. She has long, smooth muscles in her legs; her stomach is as firm and flat as a boy's. She wears white briefs and a halter, and rubber thongs on her feet. Bill is a bit shorter than she is, thickly built, very powerful, with thick wrists and a thick neck. Size seventeen. They are both so tanned that Gary feels he and Veronica must both look like invalids.

"My God! Ghosts!" Shar cries, as Gary and Veronica get out of the car. She embraces them with too much enthusiasm and warmth, and Gary can sense Veronica's withdrawal. Next to Shar, Veronica appears used up, old. She is only thirty-one, but she looks ill, as she is, and she looks frightened and suspicious, and very tired. There are circles under her eyes; he feels guilty that he has not seen them before, that only now, contrasting her with Shar does he recognize the signs of illness, remember that this isn't simply a vacation.

"Hey, it's good to see you," Bill says, putting his arm across Gary's back. "Come on in. A drink is what you people need. And tomorrow we'll get out in the sun and put some color in your cheeks."

It should be warm and friendly, but it isn't. It is like walking into a scenario where every line has been rehearsed, the stage sets done by art majors; even the sky has been given an extra touch of the brush. It is gaudy now with sunset, the ambient light peach colored, and out back, visible through a wall of sliding glass doors, the bay is brilliant, touched with gold.

"Two hundred sixty-five thou," Bill says, waving his hand as they enter the house where the furniture is either white or sleek, shiny black. He goes to a bar and pours martinis already made up, and they sit down where they can watch the lights on the bay. Between them and the golden water are red and yellow flowering bushes, an Olympic-size swimming pool, a terrace with enough seating and tables to serve as a cafe. "Too much, isn't it?" Bill says, grinning. "Just too goddam much."

"Are you hungry?" Shar asks. "Dinner won't be until pretty late. We're having a little party, buffet about ten. How about a sandwich, something to tide you over?"

"Oh, Gary," Veronica says, stricken.

"No sweat," Bill says. "It's a business party. You know, people I owe. Just happened to coincide. Don't feel you're interrupting anything."

Still, Veronica looks at Gary as if pleading with him; he shrugs. "It'll be all right," he says, trying to make his impatience sound like patience. "She hasn't been feeling very well," he adds, glancing at Shar.

"It won't be too much of a drag, I hope," Shar says lightly. "Wind us up and watch us entertain. Isn't that right, Bill?"

He laughs and pours more drinks. "You'll fit right in, Gary. Just watch how their eyes gleam when I tell them you're an investment counselor." He laughs again.

The party is little more than an excuse to get loud and drunk, Gary admits to himself later, wandering on the terrace with a drink in his hand, tired from the over-long day, bored with people he doesn't know, doesn't want to know. He knows their types, he thinks, watching a heavy-set man in a flowered shirt mock-push a nearly bare-breasted woman into the pool, laughing, leering, lusting. Shar touches his arm.

"Dance?"

They dance, his hand warmed by her golden back that is almost too smooth to be human. "Can I see you alone later?"

She smiles and doesn't answer.

He dances her to the end of the terrace, more discreetly lighted than the other areas, and kisses her. "Later?"

"Don't be an idiot. With your wife and my husband on the scene?"

"Veronica will be knocked out with tranquilizers, and Bill's on his way to passing out."

"What's wrong with Veronica?"

"Nerves, I guess. She flipped out at work. Tried to bum down the office or something." "Good God! Did she really?"

"She says she was only burning the files, but the whole place would have gone up if it hadn't been caught when it was." "What did they do to her?"

He is tired of talking about Veronica, tired of thinking about her. "Hospital. Two weeks. Now a vacation, and then into analysis, I guess. She's under a shrink's care." "Poor Gary," Shar says, her voice amused. He can't see her features, but can feel the warmth of her skin, smell the elusive scent that she wears, that she always wore. When he starts to kiss her again, she moves away and walks back toward the house. "Later," he says, this time not asking.

She smiles over her shoulder and stops to chat with a group of men standing at the sliding door to the Florida room.

Finally, Gary spots Veronica at a table by a man, clutching her glass tightly, her eyes glazed in the way they do when she drinks more than a glass of wine. He curses silently and turns to see Bill approaching with another man in tow. Bill is red faced, perspiring heavily, and the grace that he displays when sober is gone. He lumbers, stumbles into things, loses coordination in a way that seems to suggest that his limbs have different reaction times. He wards off a table before he is within reach, then hits it with his thigh, and belatedly clutches a chair to steady himself. Gary moves closer to Veronica and the unknown man; he doesn't want to talk to a drunken Bill.

". . . density ratio so fouled up that no one knows what the hell they're going to do. Six hundred units per acre. Now I ask you, does that sound too terrible to you, a city girl? You know Chicago can handle that many people, what's the difference?"

Veronica shakes her head helplessly. "Units?" "Yep. They're saying no more than two fifty per acre. Two hundred fifty! What kind of condo can you put up with only two fifty?"

Veronica looks almost desperate; relief relaxes her face when Gary draws near. "Have you eaten yet?" he asks. She stands up, nods to the man, and takes Gary's arm. Her fingers dig in convulsively. "How long will this go on?" she whispers, as they walk toward the buffet.

She looks and sounds terrible; she should go to bed. Her tension is almost a palpable thing, electric. He feels that he could touch it, be burned by it.

Bill blocks their way, still with the tall man. "Gary, want you to meet Dwight Scanlon, president of the development company I was telling you about. My good friend, Gary Ingalls, and Veronica."

"Hear you're on your way to Grand Bahama," Dwight Scanlon says, taking Gary's hand. "Lovely place. We've got a hotel over there, in fact. You have your rooms reserved? Look, cancel them, why don't you? I've got this suite, nobody in it, nobody scheduled for it until June. Yours for the taking."

Before Gary can refuse, Scanlon has turned to Veronica. "Have you seen the moon coming up over that bay yet? What a sight!" He offers his arm; she puts her hand on it tentatively, and they walk out together.

Bill downs his drink and runs his hand over his face. "Gotta turn on that air conditioner pretty soon."

The air conditioner is on, but the house is jammed with guests, and waiters and caterers. The sliding doors to the terrace have been open all evening. Gary wanders back outside where he sits down at a wrought-iron table. His head is buzzing, not unpleasantly, and there is a lightness in his legs and arms, also not unpleasant. He watches a sinuous woman work her way through a cluster of people to approach his table with evident purpose.

"I'm Audrey Scanlon," she says, and sits down after pulling a tiny chair very close to his. "You're Gary, aren't you?"

He nods.

"Perhaps you'd like to help us launch our boat Sunday," she says. She does not touch him, but he has the feeling that she is all over him.

"No way," Shar says coolly, suddenly at Gary's side. "He's ours until Monday morning; aren't you, Gary, darling?"

Audrey stands up. "Maybe we'll see you in Grand Bahama," she whispers and now she does touch him. Her hand lingers a moment on his arm, and when she moves away, she doesn't lift it, but lets her fingers trail over his skin very lightly.

"Bitch," Shar says, when she is gone.

"No doubt, they just happen to have this little company that they would love to have recommended to prospective buyers." He sounds bitter even to his ears. Shar pats his arm. Someone calls her and she leaves him.

Soon Veronica returns from the dock; her eyes are shining. "I've been propositioned, I think."

"Scanlon?"

She nods. She looks very happy.

"His wife just did the same with me. They must be fresh in from the swamps."

"Don't make it sound like that," Veronica cries. "Maybe he just found me attractive! Wouldn't it occur to you that someone else might still find me attractive?"

"He wants me to list his company," Gary says. "And he has as much finesse about it as a hippo humping a hippo."

"I wouldn't have done it." Her face twitches and settles into the newly familiar rigid lines. "I wouldn't have done anything," she says woodenly. "Why couldn't you let me have my little fantasy?"

"You should go to bed. You're so tired, you're ready to keel over."

She walks away unsteadily.

Someone falls into the pool; within minutes there are a number of rescuers in the water. After that it seems almost spontaneous, although it never really is, he knows, for others to begin shedding their clothes to jump in. Gary swims naked, as do Shar and Audrey, and a dozen others. All laughing and playing and then huddling in towels and drinking again.

Guests are leaving now, and presently there are only three or four remaining, drinking with Bill, nostalgic about old times, before the islands were bought. Veronica has vanished, possibly to go to bed. Gary takes Shar's hand and leads her to the terrace, beyond it to the velvet lawn where he spreads his towel and hers to make a bed. He lowers her to the ground; she doesn't resist.

Immediately afterward she draws away. "I have to go in," she murmurs. "I can't stay out here." She stands over him; he sits up and puts his arms around her hips, pulls her to him, presses his face into her pubic hair and bites softly. She moans and sways, but then pushes him away. "No more. Not now."

She runs, naked, gleaming in the patio lights briefly, then vanishes into one of the rooms that open to the terrace.

Gary swims again, but he knows he is too drunk to be in the water alone; he climbs out shivering, with exhaustion as much as from the cold. The guest room has an outside door, he remembers; he finds it and goes in to shower and dry himself and dress again. Veronica is not in the room. When he returns to the living room, all the guests are gone. Bill has brought out champagne that he, Veronica, and Shar are drinking.

They drink until dawn flames the sky and then they go to bed. It is eleven when Gary awakens with a pounding headache; Veronica is already up and out.

"Take this," Bill says when he enters the dining room. "Don't ask questions, just drink it." It is a juice drink, heavily spiked with bourbon. For a moment Gary feels his stomach chum, then it settles down again. The drink is very good.

Veronica looks awful; her eyes are red rimmed and bloodshot, sunken in her face. "Why don't you try to sleep some more?" he says, too miserable to care one way or the other.

From the kitchen come sounds of things being banged about. Bill winces. "Caterers' dean-up crew," he says. "Let's go out to the dock until they finish."

"I'll bring the cart," Shar says. "God knows we all need something to eat, and coffee, lots of coffee."

The sun is hot, but the breeze is refreshing. The bay is about a mile wide; there are no signs of civilization, as long as they face away from this subdivision. Now and again a jumping fish makes ripples that undulate in the water as the tide flows in like a river.

"Twelve feet deep here," Bill says. "It's shallow up in the fingers. Point's the place to be." His boat is thirty-five feet, two-forty horsepower Westinghouse . . .

Gary gazes at the gently moving water and doesn't listen to Bill cataloguing his treasures. Objects and wielders, he thinks. They all were objects and wielders of objects last night. Changing roles as easily as they changed their clothes. Even his too-brief contact with Shar was object and wielder, and he does not know who played which part.

Suddenly he recalls the scene when he first visited Veronica in the hospital. She was stupefied from Thorazine, or something they gave her. Her voice was singsong. "I don't think there are any people, Gary. Nowhere. They're all gone, and I don't know where they went. I'm so afraid." She did not sound afraid, only dull and drug-stupid. Later, Bill will make his pitch, Gary knows. *Hit a little snag, old buddy. You know how it goes.* He knows. He drinks the strong black coffee, thinking how distant his head has become, throbbing like drums not quite heard, but felt as pressure. Across the bay the land has not been developed yet and shows a low green, irregular skyline, a fitting place for the drums to originate from. He watches a boat sail up the channel, nearly all the way across the bay.

"We'll just rest up this afternoon," Bill says. "Take life easy, that's the motto down here. Not like your big city, eh?"

No one replies. Veronica is nibbling on a piece of toast; some color has come back to her face, but it is probably only the beginning of a sunburn. Shar's gaze meets Gary's and she lets her eyes close slightly, a very faint smile on her mouth.

"And tomorrow, bright and early, we'll take the boat out," Bill says. "Do a little fishing out in the gulf." He pours more coffee and lights a cigarette.

"What's that?" Veronica says suddenly, sitting upright. She points. "A shark, or something."

They all look as a dark form breaks the smooth surface of the water, arches up, and vanishes again. It is on their side of the channel, several hundred yards out.

"I'll be damned," Bill says. "One of those whales. I thought they all died." He watches and when it breaks the water again, he nods in satisfaction. "It's a false killer whale." "Killer whale? Here?" Gary asks.

"*False* killer whale. Harmless, just looks like the real thing. Listen, let me tell you what I saw a few weeks ago. Damnedest thing I ever saw in my life. Over near Fort Myers. I was driving along, heard this report on the car radio about whales beaching themselves. So I thought, what the hell, I'd go have a look. Beach was crowded with people by the time I got there, but nothing was happening. I keep binoculars in the car, you know? So I got them out, and watched. There was a line of those animals out there in the water, quarter of a mile offshore, just laying there in the water. Not moving a muscle. No surf, no wind, as calm as that bay is right now. I kept watching, beginning to get bored with the whole thing, you know? They weren't doing a damn thing. Just laying there. Then, by God, they started to move in. All at once, all together, like a goddam chorus line. And they kept coming, and kept coming until they were in water too shallow to swim in and they began to roll. People were jumping in from everywhere, yanking on them, trying to get them turned around, headed back out. Some people had rowboats, a couple of motorboats, people in the water up to their necks, just trying to get those things back out to sea. And while they're working with this bunch, another bunch was starting in, the females and young. They'd been waiting half a mile offshore for some kind of a damn signal, or something, and now they were coming in. People kept getting the first ones turned around, and those whales would just sort of swerve a couple of feet to one side or the other and back they'd come in to shore. It went on for hours. Some of the boats towed a couple of the big males out to sea again, I guess hoping that the others would follow them. They didn't."

His voice is low, awed, his gaze following the movements of the whale in the bay. "They got a lot of them out to sea again, but a dozen of them made it in. They died on the beach. Mass suicide. The damnedest thing I ever saw."

No one speaks for several moments, then Veronica says, "Why?" Her voice is tight and high. "Were they sick?"

"Marine biologists couldn't find anything wrong. No sharks in the water. No storms to mix them up, and it was too deliberate to think they just made a mistake, misjudged the depth of the water. No one knows why."

"That's crazy!" Veronica cries, jumping up. "There has to be a reason. There's always a reason!" The shrillness of her voice is startling. She clamps her lips and runs up the dock, back inside the house.

"God, I'm sorry," Bill says, his big face contrite. "I shouldn't have told that story. It... it haunts me."

"Forget it," Gary says. "What happened to the rest of the whales? You thought they all died?"

"That's the worst part," Bill says soberly. "The next day they found them down in the Keys. Beached on one of the islands down there."

Shar stands up. "I'll go do something about lunch. The caterers must be gone by now."

The whale continues to swim in great circles out in the bay, close in, then farther out again. Bill begins to tell Gary about the financial problems his company has encountered, through no fault of their own. Gary promises nothing. He will study the financial statements, the local restrictions, and so on. Bill understands. He lays his hand on Gary's arm and assures him that he understands.

Veronica doesn't come out for lunch, and after the others eat, Shar and Bill withdraw to nap. Gary puts on his trunks and swims in the pool, then stretches out under a cluster of palm trees, something *Reclinatus,* Bill said. You can transplant full-grown palm trees, instant garden, Gary thinks, listening to the wind in the fronds, a soothing rainlike sound. You dredge up the bay bottom, smooth it out, cover it with a carpet of sod, plant trees, flowers, shrubs, plant a house, plant people. Instant paradise. And there are no insects in the ground. Barren, pseudodirt. Not real.

Veronica said, after her hospitalization, "Sometimes I wonder, if I reach out to touch you when you're not looking, not thinking about me, not concentrating on being you, will my hand go through you?"

"Meaning?"

"I don't know. Nothing you do is real. You work with money—bits of paper that have no meaning. You don't even see the money. It isn't real, just figures on paper, symbols in the computer. You don't make anything, or fix anything. After you finish for the day, does the office lose its shape, melt down to nothing until you get back and give it a pseudoreality again?"

"Veronica! For heaven's sake!" He reached for her and she drew away sharply, in recoil almost.

"No! That isn't real either. A touch, a kiss, a fuck. Pseudoreal."

"I don't know what the hell you're talking about." "You can

tell if it's real. You can tell. If it's there years later. If you can go to it and find it years later." Her voice became a whisper, her gaze on something he could not see. "Money becomes figures on paper. Patients become organs that become numbers in the computer. Pseudoreal."

After she is well again, they will separate. He has already decided. She is young, pretty until she became ill. She will marry again, maybe even have children. She wants children; he said later, after we're established, a little money saved. Later. And he will find someone new, someone with gaiety in her laugh, who isn't sick. Someone who will bring fun into his life again.

He dozes in the shade and awakens to find that the sun is burning his legs. The distant throbbing has entered his head; it is his head, but there is another noise, screeching and screaming.

"Hey, old buddy, you want a gin and tonic?" Bill calls from the doorway.

"I sure as hell want something," Gary says. He feels worse than he did that morning.

Bill steps out to the terrace, shielding his eyes with his hand, looking at gulls screaming, diving, shrieking, just off the end of the dock. "Must be a school running," he says, and starts to walk toward the commotion.

Gary follows him slowly. They stop halfway up the dock. The whale is alongside the structure, the entire animal clearly visible in the quiet water. Blood is flowing from under it. The gulls wheel and scream overhead; now and then one of them dips to the surface of the water, darts up again.

"I will be God damned!" Bill says in wonder. "She's going to give birth. For Christ's sake!"

The whale pays no attention to the men on the dock. Now and then a long shudder passes through her, rippling from her great black head down to her tail. She is gleaming black, nine feet long, sleek; her blowhole opens and closes convulsively. She shudders; her body twists. She sinks, surfaces again.

"She's in trouble," Gary says. Bill looks at him blankly.

"It shouldn't take more than a minute or so. I read that somewhere. And she's bleeding too much."

The stain rises in the water, spreads like a cloud. It seems to rise like smoke signals.

"There must be someone who knows what to do," Gary says, staring at the helpless animal. "The university?"

"It's after five, Saturday," Bill says. "The Coast Guard. I'll call them. Someone there will know."

Gary stands on the dock, his hands clenched, watching the animal and the distress signals dispersing through the water. He doesn't hear the others until Shar says, "Oh, my God!" He turns to see her and Veronica staring at the whale.

"They'll find someone to send," Bill says, hurrying across the yard. "It might take a while, though."

The animal doesn't have a while, Gary knows. He doesn't say it. They continue to watch in horrified fascination as the ripples that are pain reactions spread throughout the animal regularly.

Suddenly Shar draws her breath in. "Oh, no!" she cries. She is staring out at the bay. "Sharks!"

Gary sees them, two fins moving through the water almost leisurely, as if they know there is no need to hurry. Bill turns and runs to the house. He comes back moments later with a rifle. He puts a handful of shells on the dock and loads a clip.

"Where are they?" His voice is hoarse, the words slurred. Shar points. He doesn't raise the rifle. "Too far," he says in his strange voice.

It is excitement, Gary realizes; his own mouth is dry and he feels prickly with sweat and goose bumps, as if something loathsome has touched him.

"It won't do any good," Veronica says, and her voice is different, too, high and clear, but steady. "As soon as the baby is born, she'll want to go out to sea, won't she? They'll be waiting for her."

She is looking out at the channel. There are more fins. A pack then. They must have followed the trail of blood from out in the gulf. Veronica appears transfixed, as if in a trance.

"You'd better go inside," he says. She does not give any sign that she heard him. He touches her arm and she twitches with a convulsive shudder, like the whale's. She does not look at him. "Get inside, damn it!" His hand falls from her arm and he turns away. She wants to see the blood fest, he realizes, sickened. The near rapture on her face makes her look like a transcendent Joan at the moment when the torch touches the faggots. He takes a few long steps away from her, but then comes back; he can't leave, neither can he stand still and watch. He hunches his shoulders and paces back and forth, back and forth.

Suddenly the rifle goes off and the sound is a shock that hurts. It rolls over the water, echoing.

"You can't kill them from here!" Shar cries.

"Only wanted to nick one," Bill says, aiming again. "They'll turn on one that's wounded, maybe leave her alone." The sharks move in a great semicircle, not coming directly toward the dock. They are swimming faster. He fires again.

"The bastards! The bastards!" Bill says over and over, nearly sobbing. "The bastards!"

Without warning the false killer whale moves away from the dock. She swims for about ten feet and rolls to her side. A cloud of blood spreads over the water. The gulls screech in a frenzy. They swoop down on the water, hiding the whale from view. She jerks and makes a great splash; they rise, screaming.

The baby is being expelled. Gary can see the body, the curled tail already straightening, and now the head is free. With what must have been an agony of effort the mother whale rolls suddenly, away from the infant, making a complete turn in the water in one swift, sharp movement. She has broken the cord. As she finishes the turn she comes up under the infant and nudges it to the surface. It rolls to one side and does not move. It is white underneath, three feet long, and it is dead. It starts to sink and again the mother whale nudges it to the surface of the water. And again. And again. Gary turns away. He hears Shar being sick over the rail of the dock. "They're coming!" Veronica screams. Gary swings around in time to see Veronica snatch the rifle from Bill's limp hands; Bill is staring at the whale as if in a daze. Veronica points the rifle and begins to fire very fast, not at the sharks, but downward. The sleek black whale thrashes in the water, she tries to jump, but doesn't clear the surface, and then a paroxysm of jerks overtake her; finally she rolls over. The sharks begin to hit her.

Veronica turns toward the house; the rifle in her hands is pointed directly at Gary. He does not move. Her face is closed and hard, a stranger's face. She opens her hands and the rifle falls, clatters on the shells still on the dock. She walks past him without another glance at the sharks, at him, at anyone.

The water chums and froths; it is all red. Shar staggers away from the rail. She reaches for Gary's arm to steady herself and he jerks away involuntarily. Her hand would go through him, he thinks; she begins to run toward the house.

"She's afraid your wife will bum it down," Bill says in a thick, dull voice. For a moment his face is naked; he knows. "I might burn it down myself one day. Just might do that." He walks away, his shoulders bowed, his head lowered.

The frenzied gulls, the boiling water, the heat of the sun, all that's real, Gary thinks. Veronica firing the rifle, that was real. He remains on the dock until the Coast Guard cutter comes into sight, speeding toward the dock. The water is calm again; there is nothing for them to see, nothing for them to do. He doesn't even bother to wave to them. One of the men is standing in the boat scanning the water, and suddenly he points. The sharks are still in the channel. The boat veers, makes waves as it swings around and heads out away from the dock.

They didn't even sec him, Gary knows. He is not surprised. Slowly he lifts his hands and looks at them, and then lets them drop to his sides. In his mind is an image of a raging inferno.